bounce

Also by Noelle August

Boomerang
Rebound

bounce

A Boomerang Novel

Noelle August

WILLIAM MORROW
An Imprint of HarperCollinsPublishers

HarperCollins books may be purchased for educational, business, or sales promotional use. For information please e-mail the Special Markets Department at SPsales@harper collins.com.

FIRST EDITION

Library of Congress Cataloging-in-Publication Data has been applied for.

ISBN 978-0-06-233110-6

15 16 17 18 19   DIX/RRD   10 9 8 7 6 5 4 3 2 1

To my parents, Pearl and Arnold Oberweger, for prizing playfulness, culture, intelligence, and family—and for giving me my first typewriter.

I love and miss you every day.
—LO

For my Muses—Donna, Katy, Talia, Bret—with all my gratitude.
—VR

bounce

Chapter 1

Grey

"Grey, wake up."

I swim through the blue water, following my leash to my surf-board, wondering why I hear my brother's voice. Adam sounds pissed. Maybe this dream is going to tip toward a nightmare.

"Get your pathetic ass up!" he yells, and shoves my shoulder.

I move closer to consciousness, and wish I hadn't. My head feels like a shaken soda can about to explode. I'm drooling, my neck is bent at a painful angle, and my eyes are welded shut.

Adam keeps badgering me to get up. I should face what I've done wrong. *What have I done wrong?* But right now breathing without getting sick is taking my entire focus.

"Is that how you want to do this?" Adam asks.

I listen to him stalk away, then I hear the faucet run in the kitchen before he stalks back. This can't be good.

"Are you sure?" That's Ali's voice—his superhot girlfriend. "You'll ruin the couch, Adam."

"Already ruined," he says.

Forcing my eyes open, I see him standing over me with an ice bucket. I shoot off the couch, but it's too late. The entire bucket comes down on me. The cold shock stops my heart. Every muscle in my body goes tight.

"What the hell, Adam! What was that for?"

Water drips down my arms and chest and puddles at my feet. I peel off my soaked shirt and drop it in the bucket.

"What was that for," he repeats. "Is that a serious question, Grey?" He sets the bucket down. "Are you *really* asking me that?"

In the foggy morning, the living room has a blurred, gauzy look, but my brother's immune to it. In his tailored sport coat, white-button down, and dark jeans, he looks sharp, like he has his own personal hi-def photo filter. Even his hair, which he's been wearing longer since he started dating Alison, is styled perfectly. Ali stands beside him in a tight red dress and tan heels. Way hot. Together, they're like a living Burberry ad, except classier.

"What are you guys doing here?" I'm still trying to make a full adjustment from dead asleep to freezing and awake. "I thought you were coming home Wednesday." They were in Colorado for a long, long weekend.

"I had to come home early for work," Adam says. "It's this crazy thing mature adults do."

That begs for counter on what "mature adults do," but this doesn't feel like the time. "Right."

"What the hell did you do to your head?"

"Tequila shots. Five, I think." He's giving me a funny look, so I reach up and touch bare scalp. "Oh, you mean *this*. Titus and I shaved our heads last night."

"Then someone *drew* on them with *Sharpies*?" Ali says.

"No, we did that ourselves. We wanted to beat people to it, so we drew skulls on our skulls. Funny . . . Right?"

Ali fights a smile.

Adam looks like he wants to choke me. "No. Not funny. Are you *blind*? Can you even see what's happened here?" He gestures around him, at the living room.

Finally, I do start to see.

His house is ridiculously swag. At the end of a private cul-de-sac right on the sand in Malibu, it's mostly glass, leather, and expensive wood from Bali or Nepal or something. It oozes style, sexiness. It's the kind of place that's all over home decorating magazines, and what you'd expect from a guy who starts successful businesses as casually as he drops into a wave on a surfboard. Except his house looks a little different this morning.

A girl in a short black skirt is asleep on the leather chair to my right. Nice legs. A coating of party debris—cups, crushed chips, peanuts, and beer cans—covers the coffee table and floor. Over on the kitchen island, heaps of liquor bottles, beer cans, Solo cups, and—what the hell is that? A person? Okay. Someone's asleep on the counter. That's bad.

Floor-to-ceiling windows give me an unobstructed view of the patio, which is crowded with more passed-out people. Four lucky girls took the chaise lounge chairs, and they're huddled under . . . *shit*. That's Adam's comforter. On the deck, more people, piled up like it's a refugee camp, and . . . *oh, man*. Is that homeless-looking dude wearing Adam's blue Armani?

It's only then I notice I'm not looking through glass. The door is gone. Just . . . gone.

"What happened to the glass door, Grey?"

In a flash, I remember what happened and cringe. This isn't

going to go well, but honesty's the only real choice here. "It's in the trash. We were dancing and it got crowded. The dancing got, um . . . Enthusiastic? And the glass broke. But I cleaned it up. No one got hurt."

"How would you know, Grey? How could you *possibly* know that?"

No blood? No police report? No ER visit? Not good answers. Adam's not waiting around for one, anyway.

He disappears down the hall and comes back a minute later with a shirt, which he throws at me. "Put that on. And pull your goddamn shorts up."

Whoops. I'm almost giving Alison a look at the family jewels. "Sorry, Ali," I mutter. I shrug into the shirt and tie the drawstring on my basketball shorts.

Ali gives me a quick smile back. "It's okay, Grey."

"Walk." Adam motions toward the hallway. "Let's see what we're dealing with."

What happens next is a tour of the house, Adam leading, Ali and me following. A damage assessment, basically. There are cups all over the place. Crushed chips. Spills. I mean, the mess is pervasive. It's everywhere. But there are highlights, for sure.

In Adam's room, we discover six people asleep on his bed. Four girls, two guys. In his bathtub, which is padded with towels, we find a couple—not so asleep. In my room, there are no people but somehow Adam's stationary bike is on my bed, which makes me laugh, which is the wrong thing to do, judging by the dark glare my brother gives me.

The weight room looks bad. Another broken window. The theater room looks worse. His fancy TV has some kind of drink splattered down the screen. Or, actually, that could be puke.

Adam sends people home as we move room to room. Ali peels away and comes back with a trash bag. It breaks my heart a little when she starts to pluck cans and cigarette butts off counters and floors.

"Ali, here. Let me do that," I say, taking the bag. We're back to the living room now, and everyone is gone. The house is empty except for the three of us.

Adam stands in front of the missing glass door, the Pacific steel-colored behind him. He looks from me to his beautiful girlfriend, who's picking up party funk in her dress and heels, his expression going through a cycle—exasperation, anger, and disappointment.

And I finally get it. I screwed up. Big time.

"It was just supposed to be the guys in the band," I say.

It's the truth. With Adam and Ali gone, I had my band, Welkin, over to practice last night. Which was what we did for a few hours. We sounded amazing; it was one of our best jam sessions to date. Maybe our best.

That's what got me so fired up—kicking ass. Feeling like something special was happening, like I was born to be the front man of a band—and not just any band. *This* one. These guys, who'd showed up in my life by accident. A few months back, they lost their original singer to appendicitis for a couple of weeks. I'd only partied with them before, which was how they heard me sing. I was drunk off my ass one night when Titus strummed the opening riff to "L.A. Woman," just messing around, and the spirit of Jim Morrison possessed me.

Their original singer lost his job that night.

And I became a difference-maker.

Welkin's a hundred times better with me. And they've become my saviors. I was drifting before they came around. I mean, I always knew I could sing. I've always loved it. I just never knew I'd love to sing *with a band*. Because of them, I've discovered that I love performing. They've given me direction, a dream: land a contract with a record label. And after last night's practice, I felt *unbeliev-*

ably inspired and positive we'd make it happen. So when Titus, my lead guitarist and best friend, asked if he could invite a few people over for some beers, I said sure. When Shane, our drummer, asked the same thing, I said definitely. How could I say no to Emilio and Reznick?

An hour later, a hundred people, almost all strangers, filled the house. And this morning-after disaster is the result.

Adam shifts his weight. "I don't care what it was *supposed* to be, Grey. I don't give a shit."

"Adam," Ali says, her eyes pleading with him to calm down.

He sighs and gives her a small nod back, like, *Okay, I hear you.*

That actually worries me, the effect she has on him. Ali is the sweetest girl I know. She's great for my brother. The first girl he's been serious with in years. But I wonder if she's moving *in*, which'll probably happen soon, if it means I'll have to move *out*. I don't want to move out. He was my brother before he became her boyfriend. I need him more than she does.

Adam slips out of his sport coat and looks for a clean place to set it down. There isn't one, so he slings it over his shoulder. "You're paying for all this."

I knew that was coming. "Okay. I have a gig in about a week—"

"No. You work for me now."

"What, like, a real job?"

"Yeah, Grey," he says, sharply. "Like a real job."

A wave of dizziness rolls through me. What are my options? He lets me live here. He's always been there for me. Always. And I trashed his place. Completely. I can't say no.

I adjust my grip on the trash bag in my hands. "Okay. I'll work for you. But only until this is paid off."

He rolls his eyes, which I don't understand. I just told him what he wanted to hear, didn't I? "Ali, do you mind calling a cleaning service?" he says.

"No problem. I'm on it."

"I've got it, Adam," I say. "I'll clean all of this up."

"No, you won't. You'll pay for the cleaning service, because your new boss wants you at work on time. Get your ass in the shower. We leave here in ten minutes."

I head for my bathroom, sure of one thing. This arrangement? Me working for him? Not a good idea.

Chapter 2

Skyler

*J*ust call me the yes girl, the go-along girl, the one who can be counted on to dive in first, ask questions later.

Tattoo my high school boyfriend's name on my ankle? Of course. What could go wrong?

Six days at Burning Man with a dude I just met? Sure. It's an adventure.

But this, I think, as I look in the bathroom mirror, might be my last impulsive hurrah.

Because this morning, I have pink hair.

At first, it scares the pee out of me—like one of those horror movie moments where a girl looks in a mirror, and a completely different person looks back. Luckily, my brain fills in the missing pieces as I lean in and examine my new look, a gift from my best friends Beth and Mia, who talked me into it last night after my million-and-tenth complaint about needing a change.

It's a change, all right. One in a series initiated over the last six months.

Step one, completed last week: break up with my semi-boyfriend-person Brian, who is absolutely sweet as vanilla but just doesn't make my strings quiver, if you know what I mean.

Step two, planned for today: take the six months of acting lessons Beth talked me into for a trial run with a real-life audition.

Step three (apparently): pink hair.

I have to admit, the color is somewhere between adorable and alarming, which suits me. Not quite cotton candy, not quite flamingo. It punks up my bob and gives my usual pale skin a rosy glow.

I brush the pink strands back from my face and decide I can live with it—at least for the few weeks it will take to grow out. Unless I get a part in the movie that's going to make Beth a star. I don't care what it is; I'll take "third cocktail server from the left" as long as it pays a few bucks. Anything to keep the lights on and help me get my second cello out of hock.

Beth comes into the bathroom and stands behind me, resting her chin on my shoulder. "What do you think?"

"I'm not sure," I tell her, mostly to bust her chops. In reality, I'm starting to love it.

"You wanted to do something different," Beth reminds me. "And you have to stand out from all the other BLTs who'll show up today."

"BLTs?"

"Blond, leggy, tan," she says with a cheesy smile. "You'll see."

"Well, I'll definitely stand out," I say. "Assuming my acting's on par with my hair."

"I've seen you," Beth says. "You'll get something. They won't be able to resist your look."

"Here's hoping," I say. "I've got until the end of the month before they put Christina up for sale."

"I told you I'd get her out of hock for you," Mia says from the next room. The walls are thin as tissue around here, so we don't even pretend our conversations are private. "Beyonce's lonely."

True. My poor acoustic cello's just standing in a corner of my bedroom, missing its electric buddy. Turns out that a couple of club gigs a week and busking on the streets of LA—a city where no one *walks*—does not a rich girl make. Christina is the only thing I own that's worth more than a few bucks, but it slays me to think of her gathering dust in some pawnshop.

On the other hand, there's no way I'm borrowing more money from Mia or anyone else.

Beth wraps a pink strand around her finger and holds it up to the dark skin of her cheek. "What do you think? Should I go for it too?"

"I think you're perfect the way you are," I tell her. And she is. Gorgeous high cheekbones, wide-set brown eyes, perfect glossy black hair—chemically straightened into submission for this role. "You ready for your big day?"

She pushes back the shower curtain and turns on the water. It takes about ten minutes to warm up from tepid to less tepid, but we're in a drought in California and can't waste a drop, which means a *lot* of cold showers. Then she strips out of her t-shirt and underwear and puts on a plastic shower cap.

Usually, I'd tease her about how ridiculous she looks, but something in her expression stops me. Something I rarely see there: doubt.

"What's that look?" I ask.

"What look?"

I wave my hand in front of her face. "That one."

She climbs into the shower, so her voice comes back to me muffled by two layers of vinyl, which are probably leaching fumes into the tiny bathroom and curdling our brains.

"I'm worried they're not going to cast me now," she says. "Lead's white."

"Are you kidding me? They're in love with you! That Brooks can't stop salivating."

"Oh, I know. Directors always love me. Everyone does."

"So, what's the matter? You're in, and you know it."

"I thought so until they cast the guy."

"Who's the guy?"

"Garrett Allen."

"Don't know him."

"He did that thing with the magical library, remember?"

I think I do—vaguely. Mia and Beth can deconstruct a film to shrapnel, but usually it's the soundtrack, more than anything, that stays with me.

"Looks like the guy's a shoe-in for a Spirit Award this year," says Beth. "And he's, like, twenty-four."

"Well, that's great," I say. "It helps the movie, right?"

"Right."

"And when you get the lead part, that'll mean even more attention for you too, right?"

No answer.

I poke at the shower curtain, and she yelps. "Right?"

"I really don't know," she tells me. "They cast these roles on type. Like who looks good with who. When Jon Ayers was in the lead, I had it nailed. He's a big guy. Part Hispanic. We had mad chemistry."

"Well, just go and have mad chemistry with Garrett."

She snorts.

"What?"

"Nothing. Let's just say I'm not his type."

"Well, *be* his type," I tell her. "You're an actor. Anyone who can't see how beautiful and talented you are is a dumbass, and these guys are *not* dumbasses."

"That's true," she says, and cuts off the water.

"Who's not a dumbass?" Mia asks, peeking around the doorway. Her dark curls fill the narrow space like her own personal storm cloud.

"Beth's worried she won't get the part now that they cast some-one else as the male lead," I explain.

"You'll get the part," Mia says.

Beth rolls her eyes and wraps up in a towel.

"Seriously," Mia insists. "They used you for the teaser. They al-ready *see* you in the part. And your acting kicks ridiculous amounts of ass. You light it up in there, Bets. I promise."

"*And* your best friend is Assistant Director."

"Well, *Second* Assistant Director," Mia says. "Which I think was really just Adam throwing me a bone so I wouldn't follow him around, keening."

"That Adam Blackwood could throw *me* a bone anytime," Beth mutters.

"We're getting off-topic," I tell them. "Come on! I need this. I'm seriously down to seventeen dollars and a couple of drink tickets. I don't want to have to go home to Lexington and teach music lessons. Please don't make me."

Mia squeezes my shoulder. "Chin up, Sky. Beth's going to kill it. You're going to score at least a speaking part. I'm going to AD my ass off, and it's going to be magic and sparkly unicorns for all."

She leaves.

"See?" I say, grinning. "Magic and sparkly unicorns for all. It's been decreed."

"Well, as long as it's been decreed."

"I think you're just nervous," I tell her. "Like your dream is so close to coming true you don't want to jinx it. But you'll see. It'll be just like Mia says. You'll rock the lead. I'll rock whatever job I can get. You'll become a great big star. And I'll get my cello back and serenade you on your worldwide press tour."

Beth laughs. "Way to dream big, Pinkie."

"Always."

Chapter 3

Grey

*A*s soon as we get in the car, Adam's on the phone with Brooks, his college buddy who's also the director and co-producer of the film he's funding. While Adam's more of a high-tech and financial wizard, Brooks knows everything about the film business. He's been working at the big studios for years, with the last two at Lionsgate. They're a good team. A motivated person could learn a shit-ton about The Business by listening to them. That person's not me.

As he drives and talks to Brooks, I pull the ski hat he forced me to wear down over my ears and recline the seat all the way back, trying to get some sleep.

At the Coffee Bean in the Country Mart, Adam parks and shoves a fifty-dollar bill into my chest, jarring me awake.

"Get something for Brooks too," he says, pausing his conversation. "Triple latte."

I hop out of the Bugatti and jog into the coffee shop. There's a small line, so I settle in to wait, folding the bill in my hands. Half and then half again. Smaller and smaller until it won't fold anymore. I grew up with money. Adam and I have the same entrepreneurial, restaurant- and bar-owning, deal-making dad. I have no desire to start a business, or open a restaurant or a bar, or make a film. Maybe I took after my mom. Who knows? All I know is that I want to sing. I want to make music, pure and simple. Every night, if I can.

I glance at Adam, idling in the parking spot right outside, drawing looks from everyone in the coffee shop. I also don't want to be the guy who has to jump out for a coffee he can't even afford to pay for. Maybe this job thing will be all right.

I'll work in the mailroom or something. Keep making coffee runs for my brother. Earn a few bucks during the day, and sing at night.

I can live with that.

Adam stays on the phone with Brooks until we're both walking into his fancy office at the new Blackwood Entertainment studio complex, where Brooks is waiting. They shut off their phones at the same time, preparing to continue their conversation face-to-face. Brooks rises from the leather chair in front of Adam's desk, takes his coffee, and frowns at me.

Brooks works a sort of hobo-cool look: clothes a little baggy, hair a little shaggy. Everything is designer label, but slouchy. Adam's opposite, basically. Though he's a filmmaker, Brooks looks like he'd be comfortable with a paintbrush in his hand and a cigarette bobbing from the corner of his mouth.

"Gotta say I'm surprised to see you here," he says, shooting a questioning look at Adam.

"He trashed my place," my brother explains.

"*I* didn't do it."

"So he's working for me now."

"Only until I can pay it off."

"Which is going to take months, you realize that."

I shrug, knowing I'll be able to pay him back faster. Welkin will have a record deal come April. A month, tops, and I'll be out of here.

Brooks looks from me to Adam, his grin going wider. "This is going to be entertaining." He narrows his eyes, peering at me. "What did you do to your head?"

I pull the cap off, showing him my Sharpied, shaved head.

"Nice." Brooks lets out a boom of laughter. "Must've been some night."

"Still nothing?" Adam slides behind his desk, slipping back in work mode.

In the elevator up here, while Brooks was apparently answering another call, Adam told me they have a crisis to solve. Some kind of audition or casting problem that he and Brooks needed to fix ASAP before he can get me set up. I sit and prepare to wait it out.

"His agent finally called. He's not going to make it," Brooks says, dropping into the other chair. "He was doing some intensive spa treatments. It's his typical M.O. when he gets ready for a new project. I guess he tried a deep-tissue massage and got a crick in his neck."

I cross my arms. "Is 'crick' an actual word? Like in the dictionary?"

"Yeah, it's an actual word," Brooks says. "And it's also the reason we're down a leading man for the day."

Adam sighs. "That's a hell of an expensive crick. We have a studio full of potential leading women in Studio B."

I slide out of my chair, because I have *got* to see this.

"Grey," Adam says.

I slide back.

"There's only one option that I can see," he continues. "We'll burn too much money and time if we don't go through with the audition. We need to find someone else to read his part for the day."

"Agreed." Brooks checks his watch. "And we have to do it fast."

As they discuss trying to get a stand-in actor here within the next hour, I reach for the script on Adam's desk and flip through it, looking for zombies or blood. The script, something called *Bounce,* disappoints.

"What's this about?" I ask, waving it in the air.

Adam looks at me. "It's a remake of a classic novel."

"Jane Austen," Brooks adds. "Emma's one of the most beloved female protagonists of all time. We've beefed up the comedy aspects. Brought a dating service into the storyline to make it more contemporary and tie-in with the Blackwood brand."

Sounds boring as hell, but what do they care what I think? "I hooked up with a girl named Emma a few weeks ago at a Foster the People concert. At least, I think that was her name. We didn't talk much."

Brooks shakes his head at me and Adam gets them back on track. There have to be half a billion actors in this town, but these two are acting like it's a lost cause. I mean, shit. Just go to the nearest café. I guarantee a hundred percent of the baristas are actors. With nothing else to do, I pick up the script and flip through it some more.

"Why are there so many words if it's a romance?" I say. "Isn't it pretty simple? Boy meets girl. They get it on. End of story?"

I'm talking to myself, since I'm the only one listening to me. "I mean, why do you need all this?" Opening the script to a random page, I read, " 'Emma. Beautiful Emma. I've loved you forever. I was born to love you. I've been here all along. I was just waiting for you to see me.' " I scowl, reading her reply, and then laugh when I read a little further. "*Seriously?* They *kiss* after that?" I drop the script back on the desk. "Tripe, bro. Utter tripe. You need to get a better writer, because if that's . . . if that's . . . if this is . . ."

Adam and Brooks are both staring at me intently. I feel like a mouse in an open field under the eyes of a hawk. And another, slightly more disheveled hawk.

"No," I say, dropping the script. "No freakin' way. I'm not an *actor,* Adam."

"You are today," he says, rising from his chair.

"I can't do it. I've got a crick—"

"No, you don't." He gives Brooks a slap on the shoulder. "Get everyone ready," he says. Then he's standing over me. "Let's go, little brother. You're needed over at Studio B."

Chapter 4

Skyler

*B*eth wasn't kidding. Blond, leggy girls with perfect tans occupy every square inch of seating space in the temporary waiting area of the production office, which basically looks like something Ikea coughed up after a rough night. And since most of the girls are super tiny, the ratio of butts to seating is pretty impressive.

On cue, they turn to look at us. Some give me warm, complicit smiles, like "here we go again," which makes me feel like a big fraud since this is all new to me. Most put up blank faces and then turn back to their lattes, their cell phones, or their weird little scripts, which Beth tells me are called "sides."

Suddenly, I'm extra grateful for the pink hair, if only so I can tell myself apart from everyone else. Though I'm definitely built more like an old-timey milkmaid than most of these girls, with fleshier arms and more junk in the trunk, due to my steady diet of bar food.

Totally okay in my world, of course. Drunk musicians don't judge, and neither do my cellos.

"Gonna need a shoehorn to wedge ourselves in here," Beth says, chewing her lip and surveying the room. She's giving off a weird jittery energy, which isn't like her. But then, I realize, I've never seen her at an audition before.

I'm nervous, too, but mostly because I don't want to make an ass of myself. And I really, really need a job. I don't want to go home to Kentucky to prop up my mom or fill in for my wandering dad.

It's a wonder I even became a musician, given the example he set. Rarely home. Rarely in touch. Maybe it had to do with the allure of it all, those glimpses I'd get whenever I'd tag along to a show, watch his sticks flash over the drums. Maybe it was the music that filled the house whenever he was around, telling me our family was whole again—at least for a while.

I don't know. I only know that whatever I do, I'll never let it make me abandon the people I love. I'll never make other people clean up my messes or take care of my responsibilities. Which is why I'm here today.

"I think there's a gap over there by the window," I say and start in the direction of a low tufted sofa with one free end. "You can sit on my lap."

We wind our way around the room. Beth seems to know half the girls here, and she stops every few feet to give out hugs. At this rate, it will be summer before we reach the damn couch.

"Look for someone with a clipboard," Beth tells me, picking up on my frustration because she's spooky like that. "We need to check in and get our pages."

"Okay." I look around but spot zero clipboards. I *do* see that what seemed like a homogenous mass of blondes has coalesced into something a little more diverse. A smattering of brunettes. Another couple of African-American girls. Even a redhead with a pierced septum and a trendy leather harness belt over a flowered dress.

Damn, someone else is gunning for my quirky minor character gig.

I decide to peek out into what I assume is a hallway and push through a heavy door that, instead, takes me outside onto a narrow gravel path running along the back of the building. Beyond is an expanse of brittle grass and scrub, which slopes up toward the highway where cars and trucks spew exhaust.

A younger guy, maybe eighteen or nineteen, whirls on me, throwing his arm behind his back like I've caught him with a baggie full of 'shrooms or something. He's hunky—as in substantial, tattooed and pierced, with a shaved head covered in some kind of crazy design.

Skulls, I realize. Weird.

"Jesus Christ," he says. "You scared me." He pulls a cigarette from behind his back and takes a drag before crushing it under his boot.

"Sorry." I keep the door wedged open behind me. Fanning away the smoke that wafts in my direction, I say, "I was just looking for someone with a clipboard."

He spreads his hands and gives me a grin that I'm sure makes panties spontaneously combust. "No clipboards here."

The dude's got large, rugged features but they're pretty somehow, too—thick black eyebrows, a straight nose that's just a couple of degrees shy of perfect, and full lips with a sharp upper bow. I think about music, about how sometimes unexpected notes align to make a perfect sound. It's like that, somehow. Only with a face.

"You one of the actresses?"

"Sort of."

"Sort of?"

"I mean, yes. I'm auditioning. You?"

He shrugs. "Indentured servant."

"Wow, I don't come across many of those anymore. How quaint."

"Yeah, that's me. Quaint."

His eyes are an amazing light-filled blue-gray. Like no color I've ever seen. If he was older, he'd intimidate the hell out of me, with that body and those looks. Another few years, and he's going to own the world.

"What happened to your head?" I ask. "A sign of your servitude?"

He gives an embarrassed grin and rubs his scalp like it's covered in Braille and will provide an answer. "Partied too hard and fell asleep first."

"Well, it could be worse. Your head could be covered in penises."

"Yeah, skulls are probably better."

"Probably."

Something about this guy makes me edgy, though I have no idea what it is. Maybe just the sheer size of him. Or this wiry energy he puts out, like a stick of dynamite waiting to be lit.

I don't really have time to ponder that, though. I need to get back inside and find a clipboard. Preferably attached to a person who can tell me what the hell I'm supposed to do.

"Nice hair, by the way," he says. I feel flattened by his gaze, but it's hard to tell if he's mocking me or sincere. And then I get annoyed because he's just some kid, and he's got me feeling unbalanced.

"Another late night decision," I tell him. "But at least I was sober for mine." Which is mostly true.

His features shadow, and he stoops to pick up his cigarette butt and thrust it into his pocket. "Your loss."

"No doubt."

We stand for a moment, this strange combative energy between us, like a wind that's blown up out of nowhere.

"Okay," I tell him, after a few seconds of awkward silence. "I'll leave you to your lung polluting. Have a nice life."

"Oh, I'll see you again real soon," he tells me, and there's that grin again, only less flirtatious. Also less sincere. "You'll be reading with me today."

"What?"

"Surprise."

"Very funny, but I'm reading with Garrett Allen."

"Nope. Even funnier. Garrett had some kind of spa accident. He's got a *crick,* whatever the hell that is. I'm his stand-in."

Shit. An image of Christina being thrown into some random minivan flashes through my mind, and I want to cry.

"Well, okay then. Guess . . . I'll . . . see you in there." Yeah, buddy. Take *that.*

"Looking forward to it," he says and fishes another cigarette out of his pocket. They don't seem to come from a pack. Instead, it's like his pocket's some weird dispensary of loose cigarettes.

I head back inside, and for a second I contemplate finding some way to lock him out of the building. Or dye my hair back to blond so he doesn't know it's me. Then I remind myself that he's just a kid. He's not making the big decisions. I don't have to worry about him.

Beth's waiting for me right inside the door. She's talking to Mia, who, hilariously, turns out to be the person with the clipboard.

"Well, shoot, where were you?" I ask.

Mia arches a brow. "I've been here. Where did *you* go?"

"Wrong turn," I tell them and flop down onto the sofa. I wish I had my cello with me, though it's probably not appropriate audition-wear. I just miss the weight of it against my legs, the feeling of knowing what to do with my hands.

"I got us checked in," says Beth, who hands me pages. "Want to run these lines with me?"

"Sure."

"Turns out Garrett is down for the count," she says, cheerily. "Maybe I'll have a shot at this, after all."

"Of course you will," I tell her.

Now I'm just not so sure about myself.

Chapter 5

Grey

It's eleven thirty by the time Brooks calls me into the studio. When I see the set inside the soundstage—a living room with a couch and chairs, lit up under bright lights—my stomach twists. In front of this, beyond the reach of the spotlights, is a table where I see my brother and a few people I don't recognize—an audience of one row. That makes me even more nervous. Until I remember I don't give a shit.

"You ready?" Brooks asks me, pushing floppy hair behind his ear.

He's amped up, eyes intent, his forehead a little sweaty, and working a ponytail that's only about fifty percent successful.

"Oh, yeah. Totally ready. I've been preparing for this moment for years."

"Where are your sides?" he asks, ignoring my sarcasm.

I know I'm missing something but I lift my arms up, showing him my sides.

"Your *script,* dipshit."

"Oh. I left it outside." Where I was smoking cigarettes, which I bummed off one of the sound guys, Saul, just for something to do.

People say being on set is boring as hell, and they're right. After an hour of waiting for other people to do God-knows-what, I want to climb out of my skin. The cigarettes were a dumb idea. I don't smoke, and now my throat feels raw. That's probably the last of my smoking days, right there. I have to protect my voice.

The only upside of smoking was seeing the girl with pink hair. She was something. Great style. Great body. Great everything. Really, really cute. I'm used to seeing beautiful women. LA is over-flowing with them. But she had something special. I look around for her again, but there are no girls in the studio besides Mia, who's been rushing around all over the place like the building's on fire. She's leaning over Adam at the moment, pointing at a paper in front of him.

"I'll get you another one," Brooks says. "Mia, can you—"

"I'm on it," she says, popping up. In two seconds she's handing me a fresh script, like she can telepathically identify every problem that needs to be fixed.

"Thanks," I say.

"No problem." I expect her to rush off again but she stays with us. "We're all set, Brooks. Anytime you want to start."

"Great." He looks at me. "Here's how this is going to work. First, we're screening the actors in the next room."

Mia raises her hand. "That's my job. Step one."

"We'll evaluate there," Brooks continues, "and send the actors we think have the most promise in here to read with you."

This isn't what I expected. I expected dozens of beautiful women waiting in line for me.

"You're quality control?" I say to Mia. "Then I'm trusting you. Only send the hot ones through."

She lifts an eyebrow. "Right."

"The lines you'll be reading—" Brooks takes my papers and starts flipping through them, searching, searching. After a second, Mia lifts them from his hands and turns to a page. "Right here."

"That's them," Brooks says. "These are the lines you're reading, but the important thing is to just stay relaxed, go with the flow. If you make a mistake, don't worry. This is a test for screen presence. The cameras won't even be on you. Just give these girls something to work off. Oh, and wear your ski hat. Your head's really distracting. We cool?"

Brooks levels an anxious look on me. Over his shoulder, I see my brother watching me. This whole thing, me reading lines for this audition, is sort of hilarious, but Brooks and Adam really have been working toward this for years. I can suck it up for a morning and try to do this right.

"Sure, Brooks. I've got this." I take my papers and sit on the couch under the lights.

Mia comes over and attaches a microphone to my t-shirt.

"What's this for? I thought there weren't going to be cameras on me."

"There aren't going to be."

"'Kay." She leans down right in front of me, trying to get the microphone on, and she's wearing a low-cut blouse so I appreciate the view.

"Roxanne's your first," she says.

"Actually, that ship sailed a long time ago."

"Ew, Grey. Focus?"

"Right. Roxanne."

Mia shakes her head before she leaves, like she can't quite figure me out.

There is, of course, more waiting. I'm getting hot under these lights. Hot and bored. So I take the mic and start singing "Roxanne" by the Police.

I hear a few laughs. Saul, the sound guy, pulls his headphones away from his ears. "Hey, kid. You got a really good voice."

I'm about to thank him when I see the first girl making a beeline toward me. She stops like she hits a force field, and makes a sharp turn to face the tables where Adam, Brooks, and Mia sit with a few other people I don't know.

"Roxanne Marguiles," she states, like an inmate sounding off.

"Okay," Brooks says from the darkness. "Whenever you're ready."

Roxanne walks over and sits next to me on the couch. She's wearing a bow tie, which I've never seen a girl wear even though this one is feminine, red and pink, and her platinum blond hair is perfectly smoothed, not a hair out of place. It might actually be a wig. She's also sweating so badly her makeup's running.

"Hey, I'm Grey," I say, offering my hand.

She clears her throat. Looks at my hand. "Start," she whispers.

"Oh. Okay."

I look at the pages and read the same dumb lines about *I love you, Emma, you're everything, Emma* that I read earlier. I'm proud of myself for managing to deliver them without too much sarcasm.

Then I look up, waiting for Roxanne-slash-Emma to hit me with her amazing lines back. But she just blinks at me with watery blue eyes and clears her throat. "Can you start over?" she whispers. "I forgot my lines."

"Um . . ." I look around, but get no help from the twenty people in the room who actually are in this line of work. "Sure."

So I read them again. Maybe a little more sarcastically.

Here we go. Roxanne's turn. I look up, ready for them.

Her eyes are filling with tears. She's about to cry, but then she gives me a wide, wide smile, which shocks me for a second because she has adult braces—*a lot* of them—and I didn't expect that. I had no idea.

"I am *so* sorry," she stage whispers. "I forgot them again!"

I hand her my stack of pages. "Do you want—?"

"No!" She puts her hands up, like I've just offered her monkey brains. "I couldn't. I'm a *professional*."

She's still whispering. I don't know how she's missed the fact that we're both mic'ed up *and* Saul is on a ladder, holding a boom mic over us.

"Can you start over?" she whispers. "Just one more time?"

Oh, hell no. Jesus. What the hell do I do now?

Fortunately, Mia comes over. "Roxanne," she says, guiding her off the couch like she's an eighty-year-old woman, "we'll try again a little later, okay? Nothing to worry about. Everyone gets nervous."

I shake my head. Somebody ought to just tell her. She's in the wrong line of work.

After Roxanne comes Sheila, who manages to read her lines, but with a lisp. Cute, in all honesty, but cute like a three-year-old. Then comes Amanda, a brunette knockout. Her breath smells like onions and garlic. And corpse. I almost puke when she leans in and speaks her lines. Then comes Molly, who has no visible afflictions. She's decent, in fact, but has no spark. No soul. No . . . style.

Two hours pass this way. I'm sweating under these lights, and I'm getting more tired by the second. I ask for breaks. Brooks, Adam, and Mia take turns shooting me down. This couch is my prison.

I learned the lines the first time I read them, so I make a few paper airplanes out of the script pages and try to peg Adam with them. That gets boring. So I make up a song and call it "Emma-Love." It's decent. People clap when I finish singing it.

Then I hit a wall. My hangover shows up and it's rude. It has a bad attitude, my hangover. By lunchtime, I feel like I'm dying. I get half an hour to raid the craft services table, then I'm back on. My energy's completely gone, so I start napping on the couch during the three-to-five-minute intervals between reads.

The p.m. hours drag past, even slower than morning. This was never fun, but now it's torture. My band's practicing tonight. I tell Adam I need to be there. That I won't miss it. But around six o'clock, I'm still saying that I fucking love Emma and always fucking have.

"I'm done, Adam," I say, after the thirtieth girl who looks the same and sounds the same. I lie back on the couch, closing my eyes.

"No you're not, Grey."

"Feel free to go off script if the mood strikes," Brooks says.

They're getting desperate. I don't think they've found a single girl they like. I know I haven't. They want my help in drawing these girls out, but I've nothing to give. "Must. Go. Home."

"One more hour," my brother says.

"Can't. I hate Emma, Adam. I really do. I *hate* her."

A nudge on my boot surprises me. "Hey. Could you scoot over?"

Lifting my forearm, I force my eyes open though they want to slam shut. And then they don't. Then I'm suddenly wide-awake, because what do you know?

It's the girl with the pink hair.

Chapter 6

Skyler

*T*he kid gives me the sleepy-eyed look of a sloth on Thorazine and slowly, really slowly, straightens his massive frame, scooting up and back against the arm of the sofa. There's a lot of him, filling the space. Broad chest and thickly muscled arms, long legs that spill everywhere. Giant pair of scuffed-up motorcycle boots that look to be the size of my forearm. I need him to at least make a pretense at some life here, or I'm sunk.

"Told you I'd see you again," he says, and gives me a sly grin. "Didn't get your name before. I'm Grey. Blackwood."

No.

Really?

Shit.

"So, you're Adam's—"

"Servant. Like I told you outside."

"Brother," Adam answers from behind a long table about five feet away. He and the others sit there with ramrod postures, like the panel at a parole board hearing. I can tell this guy, Grey, is working every nerve today, not just mine.

I take a deep breath and then another. The only way out is through, I decide, so I sit next to him. "I'm Skyler," I tell him. And then I smooth my skirt and glance over the pages because I have no idea what I'm actually supposed to do.

Paper rustles, and I look over to Mia, who gives me a sympathetic smile. "Why don't you start us off, Sky?" she nudges. "Start with, 'What did you come to tell me, George?' "

I nod, look over the script again, only it's like one of those anxiety dreams where words turn to squiggles and slide off the page. I can't find the line. I don't know what I'm doing. My heart doesn't speed up but makes these giant thuds in my chest—*boom, boom, boom.* Like someone's using a battering ram on my sternum.

Grey sits there, looking at me with this crooked smile on his face. That grin again. The one that says it's all just fun and games to him. I want to strangle him, but I make myself settle down, home in on my desire to wake him the hell up, make him pay attention.

Magically, the words reassemble themselves on the page, and I start. "What did you come to tell me, George?"

It sounds angry, but in the waiting area, I'd imagined delivering the line in a way that spoke of weariness, resignation. Emma's lost her chance at love, and all she expects from George is further confirmation of that fact.

Grey starts, but it comes out in one mumbled rush. *"EmmabeautifulEmmaI'velovedyouforeverIwasbornto—"*

"Whoa." I put up a hand. "Hold your horses."

His eyes go wide. "What's wrong?"

I look at the others, and the two I don't know—one man, one

woman—whisper to each other. But about Grey or about me, I don't know.

"I mean, it was a little fast, don't you think?"

"Do it again, Grey," Brooks says. "Give the girl something to work with."

"I thought you said it doesn't matter."

"Well, it matters to me," I tell him. "Kind of a lot."

He gets a chastened look, like a little kid, and goes from hard-edged to sweet in the blink of an eye. Then his expression reforms, and he shrugs. "Sorry," he says. "I'm not feeling great."

"No problem." But it feels like I'm losing control over everything here. This moment. My life.

A vision forms in my mind: me, hauling my lone cello onto a bus, bound for Lexington. Me in my little attic bedroom, listening to my parents argue as my brother's three kids run screaming around the house. My sister-in-law, Jordan, is military—deployed to Afghanistan for a fifteen-month tour.

They all need me. If I go home, I know I'll never leave again.

But if I stay, I can figure out a way to help *and* have a life. My own.

I look over at Mia, sending "help me" vibes her way.

"I've got an idea," she says, brightly, and gets up from behind the table. "Why don't you guys stand up for this?"

She looks at Brooks. "I just think it might change up the energy a bit. What do you think?"

"Good idea, Mia," he says. "Up you go, Grey."

He sighs and gets up, planting his boots like he's about to take a punch. Stuffing the script into his pocket, he tells me, "Go again."

Part of a tattoo peeks out of the neck of his t-shirt, a wing of some kind, along with a tendril that traces along the hollow beneath his Adam's apple. It looks like a vine or a branch. I can't tell, but I have an irrational desire to see the rest of it. It's like when I was a kid and took cello lessons. It used to drive me crazy to wait for the teacher to turn the page on my music. I wanted it all there in front of me. All the notes.

"Sky?" Mia prompts.

"Sorry. Okay." I'm blowing this so majorly, but at least let me get out the lines.

I take a step toward him, look into his eyes, and just let everything else go. "What did you come to tell me, George?" This time, it comes out the way I'd imagined saying it. World-weary and skittish about what I'm going to hear.

"Emma. Beautiful Emma. I've loved you forever. I was born to love you. I've been here all along. I was just waiting for you to see me."

He's not an actor, but he puts something into it this time. There's depth there and a rich timbre in his voice that weaves its way into me.

I glance at the sides and then back at him. "Don't be ridiculous. You don't love me. You told me yourself. I'm a phony. I meddle too much—"

He laughs, the perfect note. "You *do* meddle too much. And you get it all wrong, most of the time."

"*Most* of the time?" I smile at him, allowing myself—allowing *Emma*—to soften just a bit, to allow in the first stirrings of hope.

"Okay, I'm sorry." Grey comes closer. He reaches for me, a little tentatively, and the warm strength of his hands on my shoulders surprises me. It's like being anchored by a tree with roots that spread to the center of the earth. "You get it all wrong *all* the time. Because you're in the wrong line of work."

"But, I love what I do."

"I mean setting people up. Trying to fix people who don't need fixing."

"I don't do that."

"Emma."

"Do I do that?"

He nods.

"But it's just that . . ." I try to conjure all the innocence of my childhood, all of the magical thinking that kept me content in my room with my cello, while my family fell apart around me. "I want everyone to be happy."

I don't want to look away from him, but I don't remember my next lines. We're crackling now. I feel it. And I feel the focus of the others—Mia, Adam, Brooks—feel the weight of their attention on us. The room doesn't have that drowsy quality anymore. It's vital now, sharp and alive. *I'm* sharp and alive, becoming exactly what this moment needs in a way that sends prickles of euphoria through me.

"Like I said," Grey continues. "Wrong line of work."

"Well, what then? What should I be doing?" I can't bring myself to look at the words, but I think they're mostly right.

"Making *yourself* happy, Emma."

I move in even closer, because they've arrived at a moment that's been sealed for them since they first met. "I want to be happy," I say, and it comes out small and intimate, meant just for the two of us. Luckily, we're mic'ed. "You could . . . you could make me happy."

"How? Just tell me what you need."

"This . . ." I smooth my hands over his broad chest and tilt my face up to his. For a second, I wonder if we're meant to go through with it or if someone's going to stop us. And then I realize I don't want to stop. I can't. It would be like ending Beethoven's Fifth without the last movement.

He hesitates for a moment—his expression a little surprised, eyes a little dreamy—and then he moves his hands to my waist and pulls me up against him.

Is this happening?

I run my tongue over my lips, moistening them.

His face moves closer, eyes searching, asking for permission.

It's happening.

I lace my fingers around his neck and urge him the rest of the way.

"Kiss me, George," I whisper. "I want to be happy."

He leans over me. Close. Then closer. Finally, his lips touch mine, and they're warm and firm, softer than I'd imagined. They part, gently, and his mouth moves against mine, and it's liquid and hot and restrained but generous all at once.

I press into the kiss, sinking into it in a way that feels like floating. His breath tastes like smoke and mints, and I should break the kiss at some point, but it's too good. It's all too perfect. I'm myself, making out with a guy I just met in full view of a bunch of people, but I'm also Emma, finally allowing in the love I've denied myself, the love I've spent my life trying to secure for others.

Grey's tongue slips over mine, and that's probably not right, not strictly *professional*. But it sure *feels* right. I meet it with my own, fleeting, teasing—

And then I become vaguely aware of Brooks yelling, "Cut!"

Chapter 7

Grey

*B*rooks says, "Cut," but cut is not what happens between me and this girl. *Detach* is more like it. A slow, slow detach, like we're made of Velcro. Even when we finally part, I can't look away and neither can she. We're locked in, still staring at each other like the scene isn't over.

Her big hazel eyes are a little wide, surprised, and her cheeks have a pink color, just a few shades lighter than her hair. She's blushing. And I feel like I'm on fire.

I can't believe I just kissed her. *Kissed her* kissed her.

What was I *thinking*?

I wasn't thinking. I got wrapped up in the scene and just *did it*.

"Okay," Mia says. "Guys, that was . . . wow. That was really good."

Damn right it was.

Skyler finally looks away, toward Mia. "Was it?"

"Amazing, Skyler," Brooks says. "Amazing. Give us just a minute," he says, then there's the buzz of excited, hushed conversation over on that side of the soundstage.

"I think they like you," I say.

"Oh." She smiles. "Thanks . . . That was okay, don't you think?"

"Really good. You can sure fake-kiss."

It's a completely asinine thing to say. Dickish, probably. But I'm a little shaken up by what just happened. This girl just took me down to the mat. She made me forget we were in a roomful of people. She made me forget everything.

And she was *acting*.

That just ain't right.

Skyler frowns. "Thanks, I think. So can you."

I shrug. "I don't fake-kiss. You just caught me off guard when you did the line. The *kiss me* one? You sold it." I wink at her. "You're lucky we're not doing this again, or I'd be ready and bring the hea—"

"Okay, guys," Mia calls. "We're going to do this again."

"What?" we ask at the same time.

"Since we asked you to stand, we didn't have all the cameras set. And, um . . . you know, multiple takes are part of this whole movie-making deal. Right, Sky?"

"Right," Sky says. Her lips turn up at the corners in a daring little smile. "What do you say, George? Ready to bring the heat?"

"How hot can you handle it, Emma?"

She doesn't have a chance to answer because we're given the cue to start.

We're braver this time around, the energy between us more intense. When Skyler puts her hands on my chest, I grip her wrists, pulling her close.

When she says, "Kiss me, George, I want to be happy," I kiss her. But happiness isn't exactly what I'm going for. I told her I would bring the heat, and I do. I crush her soft curves against me and sweep my tongue against hers. I kiss her like I would if I were into her. Like I would if she were *my* girl.

Skyler makes a little sound and rises up onto her toes, angling her head. She tugs me down, tugs me closer, and lust spears through me.

Maybe I brought the heat, but she's giving it right back.

I take her face in my hands. She arches her back, presses against me. We make a few more adjustments to compensate for the height differential, and we're legitimately, seriously, very hotly *kissing*.

She tastes cool and sweet, but her scent is warm. Floral and soft, like a nap in the sun.

I'm pretty sure we're supposed to be stopped any second, but it doesn't happen. Then I wonder if we're supposed to stop ourselves? That's never going to happen, not from my end. But now I'm thinking too much and that makes me draw away a little, and it makes her draw away a little, and that keeps going until we finally part.

I still don't hear anyone say "cut," though, so I keep her close, and look right into her eyes. "You feel that, Skyler?" I say, studying her pretty face. Her skin is flawless. Her lips are full. "Me and you . . . we're meant to be."

I have a vague recollection of reading lines to that effect earlier, but I don't know. I never made it past the kiss, or even to it, with any of the other girls so I'm just winging it now. Ad-libbing, as Brooks said. Freakin' Robert De Niro all of a sudden, because I don't want this to end. I don't want to let her go.

For the first time since we started the scene, Skyler seems to snap out of character. Her gaze narrows, a small line forming between her eyebrows.

Then Brooks says, "Cut!" and she steps away.

Mia rushes up. "That was a-mazing! You can *act*. I had no idea, Sky! You've been holding out on me!"

"Well, I—" Skyler glances at me. "I'm kind of surprised, too, actually."

"We talked it over after the last take," Brooks says, walking up. "We want to bring you back for a read with Garrett Allen to see how you work with him. I already know you two are going to be awesome, though."

Adam comes over, and Brooks keeps talking about how great it's going to be to get Sky with a real actor. How if she could manage to have so much presence with me, a pro is going to make her absolutely shine.

Skyler frowns a little as she listens, shooting glances at Mia, who gives her small smiles of encouragement. I can tell she's overwhelmed. I notice her fingers are drumming against her leg. She's nervous. I know my brother sees everything, all the unspoken communication, too. And I wonder if he's on to me. On to how freakin' frustrated and confused I am right now. That I'm here. That I have to listen to this discussion about how great it'll be for Skyler to kiss this other guy, Garrett Allen. To see if he's better. To see if *they* have chemistry. Hearing it feels unexpectedly shitty, like I just found out the girl I kissed has a boyfriend. I didn't ask for any of this. All I did was throw a party that got out of hand. But it's the capper on an all-around messed-up day. I'm really done this time.

I catch my brother's eye. "I'll be at the car."

Then I'm outside, striding across the parking lot, the last rays of sunlight fading from windshields and mirrors. It's not until I reach the Bugatti that I realize something. I didn't call her *Emma* in that last line, my ad-lib line.

I used her name.

Skyler.

Chapter 8

Skyler

I float out of the audition space, like I'm one of those air hockey paddles, cushioned on a micron of air. Everything feels gauzy and surreal.

Who was that girl in there? The one who so completely *owned* that part? The one who kissed—*and kissed and kissed*—a boy with no concern for the others standing around, watching?

I know her from my nights playing cello, slapping out a ferocious beat, playing with the audience, feeding off them, giving back my all. But I've never felt that without Beyonce or Christina in my hands. Without the movement of my bow across strings, my body given over to its real purpose.

And the guy, Grey.

Jesus.

I bring my fingers to my lips, which still seem to vibrate, faintly, from the feeling of his mouth on mine. The power of him surrounding me, sweeping me hard against him. So confident for a young guy, but with skills like that, he's right to be. The minute I breathed him in, felt his solid arms around me, I was a goner. We could have been in an audition or in the middle of a burning building, it wouldn't have mattered.

It was only when he said my name, called me "Skyler" instead of "Emma," that it all came crashing back around me. Then it was some tattooed kid and me. A kid who can kiss like a champ but who left in an inexplicable huff.

They want me to come back again, to audition with Garrett. The *lead*.

Me. With my weird pink hair and my six months of acting lessons.

I open the door to return to the waiting room, and, of course Beth is the first person I see. She gets up from her chair, smiling and hurrying over to me.

Me, I realize, with a best friend who really, really, really wants this part.

Shit.

She looks beautiful—and nervous from sitting here while dozens of girls have their moment. Including me.

"You survived!" she says and sweeps me up into something that's half a hug and half a weird little jig. "How'd it go? Tell me everything!"

"Don't you want to hear about it later, after *your* audition?"

She makes a *pffft* sound. "Hell no. I can't wait that long, and I think I'm the last name on the damn call sheet."

"Guess they're saving the best for last," I say, and it comes out sounding guilty and insincere, though I totally mean it.

"Well, duh." She grins and leads me over to a low armless sofa that no doubt has a name like Flüg or Snöerkl. The scratchy tweed upholstery makes my skin itch, but that may be the adrenaline still coursing through my body, screaming for release. I don't want to sit. I want to jump up and down or pound my cello or spin around atop a mountain, singing.

Beth smiles with anticipation. "So . . . ?"

"Well, it actually . . ." I start, but the words stick in my throat. If I tell the truth, will it seem like I'm bragging? Or taking something from her? She works so hard at this. And I just waltzed in and nailed it.

Still, what choice do I have? I'm not going to lie to her about it. Just because it was amazing doesn't mean I'm getting a big part. And it sure as hell doesn't mean I'm getting *her* part. "It went . . . incredibly well."

Her eyes widen, and her whole face brightens with excitement. "Really? Damn, girl. Now you *have* to tell me everything!"

"I just . . ."

What? There's something so indescribable about it all. "I just *felt* it, you know? Like I got in there, and I did some lines with Grey . . ."

"That's the kid?"

I nod. "Yeah. Adam Blackwood's brother."

"Well. Shit."

"Yeah, but he's—" A really good kisser? Kind of adorable? "He was okay," I say. "I mean, he gave a good reading. He was, um . . ." I search my new acting vocab. "Present."

"Well, thank the Lord for small mercies," she says. "How much did they make you do?"

"All of it?"

"Really." She sits back and looks at me. "The whole scene?"

"Yeah, I mean everything we had. All the pages."

"How many times?"

Another girl gets up for her turn, and I watch her cross the room. She's got long V-shaped sweat stains under her arms, and has wrung her script so hard it's barely recognizable. Poor thing.

"Just . . . I guess, twice. But that's because they made us stand the first time, and they didn't have the cameras set in the right place, or the lights. So they wanted to do it again."

She nods. "To make sure they got it on camera."

"Yeah." I feel exhausted suddenly, like I do at 4 a.m., after I've dragged in from a show and from breakfast with the crew.

"Tell me how it felt," Beth says.

"Bets, it felt fucking awesome."

She laughs and sweeps me into a hug, so solid and lovely I want to cry with relief. "That's my girl," she says. "I knew you'd kill it."

"And I know you will too!" I tell her, and hug back, hard.

Other girls come and go, and then Mia enters the room with her clipboard and a giant smile on her face. "You're up!" she says to Beth.

"Finally!" Beth gets up, and brushes off her clothes, takes a few deep breaths, and shakes out her shoulders and arms to loosen up her body. "How'm I looking?"

"Like a star."

"Guess we'll have a couple in the family."

I don't know about that. But I call after her, "Break a leg."

She gives me a jaunty wave and follows Mia into the room.

The door shuts, and it's just me in this cavernous waiting area. Now I've got my choice of Flügs and Snöerkls, but I just want to curl up right here and send good intentions through that doorway. I want Beth to have what she wants. I want her to become the star she was absolutely born to become.

And I want to feel more of what I felt during that audition. Suddenly, I'm hungry for it.

Somehow, there has to be a way for us both to get what we want. Right?

Chapter 9

Grey

"How did the audition go?" Alison asks as she sets a takeout bag from our favorite Mexican restaurant on the kitchen table.

Brooks and Alison eat over so often, we all have our regular spots.

Adam's house doesn't look like a war zone anymore, but it still doesn't look normal, either. Some of the furniture, rugs, and paintings have been taken to special cleaning services, so the rooms feel empty. With so much cleared out, Adam decided to have the house painted, so a lot of what stayed behind is now in the garage or the storage pod on the driveway, where they'll be until the painters finish up later this week. And there's a piece of plywood where the new, custom glass door will go. If I didn't know any better, I'd say it looks like he just moved in.

I spoke with Ali a little while ago. Insurance is paying for the sliding door, the television, and a few minor repairs, but the total for the deductible and for the various cleaning services is twelve thousand dollars.

It's hard to believe that much damage happened in one night.

The further I get away from what happened, the worse I feel about it. I guess I thought I'd just run the vacuum after the party and wipe down the counters, and that'd be it. I didn't expect all this upheaval.

As we all take our spots around the table, I tuck into my tacos. All I want to focus on right now is getting this food into my stomach. I feel like I could eat everything on the table and still be hungry.

"The auditions were great." Adam grabs a burrito and takes the chair next to Ali. "We've got three strong contenders. Funny thing is, two are Mia's friends. Beth Pierce and Skyler Canby. Sky was a real surprise. Apparently she's only been acting for a few months."

So much for blocking out the day.

Ali smiles. "That's great! Mia must be so happy for them." She dips a chip into the guacamole. "Wait—I thought I'd heard that Skyler was a musician?"

I pause with a taco halfway in my mouth. "What?"

Skyler plays *music*? I don't have the mental power I need to process that right now.

"Yeah," Ali says. "Mia told me about her once, but I can't remember what instrument she plays. I just remember it was something I didn't expect."

Excellent. Now I'm picturing Skyler playing the flute while wearing pale pink lingerie. Weird image. Awesome and weird.

"She should be acting full time," Brooks says. "Maybe soon she will be. The girl's got serious talent." He looks at me. "Did you get a chance to talk to her?"

I stop chewing, wondering if I missed something. Was I supposed to interview her while we were acting? I swallow. "Well, we said the lines from the script. And we kissed. You were there."

Ali's eyebrows go up. "Kissed?"

But Brooks forges ahead and says, "That's okay. It doesn't matter. I'll spend some time with her tomorrow and get a good read on her. But if she's a friend of Mia's, we can count on her being smart, dedicated, and responsible. I already like what I saw."

Suddenly, I'm not loving a lot of things.

Brooks's comment, *doesn't matter,* felt patronizing. A brush-off. And the emphasis on Skyler being *smart* and *responsible* and *dedicated.* I mean, shit. Is she perfect? Because, yes, she was hot. And cute. But no one's freakin' perfect.

My nerves are shot today, no question, but all this focus on her sterling qualities isn't helping. It's making me feel pretty small—like a guy who Sharpied his scalp and threw a party that caused twelve thousand dollars' worth of damage.

Then there's the other comment Brooks made. *I already like what I saw.* What the hell is that supposed to mean? Pervert. I mean, I did too, but he's the director. Not right.

The conversation moves on without me, since it's all about the film. That's how it's been around here for months. Prior to the movie, it was all about the Blackwood/Quick merger that closed at the start of the year. Adam and Ali have merged, all right. I bet they *merge* every night.

Sometimes I wonder why I feel so much drive to get my music career going. Things can't get going fast enough for me. Then I look at the people in my life, and I get it. Overachievers, every one of them. Big time.

Which reminds me. I have to get to band practice.

"Thanks for dinner," I say, tossing my wrappers into the trash.

"You're welcome, Grey," Ali says.

I grab my keys from the hook. Adam gets up and follows me to my truck. I know what he wants, so I beat him to it.

"Ali already told me about the charges," I say, climbing in. "I'll pay them. I'll work for you and pay you back. Could you just get off my back about it?"

Adam catches the door, keeping me from shutting it. "Mom called. She was looking for you."

The blood drains out of my face. I didn't expect that. I just . . . didn't. Seems today is the day for me to get sucker-punched left and right. Still, it's been two weeks since Madeleine's last call. And here I was starting to hope she'd forgotten about me.

"*Your* mom called, Adam. Not mine."

"Come on, Grey." Adam gives me a pained expression, shaking his head. "Don't be an idiot. It's been eight months. When are you going to talk to her?"

I can't believe it's been that long, but it's true. I left home—home in Newport—in August. "Like you said, Adam. It's been eight months. What do *you* think?"

Adam doesn't move. He just watches me, waiting, I think, for guilt to work its magic on me. I know he's concerned. He's stuck in the middle of this situation between his mother—who raised me since I was five—and me. We have the same father, so the difference between us all stems from the maternal blood. His mom is a socialite; mine was a gold digger.

Is, I correct myself.

She still is.

"What happened between you two?" Adam asks.

"Gotta go." I pull the door shut. Then gun the engine and peel out of the driveway.

I sing my ass off on the way to Venice Beach. I just think of a tune and start putting words together and sing.

It's the only way I know to stop thinking.

"So?" I ask the band. "How'd that sound?"

We're in our rehearsal space—a soundproofed two-car garage a few blocks off the beach. It's Titus's sister's boyfriend's garage. Dirk charges us a grand a month, but we have a bathroom and enough space for our amps, guitars, the drum kit, a mini-fridge, a small table that seats four, and even a beat-up couch.

Titus walks over to the fridge. He grabs five beers and lobs them around the garage, keeping one for himself. "Amazing, man. Totally awesome."

Usually he has blond dreadlocks, but since we shaved our heads last night, he has a huge third eye on his forehead, moving into his hairline. It's not a bad look. It suits him. He's a visionary with melodies.

Two hours ago, I walked into the garage and hummed the tune I'd been playing around with on my drive here. Titus had it worked out in minutes. The rest of the band fell in with some guidance from the two of us. Now we have something real to work with. The song is coming together.

"There are a few things I still want to play around with," Titus says, "but it's great, bro. Really, really great."

"Agreed." Shane nods. "Badass song, Blackwood." His drumsticks are still tapping out the song's rhythm.

I nod, relaxing a little.

This is the first song I've ever written. I'm pumped. I had no idea it was going to be such a rush, this part of being in a band. Who fucking knew I'd love writing songs?

It came to me on the drive. I kept thinking about what Adam said earlier.

Sky was a real surprise.

She'd surprised me too. I hadn't expected to kiss her. Twice. And the phrase stuck with me. By the time I reached Venice, I had a few verses and an idea for a melody for "Surprised by the Sky."

Skyler inspired it indirectly, but the song isn't about her. It's about being so out of it, you don't even recognize the sky—the very thing that's everywhere. That starts at the ground, at your feet, and goes on forever. It's about making a mistake so big, it changes what you see and breathe and even move through. It's about being lost and not knowing how to *stop* being lost.

I've basically written the opposite of a love song, but it's cool. I love the song already, and it's only going to get better. And it's not like Skyler will ever know she inspired it.

"Let's play it again," I say.

We spend another hour and a half working on getting the song right. By the time we wrap it up at midnight, we've got it locked in.

Pizza is ordered. Beer and whiskey start flowing. Everyone texts their girlfriends to come over. Except for Titus and me. We're the single guys. So we hit the whiskey pretty hard, especially when the girlfriends arrive, because there's nothing else to do.

The guys are happy with our rehearsal tonight. I can tell, because Reznick sits at the table with Renee, and Emilio and Evie are there, too. They pass around a joint. Weed's not my jam, but to each his own.

Nora's practically straddling Shane, who's sitting on one of the amps.

"Whoa," Titus says next to me. We're witnessing some serious PDA.

We usually get the couch, which we call the Titanic because it's huge, grayish white, and starting to do a nosedive on one side. It's so disgusting, Titus and I are the only ones brave enough to sit on it.

"Yeah, whoa," I say, passing him the whiskey. "Musss be nice."

"Seriously. That's why you gotta land 'em when you're young. Shane hooked up with Nora when they were still in the womb or some shit."

"So they're twins?"

"What?" Titus looks at me. Then it dawns on him, and he kills himself laughing.

After a little while, he joins the others at the table, but I lay back, feeling comfortably numb. I go over the song in my head, playing around with the lyrics. My voice is a deep baritone, and I have a natural growl in the lower part of my register. There's a perfect spot in this song to dig into that.

"Grey!" Renee yells at me from the table. "Stop being so antisocial! Come join us."

"I'm good."

"Do you want me to call Jamie?"

That's Renee's best friend, who I hooked up with last month over the course of a weekend when Adam and Ali went to Vail. I got some action. I love it when they travel.

Except when they come home early and bust me for trashing the place.

Damn it. Why did I *do* that?

"She's into you, Grey. She still wants you to text her."

"Wow," I say. It's my standard answer when I want to say *no* but shouldn't. Works every time. People don't know how to interpret it. It shorts them out.

Renee looks at Titus. "What does he mean, *wow*? Is that good?"

He knows my trick but gives away nothing. "Not sure, Renee."

I have no interest in getting involved with a girl I can barely remember. But I wouldn't mind a girl's company right now.

A soft body, sweet lips.

Shiny pink hair.

Yep.

Wow.

Chapter 10

Skyler

I drag Beyonce out onto the apartment's cramped balcony, to serenade the parade of random folks passing through our little alleyway on their way to Venice Boulevard. The night sky has a reddish hue, with lacy clouds drifting above the brightened windows of the surrounding buildings. Palm trees lose their dimension in the darkness, become flattened silhouettes in the amber beams tossed up by ground lights.

Sam, a homeless dude who's gathered up our recyclables for as long as we've been here, gives me a thumbs-up as I play the opening notes of "Say Something," letting the low sad notes fill and soothe me. He sways and I smile, and we lock into a moment together that almost—but not quite—settles my nerves. Still, I can't shake free of this feeling—like my insides want to fly away without the rest of me.

"Nice job, maestro," he calls. I smile and keep playing, watching him sway, his bags stuffed full of bottles that rattle their own tune as he trudges off.

My thoughts shoot out in every direction. Part of me feels elated, almost giddy, at how well the audition went. And that kiss. Grey pulling me against him, his mouth covering mine. It keeps coming back to me, over and over.

But then came the ride home. Mia chattering at us—nervous and excited. And Beth and me, awkward suddenly. Not *ourselves*. Her audition went well, too. Mia had only great things to say. She promised they'd want us both back, but that feels so weird. It should be *Beth. Only* Beth. She's the star, ready to rise. I'm the barista. The cute one behind the counter with three lines. I'm not a lead. I play the cello. I don't act.

Only I guess I do. Or at least that I can. And that is mind-boggling and exciting and terrifying all at once.

I move into "Bittersweet Symphony," a favorite of Mia's, though it always makes me wish I had a band, something that could produce the Verve's broad, sonic sound to prop me up as I play. Alone, it sounds even more plaintive and so, so sad, even when I kick it up to a harder rhythm.

My phone brightens beside me. Mom calling. I hit a weird sharp note and stop playing to answer.

"Well, he's off again," she says, after the hellos. *He* being my dad. "A European tour, whatever the hell that means. I don't know what we're going to do."

It's always the same. My poor mom, trying to hold things down on the horse farm she inherited from her parents. Mom, who has anxiety attacks in grocery stores. Who can be fine one minute and paralyzed the next. And my dad—never able to settle. Never able to just *be* in any place for long.

"I've got the road in my bones, love," he told me about a million times when I was a kid. And I always imagined it literally—like his bones and organs were actually overlapping highways that wove through his body, filling him with this endless desire to be somewhere else.

When he came home, it felt like Christmas. He'd bring toys and postcards, matchbooks from clubs all over the world. But while he was gone, everything dwindled. The food. My mom. It would all go from sunny to shadowed to bleak until he stepped through the door once again. And we never knew, not exactly, when that would be. When he'd come or when he'd leave again.

"You'll be okay," I say, lamely, hauling Beyonce back into my room and shutting the sliding glass door. I'm done for the night.

"How?" she asks. "I need help, Skyler. I can't do it again. Not this time."

I flop onto my bed, cramming a bunch of pillows behind me to settle in for a while. Part of me wants to rush in and tell her about the audition, to assure her that I'll be able to send money soon. That I can take care of her. But I don't know that yet, and I don't want to make a promise I'm not sure I can keep.

"What about Scotty?"

"Your brother's got enough troubles," she tells me. "Three boys and no mom to help care for them."

"Maybe he could pay you to take care of the kids?" I suggest. He's got a great job, and he gets some of Jordan's benefits. "They're over at your place all the time. Couldn't you help each other out?"

I hear a harsh exhale, which means she's started smoking again. Crap. She went a year and a half this time.

"I'm not going to ask your brother to pay me to watch my own grandchildren. That's ridiculous."

"But he'd be happy to, I'm sure. If you just asked."

"Can't you just come home, Skyler?" she says. "I'm asking *you*. Help me make something of this place. It could be just like it was when I was a girl, if I just had a little help."

"Mom, I don't know anything about running a place like that, and—"

"That's not true. You're so smart. You can do anything."

Anything but avoid this conversation, which plays out once a week at least, and a hell of a lot more often when my dad's gone.

"Mom, I have my music."

"So? You can still have your music in Lexington. You can do all of the same things here. Teach. Play clubs. It's no different."

"It's completely different." But I can't tell her how, not really. I can't say it's different because here I can breathe. As cruddy as things can be, as uncertain, it's all mine. My own solo project.

We talk at each other for a little while longer, neither of us really getting what we want from the conversation. It's almost painful not to talk about the audition, to rush in with the excitement of it all. But again I can't. Not until I know it will amount to something. And besides, she doesn't want to hear it. She just wants to be heard.

So, I stay on the line, and I listen, interjecting at all the appropriate places. I stare out at the deepening evening and find my fingers moving along to a song that begins to weave through my brain. Not a song I know. Something of my own creation. Something new and original that belongs only to me.

I enter the kitchen the next morning to find myself hug-tackled by Mia, who seems to be transporting her possessions to Ethan's one box at a time.

"You got it, Sky!" she exclaims, surrounding me with a tangle of springy flower-scented curls and very nearly knocking me on my ass. "I mean, you and Beth. And someone else. A girl named Lydia Weitz, but who gives a crap about her? You got it! I'm so happy! And it's crazy, isn't it? You and Beth, I mean. The two of you."

Ethan laughs. "Hey, Curls, maybe you ought to let Sky breathe a little."

He's sprawled at our little dinette table, his long legs and broad shoulders filling half of our dinky kitchen. It's a little distracting how gorgeous he is, and paired with Mia's ridiculous beauty, it's like they're some kind of perfect relationship sun that you can't stare at for long for fear of searing your retinas. More than that, you just *feel* the way they love each other beaming at you, so bright and intense. Just being around them makes me happy and nostalgic for something I've never had.

"I'm just so psyched!" Finally, she lets go. "I'm sure you'll get some part, which is great. We'll get to work together all the time!"

Even though there are three other perfectly good chairs available, she plops down on Ethan's lap and helps herself to a bite of his breakfast burrito, which, much to her chagrin I'm sure, is a little too complicated for her to dissect before eating—one of her favorite pastimes. "You really surprised them, Sky. And me. I didn't want to make a big deal of it in front of everyone. But you slayed it. You just brought so much to the moment. Like a buttload of heart."

"Thanks," I say, heading for the coffee. A buttload of heart feels like an anatomical impossibility, but I get it.

I pour myself a cup and try to get a handle on my emotions. I'm excited, though part of me wants to tamp down that feeling, to underplay it. Maybe it's because I'm happy but not really surprised. I *felt* the energy in the room. I knew I'd done something extraordinary.

"Did it feel awesome?" Ethan asks, giving me that laser-focused look I've come to identify as his game face.

"What? The audition? Or finding out about this?"

"Either. Both."

I wave a hand. "I mean, I guess the audition felt pretty good. It was . . . It was . . . unexpected like Mia said. Like I didn't know I had it in me."

"Well, I knew," Mia says, smugly. She slides the burrito in my direction. "Want some?"

"Hey," says Ethan. "That's mine."

"Like you didn't have two on the way over!"

"I know, but"—he smiles a sly little smile and whispers something in her ear that ends with "made me hungry."

"Sorry." She giggles and kisses a spot beneath his jawline. "Not sorry."

"Where's Beth?" I ask. "Did you see her?"

Something flashes across Mia's face. I can't quite read it. Concern, maybe? "Yeah. She just went out for a run. I told her before you got out of the shower."

"Was she . . . excited?"

Mia nods. "Totally. And she was . . ." She takes another bite and chews for a second. "She was super happy for you, too."

"Really?" Why can't I believe that? I know Beth wants good things for me. She's the one who got me into acting in the first place. But I try to imagine how I'd feel if Beth spent six months taking music lessons and then got called in for principal cello at the LA Philharmonic.

"Of course, Sky," Mia says. "How can you even ask?"

I shrug.

"What's bugging you?" Ethan asks in the same tone I imagine he uses on the little kids whose soccer team he coaches. It's direct and full of concern, which makes me immediately want to blurt everything. Between the two of them, I stand not a chance in hell of keeping my thoughts to myself.

"I know it's dumb, but I feel like I'm taking something away from Beth. She's worked so hard, and I . . . I've literally been acting for like five and a half months. I don't know a frickin' thing, and she's been training since she was fourteen."

"And she's amazing," Mia says. "She killed the audition, too. It's not like your talent siphons off hers. You know that."

I nod. "I know. But it doesn't seem fair somehow. I feel like I should bow out or something."

"You can't do that," Ethan says. "First of all, it's condescending."

"Ethan—" Mia starts.

"No, I mean it. If you pull out, it's like you're saying she couldn't get the part any other way, and you don't know that."

He has a point.

"I just can't stand the thought of competing with her," I say. "Especially not for something that means so much to her."

"Obviously, it means something to you, too," Ethan tells me. "Or you wouldn't have auditioned. Right? It's not only about the money, is it?"

Good question. I think about that moment with Grey, that feeling of strength and mastery, of taking possession of another person—Emma—and bringing her to life. It felt so good, like filling myself with sunshine. It made me feel almost the same way as playing the cello does—that pleasure of being good at something, of giving other people pleasure with my skill.

"No," I concede. "It's not all about the money. But—"

"No buts. Do you want it? That's the one and only question."

"Yeah," I say. "I want it."

"Then that's it. Not competing is a cop-out. It's beneath you, and it's not fair to Beth, either. You're in it. If you don't go all in, you're half-assing it, and you don't want to play that way."

"Jesus, Ethan." I look at Mia. "Is he always this intense?"

"Pretty much. And you know he's right. Right?"

I look at the two of them, and what else can I say? "Right."

Chapter 11

Grey

It's Saturday night. The guys in the band are all going to a show at the Whiskey a Go Go. And I'm still working for Adam.

This isn't a job. It's slave labor.

Granted, the past few days weren't terrible. On Thursday, Adam handed me the keys to the brand-new black Mercedes coupe I'm driving now and told me to take our costume directors, Bernadette and Kaitlin, wherever they wanted to go, which was mostly Beverly Hills. Friday was more of the same.

It was fine. Bernadette and Kaitlin like taking long lunches to talk through all their "wardrobing strategies," and I can always get behind food. I liked driving them all over better than reading lines all day. But I also felt like I was missing out on the real action back at the studio.

I did hear about the film every night at home, though. Brooks has practically moved back in with us. If he's not at the studio, he's parked at the kitchen table with Adam going over schedules and budgets and script changes, each a million times over. All they do is work. Adam even missed our standing Saturday morning surf session today to go over casting strategies with Brooks. Again.

I guess over the past two days one of the other possible-female leads came in to read with Garrett Allen for the role of Emma Beautiful Emma. Lydia something or other. And no one liked her.

Tonight is the next audition with Skyler and a girl named Beth at my brother's house. Adam and Brooks want everyone to feel super comfortable so they had this idea to cater dinner at the house and do the final reads in a more intimate setting. Apparently, Garrett doesn't drive and he just lost his assistant, so I got roped into chauffeur-mode again tonight. Hence the Mercedes and my bad attitude. I'm literally going to be fighting traffic both ways in this ridiculous car that's completely not me. But I guess driving around in a brand-new F-150 is beneath the famous Garrett Allen.

I climb into the Mercedes and commence hauling my ass all the way down to Brentwood. On the plus side, every hour I'm on the clock gets me closer to paying off my brother.

I'm almost to Sunset Boulevard, singing along to myself on one of our demo tracks, "Sing to You," a ballad, which always makes me feel like an impostor because I've never been in love, when the song cuts out to a sharp trilling sound. The screen in the console flashes with Adam's home number so I accept the call. I'm surprised to hear Mia's voice.

"Hi, Grey. Adam said you were swinging down to pick up Garrett. Can you pop over to my place—my old place—and grab Skyler, too? I came a little early to help set up and Skyler was in the shower. I totally forgot her car is in the shop when I left."

All I hear for a few seconds is: Skyler in the shower. Skyler in the shower.

"No problem. I'll get her. Text me the address."

"I just did. Thanks, Grey. You're a lifesaver."

I hang up and the music comes back up, but I turn it down.

Skyler.

A balloon is inflating inside my chest, like I have too much oxygen and not enough at the same time. I've developed some weird crush on this girl I only met a few days ago. I mean, she's a musician. She has pink hair. She smells like sunshine. And, shit. *That kiss.*

This is bad news. It's not going anywhere, probably. What do I have to offer a girl like her? Maybe when I hit it big. She won't think I'm a loser nineteen-year-old punk when I'm accepting my fifth Grammy. Yep. A couple of years, and I'll have a shot.

When the turn to Sunset Boulevard comes up, I sail right past it. Obviously, I'm going to get Skyler first. I keep singing random words. Occasionally, some of them make sense.

"Fire's hot when you're next to it. But you only burn when you get too close. I want to get too close to you. Let's make a love that burns."

I voice message myself the lines. There could be a lyric in there somewhere.

A little while later, I pull up in front of Skyler's apartment in Venice and consider honking, because ringing the bell might make me look like a chauffeur. But Skyler comes bounding out and the blood in my veins instantly becomes Red Bull, supercharged, fizzing.

She's wearing black boots, jeans, and a black crocheted top with lots of skin peeking through. With her pink hair pulled into a sleek ponytail, I don't think I've ever seen anything hotter. Nope. I'm sure. Haven't.

She opens the passenger door and leans in and we freeze for a second, looking at each other. "Hi, Grey! Thanks for getting me!

Where's Garrett? Should I get in the back because of Garrett? So he's not, you know . . ." She shrugs. "You know?"

She's nervous. I wish it were because of me. Then we'd be even. But I know better. This audition is probably the biggest opportunity of her life.

"We're getting him next. Front seat, then you can just hop back if you think it's best."

"Right, okay." Skyler slides in beside me, and her smell moves into the car—just how I remember it. Sunshine. Summer. Awesome. My body likes her smell. A lot. I want to say something to make her comfortable, but I'm going a little haywire with her scent so I focus on getting us heading toward Brentwood.

"Sorry about the driving confusion," Skyler says. "My car's been in the shop for a few weeks. I'm saving up for the repairs."

I think about that for a few seconds. I've never really had to deal with money trouble. My brother has my back. Even this thing—the money I owe him—I know it's about the principle more than the actual money. It's not just Adam looking out for me, either. I have a trust fund I could dip into. And if I ever *really* needed it, I know I could swallow my pride, choke it down, and go to my dad for help. I've wondered before if having family money makes me soft, or spoiled. Possibly? I don't know. I don't think about it much. I don't use my family money. Like . . . ever. But I know one thing. Having it definitely makes me lucky. It's a safety net, for sure.

"What's wrong with your car?" I ask.

"Well . . . Everything. It's a million years old. Like, from the Crustacean period. I think the only thing that actually still works is the key."

"Adam's making me drive this boat around for work. You should borrow my truck. It's just sitting in the studio lot." *Stop, Grey. You made the offer. That's enough.* "It's an F-150. Nice. Don't expect to parallel park it unless you have an hour or two, but it's new and safe.

You might as well drive it." *Shut the fuck up, Grey. Please.* "You'd actually be doing me a favor. I don't like the idea of it just sitting in a parking lot. Even if it's gated at night. After hours."

Finally, I manage to stop talking. I notice that small crease between her eyebrows. I've confused her. Because she's a stranger, basically, and I just offered her my truck. Pretty overeager.

"That's really nice of you."

Kill me. Now.

"Just think about it. So, you think we'll get to make out again tonight? 'Cause that was fun."

Skyler lets out a startled laugh. "Um, no way? And we didn't *make out*. We kissed."

"Really? Then what constitutes making out for you? I mean, what's the, like, literal line that needs to be crossed?"

"No line ever needs to be crossed between us, Grey. You're the producer's little brother. Are you even of legal age?"

"Low blow, Canby." I realize I just used her last name without her ever having told me what it was. But I'm not going to explain how I know it. *Two nights ago I swiped one of your headshots from the kitchen table and put it on my bedside, where it now lives. It's not stalking, I promise. Just trying to be good at my new job that I don't want.* "And, yes. I'm above the age of consent so you might as well educate me. Tell me. What's making out, in your view?"

"Okay. Let me think about this." She's quiet for a moment. "Making out is more melty."

"Melty?" I glance at her, and see her smiling. "You were lava in my hands."

"Warm. I was definitely warm. Not lava, though."

I roll my eyes. She's downplaying it. Physical chemistry is one thing we have going for us. Or against us. We've got it, that's the point. No doubt about it. Our bodies have the hots for each other. "Okay, melty. What else?"

"It lasts longer and is private. You don't have an audience for it. And it's not acted."

"I'm with you on the first three. But the last one?" I shake my head. "I'm not an actor. Maybe you are, but I'm not."

"Actually, I'm not sure I am, either."

I pull up to a stoplight, which gives me a chance to look at her. Really look at her. She's tapping her fingers on her leg, and she's blinking just a little too quickly, like she's trying to hold back tears. We just executed a huge emotional shift, and I'm not sure why. "Sky . . . Skyler. What's going on?"

"I shouldn't have said that. I didn't mean to."

"Why did you?"

"This is all so new. I didn't expect it, and I guess I'm just a little scared." She looks at me. "Grey, don't tell anyone, okay? I really do want this. I *need* it."

The light turns green, and I have to look back to the road. The way she said *need* makes me think of her broken-down car in the shop. The word had a dark kind of ring to it. It was a kind of need that's in danger of slipping backward. It's not fair, but I compare it to the way I always feel, like I *need* to sing. Like I *need* my band to land a contract. Those feel like leaping, reaching needs. Positive needs. But I know what the backslide kind of need feels like, too. I've been there. I was there eight months ago. Almost killed me, answering that kind of need. So even though it's not the same, I think I get it.

"I won't tell anyone, Skyler. And for the record, I think you're really good."

"Thanks. And thanks for listening."

I feel like I barely did. I want to listen to more. I feel like she's hardly said anything.

I think about how Mia and the other girl who's up for Emma Beautiful Emma are Skyler's best friends. If Sky is having these doubts, it must be tricky finding someone to talk to about them. I picture what it would be like if I told Shane, Reznick, Emilio, or Titus: *Not sure about our band, you know? Not feeling a hundred percent solid.* I know I could never say that to them. If I did, it could have a lasting, not-good effect.

"How was surfing?" Skyler's question surprises me. I have no idea how she knows I surf on Saturday mornings, but I learn soon enough. Ethan, Mia's boyfriend, came out with me this morning. It's weird how many of the same people Sky and I know. Ethan's been a regular at our poker nights for months. I finally convinced him to get out on the water with me. Adam was supposed to be there, too, but he ended up having to work with Brooks.

I make Sky laugh when I tell her how frustrated Ethan was trying to catch waves. I forget how much upper body strength you need until I'm out there with a beginner. And surfing is all bend and flow. Out there on the waves, it's about feeling the ocean the same way you feel music. Ethan surfed about as well as I could probably play soccer. Sometimes passably. Most of the time hilariously. Watching him tombstone—wipe out where his board jackknifed straight down into the water and sent him flying—was pretty much the best thing I've seen all week.

We're almost at Garrett's house, according to the GPS, and I don't ever want to get there. I want to drive around Los Angeles for the rest of the night, talking to Skyler about the definition of making out, and her broken-down car, and Ethan's epic wipeouts. Thinking about all the talking I won't be able to do is depressing, which makes me quiet. In the silence that settles between us, Skyler reaches for the volume control.

She turns it up just as I pull into Garrett's street.

Time goes into slow motion and three thoughts explode in my head simultaneously.

One, my demo is still playing. It's been playing this whole time, but I didn't notice because the volume was way, way down.

Two, Skyler's song that isn't her song is in this mix. "Surprised by the Sky." I see the future unfold: she'll hear it, know I wrote it because she inspired me even though it's not about her, add it to the you-can-have-my-truck comment, and then think I'm a legitimate psychopath stalker.

Three, she's going to hear my singing voice. This scares me more than being called a stalker for having her headshot. My voice is my truth. I don't care what strangers think of it. I only cared about what Adam thought before he'd heard me. If my parents and I were getting along, if I still cared what they thought of anything I did, I'd care about their opinion of my voice. Apparently, Skyler's in those ranks, too.

Weird. I barely even know her, but I'm white-knuckling it, not breathing. Me and the steering wheel. If the steering wheel were a person, it would be turning blue.

I pull into Garrett's driveway, realizing the playlist has circled back to the ballad.

Titus strums a twelve-string acoustic, playing the short intro before I come in. This is the only song he uses it for, but he swears the instrument has the perfect tone to match my voice on this song—a ballad that Shane wrote for Nora.

When I sing it, sometimes I try to think of what they have. I picture little things, like how Nora wipes Shane's face with a napkin when we order pizza. How Shane always rubs the base of her neck when they're close, and how she leans into him, like they share feeling. Maybe they really are twins. Or more than twins. One person, two bodies. I think of how every good thing that happens to the band—a great new song or practice or a booked gig—Shane looks at Nora first.

This song, in a way, is about the person who's always your *first*.

Other times, I think of my brother and Ali. How she's made Adam happy when I wasn't sure he ever would be again. Chloe's death almost knocked me down for him. But now there's Ali, and he's good again. Better than good. One person, two bodies. Two that make one.

I've tried to imagine myself in these words a few times before, but it never sounds right. When I sing it my way, love isn't some cloud you float around in. It's not pretty and safe and neat. When I sing it love sounds flawed and dangerous, but what else would it sound like from me?

My own mother walked away from me when I was five. She left me with my dad and stepmom and never looked back. If your own mother doesn't stick around, what girl ever will?

Enough, Grey. Shit.

I cut the engine, but the song keeps playing. The spare guitar intro ends, and it's me. I come in, and I realize right away, on the first lyric, that Rez put the Grey-version on this playlist. Not the prettified version I pilfered from Shane and Adam's experiences. And I don't want to know what Skyler thinks. Not of my voice, or how I'm making a mockery of a love song. How I sound like love is fucking painful, raw and dark and awful, because, really, that was *my* first. It was *my* first taste of love.

I jump out of the car. "Be right back," I say casually like my heart isn't bleeding through the speakers in the background.

Skyler doesn't even look up.

Chapter 12

Skyler

Grey didn't have to tell me it's his voice coming through the speakers; I'd know it anywhere. It's got this wicked, velvety rasp that just grabs you—more so in song, even, than in conversation. When Grey speaks, it's a glancing thing, the dip of a word or two into this gravelly lower register. In song it's . . . it's everything. It's him.

I try to home in on the lyrics, but I'm too swept away by the tone, which is pro-level good and filled with depth. So full of wounds and wisdom, which seriously steals my breath and makes me reconsider my impression of him as just a kid, albeit one who looks delicious and flirts like a pro.

I wonder what caused those wounds.

Under all the brittle brightness and swagger, who *is* he? What haunts him to make him sing like this?

After a while, I realize I've listened to a few songs, which makes me check my watch, which makes me realize we're due at Adam's in twenty minutes, which causes adrenaline to spike through me so hard it feels like my hair's going to lift off at the scalp.

It occurs to me to go check on Grey, which also means meeting my potential costar, something that sends another surge of panic through me. But what the hell, it has to be done, and I'll feel worse if I walk in late for everything.

Coaching myself to breathe, I get out of the car and head over to the front door of a bougainvillea-draped bungalow. I climb the stairs up to a small porch, feeling like an intruder.

Just as I'm about to touch the doorbell, a voice from nowhere calls, "Come on in!" and I jump like a cat, almost tumbling down the steps.

I look around and see a tiny camera mounted under the eaves, a speaker beneath.

Opening the door, I squeeze into a space that smells like fresh paint. Tarps cover the polished wood floors and drape over mysterious lumps that I take to be furniture.

"Don't mind the mess," says a man, coming into the room. "I just moved in and am on a mission to *obliterate* every trace of harvest gold and navy shag carpet that once defiled this gorgeous space." He shudders. "Thank God I'm a master at spotting potential, or I'd have run screaming from this place the minute my Realtor brought me here."

"Hi, I'm Skyler Canby," I tell him, wondering if he'll spot my potential or want to run screaming.

"I know. I saw your screen test. *So* good." He drifts closer to take my hand. "Though you're much more adorable in person."

But, really, *he's* adorable. Blue, blue eyes. Like *blue* to the nth degree. Wavy black hair. Gorgeous skin. Startlingly good looking, even by LA standards. With an elegant posture that makes me feel like I'm looking at a reincarnation of Oscar Wilde.

He gives my hand a squeeze. "Garrett Allen."

"You're beautiful," I blurt.

Oh, God, take me now.

He laughs, and it's a big head-back, white-toothed laugh. The next thing I know he's got me wrapped up in a big hug. "That is the sweetest thing I've heard all day."

Grey comes into the room, loaded down with cloth grocery bags stuffed full of food and a sleek black leather backpack slung over one shoulder.

"Is this everything?" It's clear from the look on his face that he doesn't know what hit him, but he sure doesn't appreciate whatever it was.

"Oh, yes, thanks." Garrett claps his hands together, giving Grey an appreciative once-over. "I'm such a diva about food, it's just easier to bring my own." He peeks through the contents of the bag, trots off for a second, and returns with a small container with some kind of jellied purplish thing inside. "Pickled plums," he tells me. "Believe it or not, they help with my asthma."

"Really?"

He nods. "I know the natural cure for *everything*." Circling behind Grey, he unzips and checks the contents of the backpack, zips it back up, and gives Grey a pat on the back. "I can't believe how lucky I am. A lovely potential leading lady *and* a strapping young personal assistant. Adam Blackwood knows how to treat the talent, that's for sure."

Grey's eyes widen. "A what now?"

"Personal assistant, silly," Garrett says, grabbing Grey by the shoulders and giving him a little shake. "As in one who assists my person."

Grey steps away from him, his expression clouding. "Um. No. Sorry. I think I'm just here to cart you over to my hou—I mean, to drive you over to Adam's place. That's all. I'm sure they'll find you a different assistant."

"Nonsense," Garrett says. "I want you."

"Why don't we move this discussion to the car?" I say, as politely as possible. I don't want Grey to upset Garrett. I *need* him in a good mood.

Everything feels in suspended animation. I'll get to stay in LA, or I'll have to go home. I'll get to rescue Christina from the pawnshop, or she'll end up in someone else's hands. So much rides on these next moments.

I must be registering my panic because Grey says, "Yeah, let's go." He tries to offer Garrett a smile, and it's impressive how utterly fake it looks. "We all set here?"

"Of course. Just let me get my wasabi peas."

"Tell me where they are," Grey says, and shoots a look my way. "Why don't you show Garrett to the car? I'll be right out."

"Well, they're out on the patio, I think," Garrett says. "I was marking up the script and got peckish. So, I think they're there. Or maybe on the desk in my office. Or—"

"I'll find them," Grey says. He reaches around us, dwarfing Garrett and me, and pushes the door open. Then he not so gently shoves Garrett outside. "Go."

Garrett smiles back at Grey, adoringly. "See? He's *perfect* assistant material. Sometimes, I really just need to be manhandled. That was Avery's problem. He couldn't say no, and I just ran all over him."

"Avery?"

"The last one. Not a disciplined bone in his body." He gives me a wink and a sly smile. "Though we *did* have our moments, believe me."

"I believe you," I tell him. I suspect it's impossible to be around Garrett without having moments. "Let's go."

I don't know what laws of physics Grey breaks, but we manage to get from Brentwood to Malibu in twenty-five minutes. It's possible there's a wormhole involved.

He thrusts the car into the driveway, coming a breath away from tapping the back bumper of Mia's Prius.

Next thing I know, we're a flurry of arms, legs, and gourmet food items, borne along in a wake of Grey's impatience. He hurries us through the front door, calling out a hello and impatiently snagging everything away from us.

"I'll be right in," he says. "Let me put this stuff in the dining room where Adam's got the food."

He directs us down a long hall, past a ridiculously huge and high-end kitchen, into a vast living space. A triple set of glass doors anchors one side of the room, with tall windows on each side and a black expanse of the Pacific beyond. One of the doors is marked by a taped "X," a couple of large-framed paintings stand propped against the wall, and it looks like a couple of pieces of furniture are missing from the room, based on the square impressions etching the thick-piled cream carpet. Maybe Adam's redecorating?

"Hello, hello," Garrett says, and everyone rises to greet us.

"You made it," Brooks says. He comes over to shake Garrett's hand and then bends down to give me a hug and a kiss on the cheek. His scent is nice—like fresh laundry and the sweet tang of a stream.

"Totally my fault," Garrett says, and casts a brilliant smile around the room. "I'm such a pain in the ass, I made poor Grey schlep a week's worth of groceries over here. My apologies."

"We do have food coming," Adam says, rising. "Enough for an army."

"Or just Grey, if he's hungry," Brooks says.

I laugh but feel unaccountably protective of Grey at the same time.

Then everyone crowds around us, and we do the whole hugging and cheek-kissing thing. Mia stuffs her giant head of hair in my face and gives me a world-class squeeze, but Beth's hug is fleeting, a little chilled, and my body starts up with the adrenaline again.

I want this. But do I want to take it from her?

"You look gorgeous," I say. She's in a simple gold A-line sheath that shows off her mile-long legs. Her hair's natural and curly, pulled back loosely to accentuate her sharp cheekbones, almond eyes, and insane eyelashes. I can't imagine a camera that wouldn't love to frame her in its lens.

"Thanks," she says, and I can tell she's feeling it. As she should. She's a goddess.

"Jesus, Adam," Grey says, coming into the room. "Are you expecting a hundred more people? There's a ton of food in there."

Adam grins. "That's Alison's doing. She likes to make sure everyone's fed."

"The whole block will be fed."

"This house *is* the whole block," Mia says, and it's true. It's big enough to fit, easily, four or five of our apartments inside.

We head into the dining room, where linens cover a couple of folding tables loaded end-to-end with food, including the contents of Garrett's grocery bags and backpack. I smile when I see that Grey's made a point of propping up the bag of wasabi peas between a plate mounded with short ribs and a deep platter of truly tasty looking tomato risotto.

Brooks hands me a plate and smiles at me. "Better eat up. We'll be working you hard tonight."

I laugh. "Oh, really?"

"Really. You up to the challenge?"

Not at all. Maybe?

"Of course," I say.

"Liking that attitude, Sky," he says and gives me a wink.

I smile, but I'm distracted by the fact that he used my nickname. How strange it felt but endearing, too. There's something about him that's a little dazzling. It's like he pulses with confidence and this kind of worldliness, like he's walked the earth for eons, even though he can't be more than a year or two older than me. I know I can learn so much from him. And he'll be easy to look at while I'm learning.

I look up to see Beth watching me and feel a flush of guilt, like I'm doing something wrong just talking to Brooks. Does she think I'm flirting? *Was* I flirting?

Grey piles food on his plate and just keeps on piling.

"Hungry?" I ask.

He grins and slides a head-sized piece of lasagna onto his plate. "Always."

"You can probably come back for seconds."

"Oh, I will."

"Where the hell do you put it?"

He gives me a wicked, hilarious grin. "Well, since you asked . . ."

I blush. "I get it. Your *spleen* requires a lot of sustenance."

"Yes," he tells me. "My really big . . . *spleen*."

Brooks watches us for a moment, his look penetrating but unreadable. He turns to Adam. "Hey," he says. "When you going to have your furniture back?"

"Soon," says Adam.

"What happened to your furniture?" I ask.

Grey's lips press into a somber line, making it clear I shouldn't have said anything.

"Oh, Grey had himself a party," Brooks says. "But he got carried away."

"*I* didn't get carried away," Grey argues. "Some dumbass people I don't even know did."

"Those dumbass people trashed the place," Brooks supplies. "And young Grey here is—"

"Cut the crap," Grey interjects. "You're three years older than me. Big deal."

"Hey," says Adam, quietly. "It's okay. Grey's taking care of it. It's all good. Let's focus on the movie."

It starts to come together. The missing furniture. The new glass door. All because of some party Grey threw. Now I get why he's Adam's "indentured servant." He's got to make good on the damage.

I feel a weird sinking inside. Disappointment that seems too intense and personal for the circumstances. I liked him better when I didn't know he was reckless enough to let his buddies trash his brother's house. Maybe Brooks is only a few years older than Grey, but they seem a world apart in many ways.

Brooks turns to me. "I really want to hear what you think about Emma. Who she is to you. Have you read the Austen?"

"No. I've read *Pride and Prejudice,* of course. And *Persuasion.* But never got to that one. You have, Beth, right?"

She nods. "*Emma*'s a favorite, actually." We take our plates into the living room. Adam pours champagne and beer, but sparkling water for Garrett, who tells us he's in recovery. We sit and chat about the movie, but I don't say much. I just watch the faces of the others. Grey is closed off now. His foot taps the floor, and the plate jitters up and down in his lap.

On the other hand, Beth's got the whole room in the palm of her hand. She and Mia tell a funny story about the time Beth disguised herself to go spy on an ex-boyfriend. She's self-deprecating but hilarious. I can feel the interest in the room start to flow in her direction. Garrett's got that same big laugh, just for her. That same twinkle.

Beth and I lock eyes at one point, and she gives me a smile that tells me everything I need to know. If I get this part, it will be because I worked for it. Because I'm the best person for the role.

I pick at my food, but it's hard to focus. I'm locked in, ready to be put to the test with Garrett.

I'm ready, I think. *Let's go.*

Chapter 13

Grey

*A*fter dinner, it's audition time.

Brooks decides Beth will go first, so he and Adam retreat into Adam's office with her and Garrett. They'll work through the scenes in there.

Mia and Skyler move to the patio. Ali shows up and joins, too, ready for some human interaction after pulling a long day at the horse rescue. The girls sit around the patio table, but I park myself on the railing and keep an eye on the waves, feeling like a third wheel. Not just because I'm the only guy. Everyone here . . . they're a few steps ahead of me in Life. They have careers. They've done things. Are in the *midst* of things. It's like they've all earned a few stripes. But, me . . . what have *I* done?

I don't know why Adam wants me to be here. To serve them

drinks? Hell no. I'm not going to be a driver, a personal assistant, *and* a freakin' waiter. Part of me wonders if my brother's hoping the productive energy from these upstanding young people will rub off on me. It's not that I think he's disappointed in me. It's more a feeling like he's waiting for me to do something. I just don't know what it is. I mean . . . I'm following my dream, and I'm working to pay him back. What else does he want?

For a little while, I half listen to the girls. Ali's got a new horse she's working with, a colt that everyone wants to go and see. But my mind wanders, and I find myself thinking of the guys, who're probably still over at the Whiskey. If I left now, I could still catch part of the show.

Seriously.

What am I *doing* here?

I glance at Skyler. With only a candle in a lantern for illumination, her pink hair looks almost white. She laughs at something Mia says and I see a glimpse of that tiny gap between her two front teeth that makes her seem so rare and real and likable. She's engaged in the conversation on the surface, but I know she's thinking about Beth's audition. Probably her audition, too. Her life could completely change tonight and I think it's scaring her. It's weird that I can guess what her thoughts are. Though I could be wrong. Maybe she's thinking about Brooks. There was definitely something going on between them earlier.

Skyler notices me, and we lock eyes. I wait for her to look away, but she doesn't. We stay that way for a second, then two, three, and I feel something travel between us, zipping back and forth and back and forth. A kind of energy, like we're communicating without words. Communicating something that's maybe even a mystery to the two of us. I don't know what it is, but it makes me want to grab her hand and take her down to the beach. It makes me want to wrap her up and hold her and touch her soft mouth with my thumb and tell her *you can do this*. Because she can. I'd watch this movie if Skyler were Emma Beautiful Emma. I'd own it.

Brooks and Adam appear at the glass door. I didn't even notice them walking up. The girls all stand, going quiet, like everyone's waiting for some major announcement. You can feel the tension in the air. I'm not sure doing the audition here helped anything. It might have been easier on Skyler and Beth if they'd just done this at the studio.

Brooks claps his hands together. "Okay, round two." He goes to Skyler, stopping right in front of her. "You ready?"

"Yes," Sky says, and leaves with him. Mia's not far behind them, slipping inside. Off to find Beth and see how her audition went, I'm guessing. Adam stays on the patio, though. He gives Alison a hug and whispers something in her ear. This isn't a rare thing, but for some reason, this time it pisses me off. I already feel like an outsider. And I *live* here.

"I'm out," I say to the Adam/Ali unit. I want to find out how Skyler's audition goes, but I'll just have to get the info some other time. I can't stay here any longer.

"Hold up, Grey," Adam says. "Ali, can you give us a minute?"

"Sure," she says, and heads inside.

Adam comes over to me, propping his elbows on the railing as he stares at the black void that's the Pacific. "I checked the surf report. Tomorrow's going to be a good day. Four to six feet at Nicholas Canyon."

"Cool, but I'm out. Go without me."

I don't know why I say this. Surfing with my brother's a thing I need in life. Like singing. But Adam bailed on me this morning. And I guess I want to return the favor.

"I know things have changed since Ali, and that I've been busy with Brooks on the film stuff, but—"

"You can do whatever you want, Adam. I just don't want to surf tomorrow."

"Okay, Grey. Fine." He glances inside.

"You should go." I know he has to get to Skyler's audition.

"I will in a sec. Grey, I was going to tell you this tomorrow morning, but since you're not coming, I'm going to say it now. Mom called earlier this week and—"

The night sky folds in on me, and my lungs stop working.

"Bye," I say, stepping inside.

"She's coming out here," Adam says, following me. "She'll be here tomorrow night. Said she wanted to be here for the beginning of production. She offered to book a hotel room, but I told her she could stay here. She's our *mother,* Grey. This thing between you needs to stop. I'm done being the middleman. The two of you are going to have to figure it out."

I want to run. I want to trash Adam's house all over again, but I make myself walk. I keep going until I get to my room and swing open the door, and I'm so raged up, so deep in my own head, I'm stepping inside before I realize there are two people already in here.

Brooks and Skyler.

Brooks. And Skyler.

Sitting on the edge of my bed, with stapled pages on their laps.

They're laughing. Mid-laugh. They both stop suddenly, stunned, like I've interrupted them. Skyler stands first, her pages falling to the floor. Brooks sets his stack aside on my comforter and rises next.

She was on my bed. With *Brooks.*

I can't process this moment.

On my nightstand is Skyler's headshot, and I have the irrational urge to dive over my bed and hide it. Or tear it up.

"Sorry, Grey," Brooks says. "We were just talking through a few of the emotional beats for the scene Skyler's going to read with Garrett in a moment. Adam said it was okay to use your room."

I look from him to Skyler, whose cheeks are turning pink.

This is my fucking room, I want to say.

It's *my* room.

I wish it was cleaner, and I wish it had been me who'd brought her here, but mostly I wish it actually *was* my room. It's not. It's Adam's.

I feel like a kid. Like a little fucking kid.

What the fuck is happening?

I can't look at Skyler so I look at Brooks.

"Definitely," I say to him. "Use whatever you want. My desk. My computer. My fuckin' bed. It's yours, man. Enjoy."

When I turn back into the hallway, I almost run into Adam. He says my name, but I don't stop. I grab the first bottle of whiskey I see on the bar and head outside.

Behind me, I hear Ali ask Adam what happened.

"It's my fault," he says. "I told him about Mom's visit. I thought he was ready."

Not his fault, but he is right about one thing.

I'm not ready.

The tide is low, so I can get around the rocks on the north point. I walk until Adam's house is out of sight and there are only high black cliffs behind me, then I sit.

I open the bottle and take a long drink. After a few more pulls, I try to figure out what building a time machine would involve. Reznick was a mechanical engineering major at Cal Poly. I consider texting him, but he's probably still at the show. Where I should be.

Assuming I could invent one with Reznick's help, the question then becomes what I'd want to redo. Definitely what just happened. Brooks and my brother are assholes, but my little outburst . . . embarrassing as hell. And what if it throws off Skyler's audition? That would suck.

I want her to get the part. And I want to never see her again.

Goddamnit. It's only now that I realize I was holding some hope that there could be something between me and her. What an *idiot.* But seriously? I took her for better than a fuckin' casting couch cliché.

I can't compete with Brooks. He's a Princeton grad. A producer. He's *her age.*

Wait a minute. That's what I'd do with a time machine. I'd make myself her age.

When I'm her age, I'll be filling arenas. My band will be headlining music festivals. I'll be unstoppable.

I take another sip and my mind moves to another time machine redo. The big one. The main event. Last August, back home in Newport. I'd wipe away the fight I had with Mom. Madeleine. My stepmom. Adam's mom.

The woman who raised me and who's coming here tomorrow night.

I'd get rid of that fight because if it hadn't happened, I wouldn't have had the bright idea to track down my birth mom.

Yep. That's what I'd do.

Obliterate that day from existence.

Chapter 14

Skyler

Brooks and I stand there for the longest time, staring at one another.

"What just happened?" I ask.

But I know. The look on Grey's face stays seared behind my eyes like the afterimage of a bright light. Disgusted, angry. Disappointed. But deeper than all that. A flicker of some wild, almost animal hurt that I can't believe really has to do with me.

Brooks stoops to pick up the pages of the script, which he hands to me with an abashed smile. "I guess he didn't like us using his room? He's a little moody lately. Something to do with his mom."

I nod and smooth over the corner of Grey's comforter, wanting to do something to put things right. I pick up the headshot—my headshot—that he had propped next to his bed, and I can't decide whether to return it to its original spot or take it with me. Finally, I put it back, facedown, next to the lamp.

"And maybe he has a bit of a crush on you," Brooks adds, his eyes moving from the picture to my face. He smiles at me and holds me in the intensity of his gaze. "Not that I could blame him."

I don't know what to say to that. It's flattering. Exciting, even. But hearing it makes me feel even worse for being in his room—with Brooks.

I'm not a dummy. I know Grey had the picture for a reason. I imagine him looking at it. Thinking about me. Like I've thought of him, replayed our kiss a dozen times, his solid arms wrapped around me, the smoky sweetness of his tongue and his body pressed against me.

I've thought about our conversations, too, how quick and funny he is, thought about the sound of his voice, which I know in a whole new way now, because I've heard him sing.

Hell, if there'd been a headshot of Grey, I might have kept it on *my* nightstand, too. I completely regret not stealing the CD from his car.

But that's a fantasy—some harmless fun. He's too young and clearly too much of a mess to be anything more than that. Anything real.

"You feeling good about everything?" Brooks asks. His expression is calm, encouraging. It all feels so effortless with him, like he can take on anything, solve any problem with no fuss, no storms. "The audition, I mean. We can keep working on it if—"

"No, I'm good." I wonder if I can sneak out for just a second to find Grey. I'm itching to talk to him. To clear up whatever wrong idea he has—of what Brooks and I were doing. Of me. The injustice of it sits like a rock in my chest. "I think . . . I'm ready. But can I have just a second?"

"Sure. Why don't you come into the office when you're all set?"

"Okay. I'll be right in."

He heads to Adam's office, and I slip off in the other direction, toward the living room, thinking I might find Grey there. Instead, I come upon Mia and Beth on the couch together, and from the look on Beth's face, I can see she's unhappy. Which crushes me on the spot.

"But you can't possibly know that—" Mia's saying, though when she spots me, she falls silent, which makes me feel like an intruder.

All of this seems so unfair. Grey. Now Beth and Mia. All I wanted was a little scratch to get my cello out of hock and to keep my mom in groceries and electricity. I hate to be party to anyone's unhappiness, and now Grey's angry, and Beth's in tears.

"I blew it," she says. "It's wide open for you, girl."

Mia shakes her head. "Like I said, you can't always tell. Sometimes I think I've shot a piece that's absolute garbage. But I go back and look at it later and it feels different. So much better."

"Believe me," Beth insists. "I know." My chest tightens at the look on her face. I think I liked it better when I was nine, and everyone got blue ribbons just for participating.

"Maybe they'll let you read again?" I suggest.

She shakes her head and gives me a weak smile. "No, I kicked that door closed pretty hard. It's all on you now, Sky. Go represent for the Valencia Three."

Our nickname—the three of us in our little apartment on Valencia Court. Though Mia's moving out—slowly, eventually. And if I don't do this thing I may end up packing my boxes, too.

"Okay," I say. "I'm so sorry, Beth. I hope it's better than you think it is."

"I hope so, too," she says. "And maybe after we get a couple of drinks, I'll let myself believe it. In the meantime, there's no reason you can't kill it."

This whole night feels like one big reason, but I keep that to myself.

Garrett comes into the room. "Come on, love," he says. "Let's get this done before I turn into a pumpkin."

We go into the office, where Adam looks up from his cell phone to give me a smile and Brooks stands, holding a digital video camera like the one Mia uses. He directs us over to a cream leather sofa by a broad picture window. Outside, the evening sky is a flat somber gray, but ocean sounds spill in, giving the room a contained, soothing feel.

"Do you prefer a certain side?" Garrett asks.

"Side?"

"Of the sofa. Do you like to be filmed from a certain angle?"

"I . . . I don't know." God, could I sound like a bigger dunce?

"Skyler needs some help picking out her good side," Garrett tells Brooks.

Brooks folds his arms across his chest and considers. "I mean, they're all pretty good." Everything he says sounds like flirting but not. Maybe it's that there's nothing hesitant about it. He's just rock solid. Putting it out there so I can decide what I want to do with it. Garrett comes to stand next to Brooks, and the next thing I know, he's got his hands on my jaw, and he's turning my face from one side to the other. Then he steps back.

"You're right. They are both pretty good. Really good, in fact."

They're giving me the feeling of being a super attractive bug under a microscope. It's flattering but creepy.

"So, why don't we just, um, go with your good side, Garrett?" I say. "Just put me where you want me?"

Garrett sits right in the middle of the sofa, which is no help at all. I just choose a side, his left, and sit beside him. I spend a little time trying to get comfortable, deciding whether I should cross my legs or not. Trying to figure out what to do with my hands, which suddenly feel like lifeless lumps of clay at the end of my arms.

I can't stop thinking about Beth. And Grey. It'll be a miracle if I can remember my lines. And who knows how well I can act, really, when you put me with someone like Garrett. Someone who knows what he's doing.

I guess I'm about to find out, I think.

"We ready?" Brooks asks.

"I need just a second, please," says Garrett. He closes his eyes and leans against the back of the sofa. I watch his chest rise as he takes big, deep breaths, and a calm settles around us. When he opens his eyes to look at me, it's like I'm pulled into this tight, intimate space with him. Just the two of us in this placid little bubble.

He reaches for my hand, and I give it to him. His palm is warm and solid.

"You're going to nail this," he says, and it's not a question or a demand. Just a statement of fact. He releases my hand with a wink and turns to the others, patiently waiting. "I'm ready."

We play the scene, another argument between George and Emma, but this one's from earlier in the script. It's playful. It doesn't have quite the heat of the scene I played with Grey—for a lot of reasons, I guess—but I can still feel this crackle in the air between Garrett and me, this ease that makes it feel, truly, like we've known each other forever. It's everything I thought it could be.

At one point, Garrett goes off script a little, teasing me. No, teasing Emma. Digging into her character flaws, challenging the way she likes to meddle, the way she thinks she has all the answers. I improvise back, my brain calculating all the possibilities for how to play it—angry, sad, strident—but I come back a little softer, more vulnerable.

This confidence of Emma's is a mask; I know that somehow. She gives it right back to George, goes toe-to-toe, but I let the insecurities show, just a bit. Let the hurt show, the feeling of casting about in life, of trying to find her rudder by steering the lives of others.

And then Garrett moves us effortlessly right back to the script. Damn, he's a pro. The scene seems to move us through dozens of emotional beats—flirting to serious to funny to wistful, and I ride along with it all, anticipating, more with my body than my mind, how to play each moment.

Everything else falls away, except Garrett, who's right there with me, ahead of me sometimes, guiding me with his eyes, micro-movements of his body that I can read like I've studied him forever. It's magical, the best kind of harmony

We finish, and there's a second of silence in the room. And then applause.

"Wonderful!" Brooks exclaims.

I look over at Garrett, who gives me a wide, wide smile, those blue eyes alive and captivating. "Just like I told you," he says. "Nailed it."

Chapter 15

Grey

*T*he first thing I see when I wake up is Skyler's headshot on my nightstand. It's facedown, and I know I didn't do that, so there's really only one explanation: she saw it. And didn't like that she saw it.

I press my eyes closed, anger moving through me like a hot sting. It's not like I meant for her to see it. *I* didn't invite her in here. Images flash through my mind. Skyler's soft lips just after I kissed her during our scene. Skyler jumping into the car when I picked her up at her place last night. Skyler sitting on my bed right where my left hand is.

With Brooks beside her.

I grab the headshot and rip it up. I can't make myself throw the pieces in the trash, though. I toss them back on my nightstand. It was just a stupid infatuation. It's not like anything was going to happen between us, and there are plenty of other girls out there. Whatever.

The time on my alarm clock flips to 6 a.m. My bedroom door is cracked and I hear the soft whir of the espresso machine brewing from the kitchen. It's Sunday and on Sundays we get up and surf. Not today, though. Today, our mom arrives. *His* mom. Madeleine only raised me from the age of five, which shouldn't even really count. Don't they say the first five years are the most important in a kid's life? Well, she had nothing to do with those. Not that my birth mom did, either. All I remember from those years was the smell of cigarettes and booze—and fear. Just a constant, constant fear. Of going hungry or getting hit. Of watching my birth mom drink. Worst of all, watching her let some new asshole into our lives, which would mean more getting hit and more going hungry for both of us.

The espresso machine shuts off, and I hear Adam moving around. I can't believe he's letting her stay here. He knows how things stand. Mom and I haven't talked since August. I never want to talk to her again, and my head hurts, and there's no way I'm staying here with her. Getting out of bed, I reach into my closet for my duffel and start throwing some clothes into it.

"You're up. Are you sure you don't want to—" Adam says, appearing at the door. He lowers the espresso cup, his eyebrows drawing together. "What are you doing, Grey?"

"Packing. Titus invited me to go on safari with him." I mean, shit. What does he think I'm doing?

I head to the bathroom, grabbing my things from a drawer. I catch my reflection and see hard, pale eyes like concrete. My dad's eyes. Adam took after Madeleine, in almost every way. Their calm temperament and long fine bones, like if they just ran fast enough, they'd take off flying. But I'm like our dad. Hard, volatile. Brawling stock. Husky. Big. Built to survive the back alleys of the world.

Dad's wealthy now but he grew up that way, on the streets, and still has some shady back alley running through his veins. I'm a souvenir from that part of him.

"You're seriously leaving?" Adam says. "Where are you going to go?"

Wrong thing to say if he's trying to stop me. I have no idea where I'm going. All I know is I'm not staying here. That's as far as I've gotten. But the insinuation that I'm homeless without him, worthless without him, only makes me angrier.

"A hotel," I say, though I know that's a lie. That's depressing, like something people do during a midlife crisis. Then it hits me. The band's rehearsal garage. I'll go there. It's already my second home anyway.

I head back into my room and grab my keys off the dresser, then stop. Adam is still at the door, blocking my exit. "When is this going to end, Grey? What the hell happened between you two? What did Mom do?"

For the first time in the eight months since I left home, I actually want to tell him. I don't know if I'm just tired of dodging his questions and her calls or what, but I hear myself say, "She didn't do anything, Adam. *I* did. I screwed everything up."

He's silent for an instant, as surprised that I answered him as I am. "You couldn't have. She's been trying to talk to you since—"

The storm inside my head's reaching hurricane levels. Time to go. I push past him, shoving him out of the way as I step into the hall. It still surprises me that I'm bigger than him, stronger, though I have been for years.

"Come on, Grey. Enough of this shit." Adam follows me as I head for the garage. "If you're going to run every time you don't like something, you're going to spend half your life running. Can't you see that? Whatever it is, you need to *stand* and *fix it*."

In the garage, I'm momentarily caught off guard when I see the

Mercedes parked in my spot until I remember that's my new work car. I hate that my truck is still sitting at the studio parking lot. Suddenly, it just seems too damn easy to get rid of important shit. You shouldn't just be able to ditch things like a truck or a kid like some travel coffee mug you forgot somewhere then decide you don't really need. My throat tightens, and my eyes blur as I throw my bag in the backseat. I have to get out of here *now*.

I hit my head as I climb into the Mercedes and it takes everything I have not to punch the car in retaliation. "You said she'd be here for two weeks, right? I'll probably be back once she's gone."

Adam runs a hand through his hair in frustration, making it stick up. I can't see inside the house anymore, but he sends a quick look that way. To Ali, I'm positive. We've woken her up, and he's telling her to stay where she is.

That's right. Stay away from Grey. He's a hazard.

It feels like it's taking a year for the garage door to open. Adam comes over to the car, and I hate that I left the window down because he props his hands there, and I can't pretend I don't hear him.

"I was trying to help," he says. "I thought this would help."

"I know. It's fine, Adam." I turn the engine. "You mind?"

His hands come away, and he straightens. I glance up for confirmation, and sure enough, there's more pain than frustration on his face.

That's what I wanted. I knew exactly how to play this so it would inflict maximum damage on him. It feels familiar. A lot like what I did with Mom. Madeleine. With people close to you, acting like you don't give a shit is the worst thing you can do. At least a fight has meaning. There's feeling in a fight.

"I'll see you at work," I say, and back out.

On the drive, I call Titus and have him meet me at the garage. I don't want to sit around alone. I can't.

He's waiting when I get there. His bloodshot eyes take in the duffel I toss on the Titanic, my new bed, but he doesn't say anything. All he says is, "You hungry? 'Cause I'm starving."

We walk down to the coffee shop and order breakfast sandwiches. I look outside as we wait for them, feeling like a vagabond. I know this neighborhood, but it looks different to me now that I won't be leaving it tonight. I try to figure out if it's a place that feels like me, reflects some part of me. Rhode Island never did. Malibu hasn't either. But Venice, for all its funky shops and low-key vibe, doesn't feel like me, either. I wonder if connecting with a place is a real thing that happens to other people or if I'm just making it up in my head, like a myth. Some kind of physical plane I'll never reach.

Titus starts to tell me about the show I missed last night. Blake Vogelson was there to check out the opening band, Heydey. Vogelson's a producer at Revel Music. He's pretty new on the music scene, but he's already big time. He's a genius at spotting talent, so everyone in the band—in *my* band—was buzzing. Just knowing that magic of discovery might happen—even if it's for another band—had them all pumped. I know exactly what he's talking about. That kind of energy, like life is happening, like moments are significant, is what I feel around Skyler.

"I'm not sure they had enough," Titus continues. "The songwriting could've been better and the lead singer had a decent voice, kind of reedy, but she looked terrified up there. I felt bad for her. She forgot her lyrics a few times. It wasn't easy to watch. But the cool thing is Reznick talked to Vogelson for a while. Rez managed to get his card. Vogelson said he'd take a listen to our demo."

It's good news. Normally, it would give me a major bump of adrenaline. If Vogelson actually listens to our stuff and he likes it, it could be life-changing. It could lead to a record contract, which is everything I want. I don't know what's wrong with me. Why I can't seem to get as excited as I should be.

"Revel. Cool," I say.

"Yeah. I think Rez was going to email him this morning."

"Nice."

Titus lifts a pierced eyebrow at my lame reaction, but he doesn't say anything.

We get our food and grab a table outside. Titus tells me he thinks he's going to keep his head shaved because this girl he likes commented on it last night. He's not sure if it was a complimentary comment or not, but he's guessing it was.

It's an effort to follow along. I'm halfway here and halfway nowhere. Maybe my place is nowhere. Maybe I'm like a GPS that's always recalculating routes, never setting a firm point on the world.

I'm being an asshole, I realize. I make myself respond.

"Wrong, dude. You have huge ears. Let it grow back," I say. It's actually the truth, and he had a pretty cool look when he had blond dreads. He kept them short, which gave him a sea-anemone-head look that was pretty unforgettable.

Titus runs a hand over his scalp. He smiles and tells me to go to hell, then keeps bringing the bullshit. Shane and Nora found a scrawny black kitten in the Whiskey's parking lot after the show. Nora begged Shane to take it home because she can't have pets at her apartment. Shane put up no resistance, and by the time they got it in the car, they'd named it Thor. Titus thinks it's the first step in them settling down. He thinks they'll be living together, with Thor, by summer.

"Sucks for them," I say.

"Totally. Dude's practically married," he agrees, but we're both lying. We'd both take what Shane and Nora have. Like, easy. Easy decision.

When we're done, we head back to the garage. Titus picks up his guitar and sits at the table while I open the garage door. The morning fog is burning off. A homeless guy wearing piles of oversized clothes shuffles his way across the street with a gray pit bull in tow.

"Check it out, Blackwood," Titus says. I join him at the table and rub my eyes, trying to make them focus on Titus's fingers, hovering on the guitar strings. "I thought up this melody last night," he says. "I think we could build it out into something."

He bends around the instrument and attacks it, his head bobbing to a rhythm that's driving and urgent. With every chord change, I can feel myself coming back to life. I don't think he just thought it up last night. What I think is that he's probably had it and realized this morning that it's the one thing I can actually lock into—and I do. The melody puts me back together, limb by limb. It makes me want to yell and laugh and break shit. It takes away the feeling I've had since I left home that I'm floating.

You're right here, it says to me.

You're right fucking here, and here is amazing so snap the fuck out of it because life is amazing. Feeling—feeling anything—is incredible.

Titus's hands finally still, and it's quiet for a beat. Then sounds come back. Cars driving. Birds arguing. A street cleaner cleaning. All of it. All the life in the world seems brighter, sharper, better.

Music is where I belong. Music is my home. Music doesn't ever leave, or give you up, or smack you around, or treat you like someone else's dirty laundry. It doesn't want you to be better than you are. It doesn't make you feel forgotten, or unimportant, or ashamed. Music is all. It's everything. Home.

"What do you think?" he asks, peering up at me.

I nod, because saying *dude, you just brought me back to life* seems a little over the top. "We'll call it 'Runner,' " I say.

Titus slides my notebook over to me. "You got a pen?"

I do. And we're on our way.

Chapter 16

Skyler

I wake to the sound of a cello being tortured. Opening my eyes, I find Mia posing in my bedroom, my beautiful Christina in her arms.

"Ta-da!" she says, and drags my bow across the strings, creating a sound like someone strangling a cow.

I sit up, feeling nauseated from too little sleep. I didn't conk out until around four, amped from the audition but also worrying, worrying, worrying—like I do—about Grey, Beth, my mother, children in impoverished countries, whether the music store down the street will make it to the holidays. Everything. My brain a churning, discordant symphony until, finally, I wore my consciousness down to a sleepy nub.

"Hey, I told you not to pay to get her for me," I say, trying not to sound pissed.

Mia hefts the cello onto my bed, basically onto *me*, and then climbs in beside me.

"You'll pay me back," she says.

"How?" Then I see how bright and expectant her green eyes are, and, finally, I get it. "I got the part?"

She nods and breaks into a huge grin. "You got the part! Adam told me I could deliver the good news, so I picked up Christina to celebrate."

"I . . ." Don't know what to say or think. It shouldn't be a surprise. I *felt* how well the auditions went. But now that it's here and mine, it feels as likely as winning the lottery. "Wow."

"Total wow," Mia agrees. "They love you, Sky. Like *loooooove* you. Garrett can't stop talking about you. Brooks is so ridiculously into you. Everyone thinks you're made for the role."

"It just feels so . . . crazy." I get out of bed, pulling Christina's case out of my closet and tucking her inside with a little pat. The whole family together again.

"Not crazy. Earned."

I did it. I'm going to star in a feature film. I can help my mom, pay my rent. Stop being the deadbeat roomie. Beth should—

Shit.

Beth.

Sounds come from the kitchen, and I can smell coffee and hear the old linoleum floor creak as she moves back and forth between the stove and fridge.

I turn back to Mia. "Does Beth know?"

She shakes her head. "Not yet. They want to offer her the part of the barista. But they said they'd beef it up for her, make her more of a best friend. They liked her a lot, too. It was close. They just felt you were a better match with Garrett."

I nod. "Beth called that the day of our first audition."

"Well, she's a smart one," Mia says, and gets back out of my bed. "Let's go tell her."

Panic creates a weird flood of saliva in my mouth, and I swallow. "Me? Why? I mean, shouldn't it just be you?"

"No, it should be the two of us, because we're friends, and this is exciting!"

"But she's going to be disappointed."

"A little, sure." Mia leans down to look in my vanity mirror, trying—and failing—to tidy her curly hair into some kind of ponytail-like thing, which just makes her head look like a weird topiary. "But you know Beth. She's strong as hell. And she'll be so happy for you." She turns to give me a look. "You do know that, right?"

"Of course." I know I'd be ecstatic if our roles were reversed. But then it wouldn't bother me at all if she got the lead. This has always been *Beth's* dream, not mine. It feels like I snuck into some fortified compound where she's been pounding away at the gate for half her life.

"Well, gird those ovaries, and let's go."

I breathe. Do it another couple of times. "Okay," I say. "Girded."

Out in the kitchen, Beth's in a long t-shirt and basketball shorts. Her usual Sunday attire. A stack of pancakes sits on the counter beside her, and she'd laid out three place settings. Which makes me equal parts guilty and hungry.

"Oh my God, are those banana pancakes?" Mia says. "I miss these so much."

"Miss them?" Beth says, turning toward us. "You haven't even moved out yet."

"I've moved out," she protests. "I mean, mostly. Sort of."

"Sort of is right," Beth says. She nods toward the table. "Sit."

We obey, and Beth slides a gargantuan tower of pancakes in

front of Mia, along with strawberry syrup and butter. Mia starts to doctor her pancakes, separating them from the stack so she can add appropriate amounts of butter and syrup to each one before reassembling them into a pile.

I give her a look and nod toward Beth. "Tell her," I mouth.

She shakes her head and holds up the one-second finger. "Relax," she mouths back.

I groan. Now that we're here, I want to get it over with already, but it doesn't feel right coming from me. The tension makes me want to throw up, but Beth just hums and cooks, and for a minute, the kitchen's quiet.

Finally, she comes over and sets a plate down in front of me.

"Congrats, roomie," she says and gives me a resounding kiss on the cheek.

I look down to find she's cut the top pancake into the shape of a star and spelled out the name "Emma" on it with M&Ms on a whipped cream cloud.

My throat tightens. "Oh, Beth . . ."

"How did you know?" Mia asks.

Beth plops down with her own plate of pancakes and raises an eyebrow at Mia. "Girl, you dragged that cello in here with a big old grin on your face. And you know these walls are made of spit and tissue. I could hear your whole damn conversation."

Including the part where we talked about how she'd respond to the news. And now we know the answer: with pancakes. So like Beth. Always surprising in the most magnificent, big-hearted way.

I'm relieved and overwhelmed, and for about the sixteenth time this morning, at a total loss for words. Everything hits me, in this sharp and dazzling way—like sunlight bursting through fog. I'm going to be the lead in a movie. I'm going to live out this amazing dream. My whole life's about to change in ways I can't even begin to imagine.

"So, you know they want to give you the barista part?" I ask. "Mia says they're going to expand the role for you."

"They really loved you, too," adds Mia.

Beth nods. "Damn right they did." We laugh, and she spears a chunk of pancake and smiles at us. "We are going to tear up that set."

Something's a little off; I can see it in her eyes, and the smile comes and goes a beat too quickly. But I can see how hard she's trying, how much she wants this to be a celebration. Not just wants it. *Needs* it.

So, I smile back and dig my knife and fork into the "E" in "Emma."

"It's going to be perfect," I say.

As I take the stage at Maxi's that night, I see the crowd's a little heavier than usual for a Sunday. Mike, the owner, gives me a thumbs-up from his usual spot by the bar. He's thrilled for me, even though the movie means I'm not going to get to come around here for a bit.

I plug Christina into her amp, so happy to play electric again. It occurs to me that Mike's going to find someone to fill my Sunday and Thursday spots. I wonder who. And then I wonder if the custom-ers will love that person more than me. And if they'll kick me off the film on day one—like the second I open my mouth, they'll know it's all a big mistake, and that will be that. Hello, Kentucky.

I settle onto my chair and look out at the crowd, trying to absorb their energy. Silently, I ask them what they'd like to hear, plucking at the strings to warm up my fingers. The vibe is awesome. Light and spirited. The air thickens with expectation, the anticipation of pleasure I'm dying to provide. So, I decide to go right for the good stuff, plunging into the first notes of "Smooth Criminal."

Some nights, I close my eyes when I play. It helps me to feel the music more, connects me in some way with my fingers, the string, the sounds I'm coaxing out of my cello. But tonight, I keep them open, watch the crowd, and think about how much I'll miss this—these moments when I can see how my music moves people. Watch them nodding their heads, tapping their fingers against the tabletops, keeping time with their feet, so many of them, like rows of factory workers operating imaginary treadles.

Even when they're jerks and talk through my entire set, I know my music means *something* to them. Main attraction or soundtrack to their conversation, we need each other. We move each other. And I love that feeling so much I could kiss it.

I think about how acting offers some of that same thrill, how a character is a conduit for emotions, like music is, all of it about this energy moving back and forth, delicious, powerful, connecting us in this place that's so real and deeply true.

God, it feels so good to put my whole body into it, to feel my muscles burn, sweat drip off me. I feel like a beast in the best possible way, which makes me wonder if I can love two things—two completely different art forms—equally. Can I give my passion to both?

I move into "Rock You Like a Hurricane," which is guaranteed to peel the paint off the walls and wear me out completely. But I want to be exhausted. I want to ride the music and the night and put off thinking about anything else.

Movement catches my eye, and a group of people slips into the café, taking seats in the back. It takes me a second to register that it's Brooks, Adam, Alison, Garrett, and a few other people I don't know. One woman and two other men.

I can't make them out that well under the lights, but I see Brooks shoot a smile my way. I nod, trying not to get flustered.

This isn't a film set, I tell myself. This is *my* house. I know what I'm doing here.

To punctuate that idea, I power my way through a few more

songs, "Seven Nation Army," "Purple Haze," "In the Hall of the Mountain King," which puts me into a wild, hypnotic state until everything else drops away but the music. I hope it's okay for Emma to have shredded fingertips, because that's what they're getting to-morrow for the first table read and wardrobe fittings.

Finally, I slow it down, playing through a few ballads. I even do Bon Iver's "For Emma," as a private joke to myself, though Brooks catches it and gives me a little salute with his glass. He's sharp, that one. He watches me in a way that makes me want to show off a bit, but I've already blown it out tonight, so I just settle into the rest of my show, taking a few requests and ending with "Viva la Vida" and wild applause.

Afterward, I spend a few minutes in the greenroom, trying to do something with my sweaty, blotched-out self, though it's pretty much a lost cause. I fluff up the pink strands, the ends now a sodden magenta, throw on a little lip gloss, and decide that's as good as it gets. My fingers burn from how hard I played, and I still feel drunk on the music.

Back in the main area, Brooks comes up to me and sweeps me into a bear hug.

"Holy shit," he says. "You're amazing. I've never seen anything like that!"

I grin and push away gently. "I had no idea you were coming out. I could have comped you guys."

He waves a hand. "Just a spontaneous impulse. I wanted to see you play." His chestnut hair is pulled back from his broad face, and in the café's dim light, his brown eyes look deep and soulful, softer than usual. He's also got an amazing smile, broad and bracketed by deep dimples. He usually looks so intense. I decide this is a better look for him.

"That's really sweet of you."

"And Garrett wants you to meet someone. His agent?"

I look over at the table where the others sit and try to guess which of them is his agent. I settle on the woman with an auburn pixie cut, her long neck swimming in the cowl of some kind of cape-blouse combo.

It turns out I'm completely wrong. His agent is the older man, introduced as Parker, though I don't know if that's a first name or a last. He's got a head of thick silver hair, like a mane, and a precisely groomed goatee. He kisses both my cheeks when we meet and holds on to my hands for a really long time.

"Garrett told me you were special. And he was right."

"What did I say?" Garrett asks and gives me a quick hug. "I told Brooks he has to work in the cello somehow."

"Into the movie?"

"Absolutely! You can't let a talent like that go to waste."

Brooks laughs. "I'm pretty sold on the idea, actually. Just have to convince Leigh to work it into the script. Lucky for us, she's a total badass, like our Skyler here."

Even though I'm used to people watching me, all this focused attention at close range makes me blush. And the thought of them rewriting the script to feature this part of my life? Amazing.

"Come," says Parker, pulling me toward the table. "Sit."

I'm introduced around to a couple of friends of Garrett's and to the woman, Jane, who's his publicist, apparently. "My port in the storm," Garrett says, grandly. "Basically, she keeps me from looking like a prick."

We sit and chat, have a few rounds of drinks. The high from being onstage mellows into this sheltering warmth. Parker, especially, is full of compliments, commandeering the conversation to keep it focused on me, though I'd much rather talk about anything else.

"You're going places," he says, tipping the last of a bottle of champagne into my glass. "I want to help you navigate."

"I'm sure a lot of people want that spot," says Brooks, smiling. He takes my hand beneath the table and squeezes. His touch feels firm, reassuring.

"Well, I'm here *now*." He leans in, and the spicy smell of his aftershave surrounds me. "Listen. Garrett can tell you, I fight for my clients, I keep them working. And I get them what they deserve. Our agency's boutique, but we're formidable."

Finally, it penetrates my thick skull that he's asking to be my *agent*. That he's *wooing* me, not just making small talk. The idea feels so surreal, I don't even know what to do with myself.

"Do I really need an agent?" Probably the exact wrong thing to say, but I can't see beyond the first day of filming, let alone to a whole career.

"Honey, you're poised to break out in a major way," Garrett tells me. "This is *exactly* when you need an agent. These first steps are critical. You have to be smart and make sure someone's got your back."

"I've got her back," Brooks says.

And I've got my own back, I want to say. But in this case, I really don't. How could I? I don't know anything about this world and how to negotiate it. Maybe I do need a navigator.

Parker pulls out his cell phone. "Give me your number," he says. "I'll call you for lunch this week."

I do, and he thumbs it into his phone.

Garrett picks up his glass and proposes a toast. "To Skyler, and her first Hollywood lunch."

I laugh, but he gets a serious look on his face.

"Seriously, get ready for liftoff, girl. You're going to do great things."

"To Skyler," Brooks says, giving me a look that sends warmth through me. "And to all the great things we'll do—together."

Chapter 17

Grey

So, Blackwood gave me his little brother for the duration of the shoot."

"I'm your assistant, Garrett," I say. I don't like sounding like I'm a present.

We're in Garrett's trailer on Monday morning, on the first official day of production. *Yayyy.* I'm in the movie business.

Garrett turns on the illuminated mirror. "Same thing, pretty much!" His reflection smiles at me. "I'm *so* happy about this. I asked for you, you know. We didn't have much chance to talk Saturday night, but I'm a great judge of character and I like you, Grey Blackwood."

"Huh," I say, because it's early, I slept like shit on the Titanic, and I don't know how else to react to that. Until I earn enough to pay Adam back, I'll be stuck driving Garrett around and basically being at his every beck and call. I already had no desire to be down here at the studio. But now with this new assistant position, and now that my mom—shit, *Madeleine*—is going to be here, it's going to be agony.

Garrett shuts his mirror off and turns to me. His skin is so pale and his eyes so blue, he looks like he could be one of those deep-sea creatures that've never seen a day of sunlight. Except instead of weird tentacles and rows of sharp teeth, he looks like he's been sculpted by Michelangelo.

"You don't look anything like Adam." Garrett looks me up and down.

"Different moms." *Very* different moms.

Garrett blinks. "Ah, I see. And how old did you say you are?"

"I didn't. Nineteen."

His jaw literally drops. "Youngster!" he says, though he's only five years older than me. "You seem older because you're so . . . big. I'll be kind, don't worry. Well, time to get working! We start in half an hour, and I haven't had a drop of caffeine yet. Could you wrangle some for me?"

I'm going to kill Adam. I'm going to kill him for making me do this. I haven't seen him since yesterday morning when I left his place, but I did hear from him last night by text.

His message was: *You're Garrett's assistant for the shoot. Try and back out of this.*

I shake my head. I'm not backing out. How can I, when he accused me of always running out on things? He could be right, but it doesn't matter. Proving him wrong is my top priority. I am *not* quitting this job.

Then it hits me . . . If I got *fired*, then it wouldn't exactly be like I *quit*. Adam couldn't blame me if Garrett and I just didn't get along.

Yes. That could work!

A brand-new Keurig coffee machine sits on the small kitchen area in the trailer.

"Sure, Garrett. I'll make you a coffee." I step toward the machine, already thinking of the chemistry experiment I'm going to put together.

"No, no, no," Garrett says, laughing at me. "Not *that* coffee, Greyson von Blackwood. That coffee isn't edible."

Here we go, Grey. Roll out your weapons.

"Edible is something you eat. I'm pretty sure you mean potable."

I cross my arms and wait for him to tell me I'm being a superior smartass.

Garrett stands and faces me, beaming. "What a smarty-pants! I love it! Okay, I want a *potable* triple macchiato, extra whip, extra caramel, extra hot."

"Sorry, dude. I don't think they have that over at craft services."

Garrett play-punches me on the shoulder. "Well, *dude,* you'll just have to go get it! I'm sure there's a Starbucks around here somewhere."

I play-punch him back, except with less playing. "Are you sure you want that kind of coffee, Garrett?"

"What do you mean, am I sure? That's my drink! I have it every morning and sometimes in the afternoon."

"Obviously."

Garrett's eyes go wide and his hand comes to his chest. "You're saying what, exactly?"

I cross my arms. "I'm just saying that I wouldn't drink that sugary shit if I were you. If the camera adds ten pounds, you could lose about twenty. I'd do straight black coffee if I were in your shoes." I look him up and down. "Yeah. I'd even skip adding milk. No offense, Garrettson, but you really can't afford it."

Garrett's narrow shoulders press back and he draws a huge breath. He's about to go ballistic on me, and I am ready for it. Bring it, Allen. Fire me. Toss my disrespectful ass out of the trailer.

He steps forward, and next thing I know, his hand is on the

back of my neck pulling me toward him, bringing our foreheads together.

Our heads are bowed, like we're praying together.

"Thank you," he whispers. "Thank you for your honesty."

What. The. Hell?

I can't speak, but he doesn't need me. He keeps going.

"I'm a stress drinker. But not alcohol. Not anymore. Sweet drinks. Milk shakes. Macchiatos. Smoothies. It's the sugar I need. I'm worse than a hummingbird with it. I mean I have the best diet, but the sugar . . . It's my Kryptonite."

"Wow."

"I know." He nods, and my head goes up and down, too. "I know. It gets worse right before I start a shoot. I can't stop myself. It's the stress . . . it ruins my regime."

"That sucks, Garrett. But you need to let me go."

"I'm almost done. I really do like you, Greyson."

"My name's not Greyson—"

"That's okay. You know I mean you. As I was saying, you're honest. We're going to make a great team." He takes a deep breath. Then he kisses my forehead and steps back. "Black coffee." He claps his hands together. "Let's do it!"

I flee for craft services, trying to shake off what just happened. I feel so confused. That did not go the way I thought it would. Not even close.

As I step out of the trailer, I see Adam and Madeleine, my Not Mother, standing in front of the next trailer over. Freakin' perfect. My body goes cold, and I freeze.

Mom looks like an old-fashioned movie star, with her fitted blazer and skirt. Red lips, her blond hair in neat waves. They're clearly having a tense conversation, which is probably definitely about me. And then they both look at me, and their matching expressions of surprise and concern confirm it.

"Grey," Mom says.

The feeling of betrayal is like fire moving through me, thawing me. I can't believe my brother did this. Let her come here. I pretend I didn't hear her. I turn and walk away.

"Give him time, Mom," Adam says behind me.

"Just give me some fucking *space,*" I mutter.

I'm so rattled, I can't remember what I'm supposed to be doing. I just keep walking. And then I'm walking past a trailer and catching a glimpse of Skyler, Mia, and Beth, sitting at the small booth inside. I only see them for a fraction of a second, but Beth looks over and sees me. In that second, I feel a sort of connection with her.

Garrett told me earlier that Skyler got the part of Emma. Beth got some kind of consolation friend role. Maybe nothing's actually going on with Skyler and Brooks. I mean, I'm assuming a lot. Though I *did* catch them in bed together. Hah, funny. But I definitely don't feel like I'm getting the starring role with her.

Jesus. I can't even get my head around what these next few weeks will be like. It's easier to count the people I *don't* need to avoid. Saul, the sound guy. Bernadette and Kaitlin, from wardrobe. That's about it.

When I get back to the trailer with coffee, Garrett is talking to Bernadette about wardrobe. They're looking at photos on Bernadette's iPad, so I sit on the trailer's steps to await my next orders. This is a risky place to be. I want to see Skyler and I don't want to see her. I want to see Mom, and I don't want to see her.

The whir of generators surrounds me. I don't know why we had to be here so early. It seems like no one's actually *working.*

"This coffee tastes like shit, Greyson!" Garrett calls from inside.

I laugh, despite myself. "You'll get used to it."

"If you say so!"

I shake my head. Maybe I can work with the guy after all.

My phone buzzes in my pocket. I fish it out and see a text from Titus.

Vogelson/Revel just emailed Rez back. He liked our demo. Call me!!

I read it twenty more times. I'm still sitting there, staring at my phone, as Bernadette slips past me.

Over and over, I think this is it. This is it. I've always felt like all we need is a chance and now we have it. If Vogelson likes the demo, we're ninety percent there. I can perform the shit out of our songs. I can get better, too. I'm only a few months into performing. With a producer and more experience, we'll only improve.

I want to sprint to Adam, to Mom. I want to tell them what I've done, me and the band. What I've achieved, what I'm going to achieve, on my own merit. Without their money or support. I did this, I want to say.

I want to grab Skyler and tell her, too, because she'd understand. This is happening to her, too.

But I don't move.

I don't move.

I want to tell someone, but there's no one I can tell.

"Greyson," Garrett says from inside. "I'm not very fond of alone-time. You should probably know that up front. Part of your job is going to be keeping me—"

Garrett takes one look at me as I enter the trailer, and his smile disappears. He pats the table, indicating the seat next to him. I guess I have no poker face.

"I'm listening," he says simply, his blue eyes unblinking.

"I'm going to be a rock star."

"Of course you are."

That surprises me. It makes me laugh. And then I can't seem to make myself stop.

Garrett sits back in his chair, smiling as I laugh until my stomach cramps and my eyes sting. And when I finally settle the hell down, I tell him about the band and Vogelson, and Titus's text.

Garrett listens quietly, his eyes sparkling. I bet he knows tons of famous people who've starred in huge movies and maybe even filled arenas, but he's grinning like it's his big moment as much as it is mine.

When I'm done, he stands and goes to the kitchen area and pulls a bottle out of the mini-fridge. "This calls for some potable champagne, Greyson. How incredible and wonderful," he says, and I know he means it. His smile takes on a wicked tilt. "But don't think I'm letting you go anywhere until this shoot is done."

Chapter 18

Skyler

Mia, Beth, and I get to the studio at 8:45 a.m., which I've been told is a late start. But I couldn't sleep again, revved up from the night at Maxi's, all the attention from Garrett and his agent, Parker, and the . . . whatever it is . . . with Brooks, who drove me home on his motorcycle, gave me a tight, long hug at the door. I'm not going to lie; he feels good, smells better. There's something so sturdy and adult about him.

Which, of course, makes me think of Grey. Who doesn't seem sturdy and adult at all, but who feels so *alive,* somehow, super-heated where Brooks is a slow and steady warmth.

I push all of that aside to focus on the day in front of me.

"Why don't we grab something at the craft services table before your fitting?" Mia suggests. "I have to head over to Boomerang for a bit and then run Nana to an appointment."

"You're not going to be around today?"

She shakes her head. "I'm going to meet with Adam and Brooks to go over reels from prospective DPs, but I have to finish work on some TV spots for Boomerang. I'm holding down the fort there until production really gets going. And Nana has physical therapy."

"How's she doing?" asks Beth, making me feel like a jerk for not asking that first. Mia and her grandmother are so tight, I know it kills her to see Nana wheelchair-bound after the accident she had a few months ago. The last time I saw her, she didn't remember me at all. She seems to be slipping away, faster and faster. I wish I could do more for Mia. Anything to soothe the pain she admits to only rarely.

"She's a trooper," Mia says with a sad smile. "Come on. Let's eat."

After we throw down some coffee and bagels, we go our separate ways. Beth's got to fill out some paperwork, and it looks like I have hours in wardrobe ahead of me. The table read is scheduled for 3 p.m., so I'll see her again then. Since she's in a supporting role, she's got a lot of off-days, so we won't be together as much as I'd hoped. But she's already lining up other auditions, which I take as a really good sign. I want something amazing to come her way so badly, I can taste it.

I spot Garrett and Grey in some weird tête-à-tête where Garrett is hanging on to Grey's arm, and gesturing madly, while Grey looks like he wants to fade through the floor. Garrett catches my eye and blows a kiss. I pretend to catch it and plant it on my lips. He laughs, but Grey just gives me a strange look that I can't interpret from a distance. We've barely spoken except to mumble "good morning" at each other.

I head off to one of the production offices, where I'm supposed to meet Kaitlin from wardrobe. I find the room already filled with racks of clothing, more than I've ever seen in one place, outside of a department store. Kaitlin and Bernadette have shown me sketches for how they want Emma to look. Modern, super chic but with a little whimsy.

Running my hands over the garments, a little thrill pulses through me. There are so many beautiful pieces here, of such high quality. All so different from my usual slouchy sweaters and jeans, peasant dresses over funky leggings. Even before I've put anything on, I'm convinced of how much costumes can make a character. I can *see* Emma, looking at these racks. See her in a way I haven't before now.

"Killer, aren't they?" Kaitlin asks from the doorway. Her clothes and makeup are so on point, she makes me feel like a bridge troll by comparison. She's loaded down with supplies, and I take a sketchbook and sewing box from her, as she sets a roll of measuring tape and her laptop onto a table by the windows.

"They're beautiful."

We chat about the character for a bit while Kaitlin gets herself together. "What are you?" she asks. "Size six?"

I laugh. "Not since junior high. More like a ten on the bottom, eight on top."

"Well," she says, with a little frown. "Some of these are a bit smaller. Some designers don't go up past a six."

"Really?" It hadn't even occurred to me that I might not fit into the clothes. I assumed the clothes would have to fit *onto* me.

"Yeah, but let's not worry about that. I think the tops will be fine, and we'll swap out anything we like for larger sizes, if we can find them." She pulls out the measuring tape and starts to unspool it. "Why don't you take off your clothes, so I can get firm measurements?"

I look at the open windows, the open doors out into the hallway. "Uh, sure."

"Don't worry. Everyone's tied up with meetings."

I unzip and step out of my jeans, pull my shirt up over my head.

"I'm going to measure everything," Kaitlin says, getting down on the floor. "So, we're going to be really good friends by the end of this." She pushes her silky brown hair over a shoulder and curls the tape around my ankle, then makes a note in her sketchbook. This goes on for every part of my body—from toe to head with about twenty stops in between.

"Don't suck in," she says, when she goes to double-check my waist.

"Sorry. Didn't realize I was." But the more that tape cinches around me, the more conscious I am of my size. Not that I'm big, but that my proportions maybe aren't the greatest. My hips and thighs are fleshy compared to my narrow shoulders and completely average breasts. I've never thought about it much, but seeing those measurements go into her book makes me wonder how I compare—to the clothes on those racks and to all the other girls trying to make a go of it as actors.

"Am I . . . Is there a problem?"

She makes a last notation in her book and looks up at me. "Problem?"

"I mean, with my size. Or . . . measurements. I mean, should I try to lose some weight?" It kills me to even ask the question. It makes me feel needy and insecure. But this is all such new territory. I want to look good for the part. To be able to wear those beautiful clothes of Emma's like I truly own them.

Kaitlin hands me a shirt to try on—a tailored blouse in navy, which I'm relieved to find fits perfectly. "Well, you are a bit bottom-heavy. Which we can totally work with, of course. Though the camera does add . . ."

She doesn't finish, but she doesn't really have to say more.

I step into a gray wool skirt with a ruffled, asymmetrical hem. It's definitely a tight squeeze. We can zip it, but it bunches at my thighs and wouldn't be great if I actually plan to breathe. I feel a zing of panic. Maybe they should have tried to dress me before giving me the part.

"What do you think I should do?" I ask.

"Well, just lay off the bread and pasta. Try to cut down on alcohol. All of that makes you look bloated. Just go a little easy."

I nod and step out of the skirt, relieved. Probably just cutting beer and chicken wings from my diet will go a long way. Having fruit and yogurt instead of the bagel I just slathered with a metric ton of cream cheese.

This is manageable.

"You know, I've got these supplements you might be into," Kaitlin says, heading over to her sewing basket. She comes back with a couple of blister packs filled with what look like vitamins.

"What are they?" I sniff the plastic, which smells like every other vitamin supplement I've ever smelled. Herby. A little like dirt.

"They're all natural. A little bit of a water pill and then some goodies to rev up your metabolism. Totally safe."

"Do you know what's in them?"

"It's a long list, but nothing crazy. Amino acids. That kind of thing. They should definitely help. Here. Try a few of mine and see what you think. Even if you can just lose a few pounds before filming starts, you'll probably feel better."

I nod and take the pack from her. I'm sure they're fine.

We try on a dress that's beautiful but also tight. Next time, I'll definitely skip the bagel.

Chapter 19

Grey

Wednesday afternoon, Bernadette sends me back to the costume trailer for a fresh shirt.

"That one's history," she says, shaking her head at Garrett. He's sitting at a desk in an office set up in the studio, coffee stains splattered across the front of his button-down. Today, we're shooting footage of his character, Mr. Knightley. He's supposedly some kind of real estate tycoon who rarely works. My dad's friends with a couple of real estate tycoons and those guys *never* stop working, but this is the Hollywood version, I guess. In the film, Knightley mostly just lounges around and gives Emma Beautiful Emma a hard time as he struggles to hide his ardor for her. Painful.

"It most certainly is. We can't take me anywhere," Garrett says, with a big smile.

You can, but it's a hazard. Turns out he's super accident-prone.

The problem is he thinks he's a multitasker, but he's really not. Earlier this morning I stopped him from smashing into a car as he was walking, texting, and talking to me. Part of my job is turning out to be making sure he doesn't kill himself. I'm babysitting a toddler.

"Just try talking before or after you drink next time," I tell him.

"Not during, Greyson! I'll remember that!"

He won't.

As I'm heading outside, I hear my name. It's Brooks, who's standing with the director of photography. "We're on a shooting schedule so make it quick, please," he says.

I nod, but as I step into daylight, a surge of anger shoots through me. The dynamic over the past couple of days makes no sense. Garrett orders me around, but it doesn't feel disrespectful. It's light and joking. He loves it when I shut him down, or call him out on behaving like a princess. He thinks it's hilarious, which somehow makes it easier for me to schlep around and do shit for him. With Brooks, it's been the opposite. Whenever his assistant director is busy, he asks me for things. He'll say please like just now. All proper and nice. But I still feel like he's ordering me around.

I've been trying to tell myself it's because we were friends before this. I've known him since he and Adam were at Princeton together, and we were roommates for a few months. But I think it's more than that. It feels like he's making a point of letting me know where I stand. Which is about a thousand pegs below him.

As I head to the costume trailer for Garrett's replacement shirt, I think about last night, when I saw him in the parking lot with Skyler. It was late and almost everyone else had already gone home. I was in the Mercedes, and I had Garrett with me, as usual. He was talking on the phone and checking his schedule for the night on his iPad, so I'd know where to drop him off. I watched Skyler snap a helmet on and climb onto the back of Brooks's bike. I watched her wrap her legs and arms around him. She didn't see me, but Brooks did. Brooks looked over but he didn't tip his head or smile or anything.

It was more like we just looked at each other, acknowledging the situation. He got the beautiful girl on the back of his motorcycle. I got the gay actor who couldn't remember his iPad pass codes without my help.

I've only seen Skyler one other time this week. That was also yesterday, when I ran into her at craft services after lunch. She had a tray with an apple and some kind of smoothie on it. When she saw me, she set it down and the apple rolled off the tray, but I caught it.

"Congrats," I said, setting the apple back on the tray. "On getting Emma Beautiful Emma. I haven't had a chance to tell you yet . . . I'm happy for you, Skyler." I'd stepped in to give her a nudge on the shoulder, just needing to touch her. But she must've thought I was moving in for a hug because that's what we ended up doing. Hugging right by the fruit bar.

It was amazing and unexpected. But later, when I saw her straddle Brooks's bike and leave with him, that hug lost the *amazing* part.

I'm so tied up in my head that I'm not prepared when I jog into the wardrobe trailer and see Skyler sitting on a long bench. With *my mom*.

"*Shit . . . shirt.* I was sent to get a shirt," I stammer. "Garrett spilled shirt on his coffee. I mean coffee. It's what he spilled."

No idea what I just said. My body temp is skyrocketing. Mia's here, too, standing by one of the clothing racks. I focus on her because she's the safest.

She lifts a white men's button-down. "Bernadette radioed me. I'm on it." She disappears outside before I can say a word.

"Hey." Skyler smiles at me, tucking her hair behind her ear. "I just met your mom. We were just—"

"Stepmom," I say, and almost cringe. I don't want Skyler to see this. She doesn't need to know about my family issues.

Madeleine rises and steps toward me like she's approaching a wild animal. "Hello, Grey."

I haven't looked at her in months, and she looks different. Older. Prettier. Thinner. Happier.

Growing up, people would always tell me how pretty my mom was, mistaking Madeleine for her. My real mom doesn't look anything like Madeleine. My real mom looks like she's lived a hard life. She *has*. And I wish I didn't know that. I don't know why the hell I had to go see what I thought I'd been missing. I ruined everything.

Mom gives a shaky smile. "Adam and Skyler were just telling me about your singing. I'd love to hear you sometime."

For a second, I think she's heard about Revel, but she couldn't have. I made Garrett swear he wouldn't tell anyone, and my band is a pretty isolated part of my life. Adam hasn't even met them. Then I wonder: Is this how Mom thinks this is going to work? That we can just skip eight months and pick it back up this easily?

You can't hear me sing, I want to say. But I glance at Skyler, who's definitely aware of the tension now. "Someday . . . maybe."

Madeleine's smile goes bigger. It's too hard to look at. She hasn't earned that kind of happiness. How can she be that happy just because I told her she can hear me sing? It doesn't seem right. It seems like too much. I don't know why she's not yelling.

"So . . . uh, the bedroom door in my trailer keeps jamming," Skyler says. "Do you mind if I borrow him for a minute, Madeleine?"

Mom is in some euphoric alternate dimension. Hope is marching all over her face like a parade. I want to shut it down. I want to squelch it, but Skyler's hand closes around my wrist, pulling me toward the door. She lets go outside, and we say nothing until we reach her trailer.

"Family problems?" she says, stopping in front of it.

What's the right answer here? Deny it? That'd be lying. Tell her yes, she's right? She already thinks I'm a stupid kid. I take a pass, going with silence.

Skyler nods. "I've got those, too."

"You said you have a jammed door?"

"No. That was improvisation. You looked like you needed to get out of there."

"You rescued me?"

"I think so."

My chest relaxes, and my breathing flows back in and out. *You did,* I want to say. *Thanks,* I want to add. But I don't.

"Come on." She opens the door to her trailer, and I follow her inside. Skyler grabs two beers out of the mini-fridge, pops them open, and holds one out to me. "Don't report me to the authorities, okay?"

"Skyler . . ." I can't handle the young jokes right now. I need to get out of here. Hanging out with her when I'm this shaken up is a bad idea.

I turn to go, but she takes my hand and places the beer there. She doesn't say anything but there's warmth in her eyes. She taps her beer against mine, then climbs up onto the kitchen table, which is affixed to the trailer floor on a pedestal.

I stand in front of her and we drink our beers. Skyler swings her legs a little, back and forth. Other than that, we're quiet. The incident with Mom recedes with every sip of cold Mexican beer. It hits me: I'm alone with Skyler.

"So, Greyson." Her mouth transforms from a faint smile to a wide grin. "How's it going with Garrett?"

"We're best buds. How's it going, being a movie star?"

"Great. Except I have no idea what I'm doing."

"You look the part."

"Hah," she says, because she's in Emma wardrobe, a white shirt with pink flowers that scoops down. I don't even tell myself not to look. She's gorgeous. Full breasts, pale smooth skin. She looks like a woman, curvy, where a lot of girls in this town are so thin. Origami sharp.

. I step closer and set my beer down. Then I reach out and run my fingers over her collarbone, a brush against her skin. She's so warm and soft.

I look into Skyler's eyes, and see her surprise. That makes two of us. I have no idea what's gotten into me. But there's something in her expression, an eagerness and invitation. She's drawing me in. I run my fingers up her neck, to her soft pink hair. She leans into my hand and my body goes electric. How can such a small thing feel so big? She blinks at me, and I freeze the moment, her leaning into my hand. She's the most feminine, perfect thing I've ever seen.

"You're beautiful." I don't care if she knows I think that. She has to know she's beautiful. And I have nothing to lose. She's not mine. She won't ever be.

I sense the shift between us before Skyler straightens, moving away from my touch. "Grey," she says.

I snap back to reality, withdraw my hand, step back.

What *the hell* did I just do?

"Thanks for the beer," I mutter.

Then I'm gone.

It's past seven o'clock by the time Titus and I haul ourselves out of the Pacific. The shoot ended early today, and we got a long session in. The surf was awesome. I prefer the breaks in Oxnard and north Malibu, but Venice delivered tonight.

Titus peels off his wetsuit and racks his board. He's supposed to meet his parents for dinner at seven, so it's a lightning-quick change. He jumps into his Jeep dripping wet.

"Maybe tomorrow?" he says.

"Maybe tomorrow."

It's become our refrain in the band. We're in a holding pattern. Vogelson told Rez he wants to hear us play live to get a feel for our performance quality. So Rez ran some of our booked gigs by him, but apparently Vogelson had something else in mind. He didn't say what, exactly, only that he was working on something and would send more details soon. So "maybe tomorrow" has become our constant hope. Rez, our worrier, is paranoid Vogelson will back out even though the guy said he loved our demo. None of us will relax until an audition gig is officially locked in with him.

With Titus gone, I head for the outdoor showers. They're for surfers and beachgoers, but who says they can't also be for guys living out of garages?

I rinse the sand and salt water off my board and wetsuit and set those aside. Hardly anyone's on the beach anymore, but the foot traffic around the restaurants is picking up. The sun's setting over the ocean, pink and blue and purple, and I wonder if Adam, Alison, and Mom are seeing the same thing twenty miles north of here, on the back patio at Adam's house. I remember the text I got earlier today from him.

Adam: Dinner, just you and me?

And my reply.

Grey: Can't.

I don't know if I'm pissed at him for letting Mom stay at his place, or because I work for him now and it feels . . . demeaning. But I'm not up for seeing him. *Not* seeing him doesn't feel great either, though. I can't win.

With my gear clean, I grab a bottle of shampoo from my backpack. It's more out of habit than necessity, since I have almost zero hair. But strange things that seemed insignificant before matter more now that I'm homeless-ish.

Sleeping on the Titanic in the garage has been uniformly depressing. I've done it three nights, and there's nothing about it I like. It's worse on the nights the band doesn't practice and I'm there alone. Sunday was one of those.

Tonight's one of those nights, too, but this time I have a plan. Surf, which always boosts the mood. Shower, also a mood-booster even if it's a cold, outdoor shower. Burrito and beer at the corner taqueria, after I drop off my board at the garage. Then friends. Rez teaches music lessons to little kids on Wednesdays, so he's out but I'm going to try to hook up with Titus again later. Or maybe I'll go see what Shane, Nora, and Thor are up to.

I went a little overboard on the shampoo and some runs into my eyes. I tip my head up and let the water flush the sting out. An image of Skyler earlier appears in my mind. How she looked when I'd touched her neck in her trailer. She'd liked my hand on her. I *know* she did. I imagine what would've happened if we'd kept going. If we'd both stayed in that suspended place, where it was just me and her and nothing else. I picture myself kissing her, my hands on her hips. My fantasy ends there, because I hear something that sounds like my name. *A lot* like my name.

I step out of the shower and grab my towel, wiping my eyes.

"It *is* you!" Mia says. "See, Sky? I told you it was him."

Chapter 20

Skyler

Good lord in a basket, it's him all right. Grey. Illuminated by the golden lights coming on along Venice Boulevard. With suds and water sluicing off his ridiculously ripped body, cascading from his massive tattooed biceps, running down his taut muscled abdomen. His swimsuit sags dangerously low, clinging to his sturdy thighs, making, um, *everything,* pretty evident.

And evidently pretty impressive.

Probably, this would be a good time to actually speak some words, but even in a town full of hot, hot people, this is kind of stratospheric.

"Yep, it's me." Grey reaches back to turn off the shower, which breaks the spell, so I can at least avert my gaze like a decent person. Then he rubs a towel vigorously over his gleaming body and tucks it around his waist.

He has a strange look on his face—peevish, embarrassed, and it feels suddenly like we're intruding on something. Or maybe it's just me. I think about that moment in my trailer. His fingers on my skin. My wanting and not knowing what to want.

"Uh, so, what are you up to?" I ask in an effort to win the prize for most obvious question ever. "I mean, I can see what you were up to." Seriously, Sky? "But, uh, were you just in the water? What brings you out here?"

"I'm crashing nearby. At the garage where my band rehearses."

"Really?" asks Mia. "Why?"

Grey looks from me to Mia and then back to me, weighing something. Maybe whether or not he can trust us. He's got this hot, coiled energy all the time, like he's always holding back. Like he's an animal caged inside a human body.

"Just staying there for a few weeks."

"Because of your mom?" I ask. It was obvious from their interaction on set that there's some bad blood there, though compared to my mom, she seems kind and thoughtful, whip-smart and curious without being overbearing. Which makes sense, given her offspring.

Then I remember that Grey's not really her offspring. He said "stepmother," and the way he said it really answers my question.

Which is good, because *he* doesn't actually answer it. Instead, he gathers up his stuff—surfboard, wetsuit—and gives us a grin. "I gotta head out," he says, as though nothing's hanging there between us. He looks away for a second, following the path of a guy in an Obama mask as he weaves his way up the boardwalk on a ribbon-festooned unicycle. "Told some friends I'd hook up with them tonight."

"Wait," says Mia. "So, you're just sleeping in a garage? Like on an air mattress or something?"

Grey shrugs. "A couch. It's okay."

"And taking freezing-cold showers out on the beach? That doesn't sound great, does it, Sky?"

"No, it doesn't," I say, but I'm afraid of where she's going with this.

"Can't you stay at a hotel or something?"

He shakes his head. "Money's a little tight right now. I'm giving Adam almost every penny to pay him back for the house, and I don't really have . . ." Again, he goes silent, and I can *feel,* literally, the tension of him wanting to talk, wanting to say more to someone. Needing it.

"Why don't you come stay at our place?" Mia blurts. We have that in common. The blurting thing. "I mean, I'm just about all moved out, so there's room."

Ay, dios. No. No.

But I can't say anything. I can't tell my best friend, who knows I'm talking to Brooks, starting to maybe, sort of, think about where that could go, that having Grey in my apartment, so close *all the time,* is a very dangerous, very bad idea.

Grey shakes his head. "Nah, I appreciate it, but I'm cool here. I promise. Thanks, though." He takes a few steps toward a squat gray building with weather-beaten shutters and a tiny, shed-like garage in the back. "I'll see you guys tomorrow."

"Hang on," says Mia, pulling me along. She gives me a look, tipping her head in his direction, like she's tapping me in for the debate. "You're cool with it, right, Sky?"

"Of course." Not. In no way. "But it seems like he's got it under control here. So, if—"

My words disappear, though, because Grey's pulled up the garage door, the muscles of his broad back and shoulders shifting smoothly as he thrusts the door up along its rusting track.

"See?" he says, pointing to a lumpy white couch sporting what looks like a half-century's worth of mystery stains—a perfect complement to the funk of beer and weed and sweat potent enough to make my eyes water. "Perfectly fine, right?"

But, like me, he's lousy at hiding his feelings. Even turned away to shove some empty beer cans into a garbage bag, his body language tells me everything.

He doesn't want to be here in this musty space, crowded with furniture and audio equipment, the only natural light coming in from the tiny half-moon windows set into the garage door, which faces a dim alleyway.

"You should come stay with us," I say, surprising the hell out of us both. "I mean, this is . . ."

"It's fine," Grey insists. "I don't need much, and I'm hardly ever here."

I think how different he is from Brooks, who says what he means, tells you—without hesitation—what he wants.

"Come on," says Mia.

"Seriously," he tells us. "It's really nice of you to ask, but I'm fine. I can't afford—"

"I paid up on the place through the end of the lease," Mia says. "You can just chip in on food and utilities. I'm sure you can manage that, right? It's only for a few weeks. *And* you'd be rooming with two awesome, superhot girls. How can you say no to that?"

He looks at me, and I can see he's worried about the same things I am. Rooming together. Being too close, constantly one second away from making a really dumb choice. He's young and too reckless for me. And a musician, on top of it all. He's everything I don't need sharing my space.

But something tugs at me, makes me put all of those concerns aside. I see it in his smoke-gray eyes, which are so alive, so deep and full of thoughts. Some pain or fear lives there. Something that makes it so hard for him to accept. To take a simple kindness. It's not just about me but about trusting. Anything.

Seeing that, I can't let him spend another night in this crappy place. Just . . . alone.

"You should come home with us," I say. "It will be . . . a lot better than this, I promise."

He moves around behind a low table and starts in on clearing away takeout bags, emptying ashtrays. "I can't contribute much. It just wouldn't be cool."

God, he's so stubborn.

But then so am I.

"Well, how about a trade?" I suggest. "My car's never coming out of the shop, and it's going to be a while before the money stuff gets sorted. So, how about I take you up on using your truck? In exchange for you coming to stay. That's fair, right?"

"You can use my truck anyway. I already offered."

"I know. But that didn't feel right to me, either. This does."

"What about Beth? Don't you have to ask her?"

Mia waves a hand. "She'll be fine. You don't know how many people come in and out of that place. She won't care."

He looks at me for confirmation.

"It's true," I tell him. "It's practically a flophouse. One more body will hardly register."

Which of course makes me think of his body under the shower. His hand on my throat. That kiss. I may be signing up for a lot of temptation, but it just feels—so much—like the right thing to do. And I'm a grown woman. I can keep my hands to myself.

"Please, Grey. It'll be fine. I promise."

"Okay," he says. "Okay. That would be great. Let's do it."

Chapter 21

Grey

"We're ordering pizza from Johnny's," Mia says, dropping her purse on the kitchen counter. "Are you okay with pepperoni and pineapple?" she asks me.

"Um . . . on the same pizza?"

Beth's sprawled on her back on the shag area rug, her feet propped up on the coffee table. She's been on the phone since I walked in five minutes ago. She didn't even bother to hang up when Mia and Skyler explained that I'll be staying here for a few weeks. She just held the phone away from her head, then said, "Sup, roomie," and went back to her conversation. She seems pretty chill.

"It's a good flavor pairing, trust me." Mia fishes her phone out of her purse. "The pineapple is a perfect foil for their spicy pepperoni. I'll order a combo, too, in case your friend wants to come over. There are drinks in the fridge. Help yourself to anything."

"Great." I shoot Titus the address, telling him to get here now. The dinner with his parents fell through. They're both lawyers and neither of them could get out of the office in time, which works out for me. I'm out of my depth and I could use him as backup. This is where I'm living for a few weeks, but I don't actually know where I *go*. I feel like a suitcase someone hasn't bothered to unpack and put away yet.

Skyler plops onto the couch and smiles at me. "Don't worry. You'll get used to it."

I think she means the funky pizza, but maybe she means being swallowed into the Mia-Beth-Skyler vortex. Mia just finished telling me I can use her bedroom furniture, since she and Ethan want to get some new things. Things are changing fast around me. I'm starting to worry there'll be a Grey makeover in my future.

While Mia orders the pizzas, I head back into the adjoining living room. Beth's blocking access to the only unoccupied chair. The girl's got legs. And sitting next to Skyler on the couch doesn't seem like a good call. It's not that the couch is small. It's more that I'm big, and that she sat in the middle, kind of monopolizing it. Why am I analyzing this? Screw it. I sit down next to her.

"So here we are," she says, without looking at me. "In my . . . I mean *our* apartment."

"Yep." There's a framed picture of her with Beth and Mia on the wall, from when she had blond hair. She looks great. It makes her more wholesome, more Kentucky. But I think I like the pink better. She's damn hot, either way.

Skyler drums her fingers on her jeans. "It's nice to be away from the studio. We're there so much."

"Except no craft services."

"True, but no spotlights, either. That's a plus."

"And fewer people."

"Well, Beth."

"Right. But she's not listening to us."

I'm not even sure *we're* listening to us. Why is this so awkward? Why did I tell her she was beautiful earlier, in her trailer?

This is painful. What's the right move here?

I turn toward her, because it's weird that we're both facing forward. Now her face is only inches from mine. Now I'm trying not to look at her mouth, and trying not to stare into her eyes, and trying not to look like I *can't* look into her eyes.

It's cool. No big deal. I'm just going to be living in her apartment. I might get to see her step out of the shower in a towel, or in her pajamas. Maybe they're tiny pajamas. Maybe she sleeps in one of those shiny, nighty things. Or a t-shirt. That seems more her style. Something soft and pink, like she was wearing in her headshot.

Shit. I've been staring. "So, um . . ."

"Yes?"

"You're kind of a couch hog." My shoulders are tight from surfing, and I want to sprawl out, stretch them, so I lean back, extend my legs, and drape my arm over the back of the couch. Better. "You're going to have to work on that, if we're going to be roommates."

I weigh so much more than she does that the cushions sag my way and she becomes a sort of Leaning Tower of Skyler.

"I'm not a couch hog," she says, scooting away from me. "It's your fault for being so big."

"Most girls don't complain."

She laughs. "You really should get over yourself."

"I will if you will."

"Deal."

"Wait, hold up. I don't like that deal."

She smiles. "Too late."

I feel like we're finally getting over some nerves here. Getting back to feeling comfortable around each other. Beth is talking to someone about eyebrow piercings. She's pinching the skin over her

eye to test how much it would hurt. Mia's disappeared. The bathroom fan is on; she's in there. I don't think I've ever been this aware
of where people are. I'm like an air traffic controller for girls.

I bump my knee against Skyler's. "So you got your first week out
of the way. How do you feel?"

"Honestly? I'm hanging in there, but . . . I'm tired."

I've noticed her eyes are glossy tonight, and there are faint shadows beneath them. They weren't there the day of the first audition.
I can't imagine pulling her hours. The time she's shooting is only a
fraction of it. Even when she and Garrett are in their trailers, they're
running lines or doing publicity stuff, or waiting—which isn't relaxing. When I perform, it's a huge rush while I'm onstage. It's a
two-hour sprint. Sky and Garrett, they're on all day. They're doing
daily marathons.

"Anything I can do?"

"*Would* you? Do something, I mean?"

"I offered. Name it."

She shakes her head. The way she's looking at me, it's like she's
measuring me. Trying to figure me out. She's the only person who
makes me feel young, and it's when she looks at me this way. It
sucks. I've lived a lot for nineteen. I've seen a lot, been through a lot.
If age is experience, I'm at least her age.

"Sky, stop looking at me like—"

Someone knocks on the door, and Beth jumps up to answer it.

"Hey, is—" Titus almost drops the twelve-pack under his arm
when he sees Beth. "Whoa . . . Hi."

"I gotta go," Beth says into the phone and stuffs it into her pocket.

If love at first sight were something I believed in, it'd be happening right now. Neither one of them says a word for five full seconds while their pheromones introduce themselves, chat it over, and
decide, *yes. Yes, I find you very attractive.*

"I'm Titus," he finally says. "Grey's friend. We're in a band together. I'm lead guitar. Backup vocals sometimes, for songs that need backup, uh, vocals. Hope it's okay I'm crashing. I brought beer for . . . for us to drink."

Beth fills in her half of the equation with the roommate info, the acting info, the college info, and then double rainbows arc over their heads, and they're both laughing at nothing—seriously, *nothing* funny. Something about the beer Titus brought.

"My ex hated it," he says, "and we broke up a year ago."

"That's so weird!" Beth says. "My ex hated Dos Equis, too! Like, *hated* it. How can beer fill someone with wrath?"

And they make some kind of instant pinky-shake pact to forevermore call it *Dos Exes*.

Titus barely nods my way as he steps inside. He and Beth move into the kitchen like a developing hurricane, where Mia's opening a bottle of wine.

Skyler leans toward me. "What. Just. Happened?"

That tiny gap between her teeth kills me. It gives her the sweetest damn smile. A smile that makes you smile back.

"What we just observed were literal sparks flying. Kind of like when we first met. Except we were sparkier."

"You really think so?"

"Yes. I already told you so. I made you melt, remember?" We both know we had mad chemistry. *Have* it. Her sunshine scent is driving me crazy. I want to brush the hair away from her bare shoulder. Kiss her. Being this close to her, it's like the rest of the world goes out of focus.

She must see something in my face because she frowns. "Grey, we should talk about something. Now that you're living here, we need to—"

"Hook up immediately. Agreed."

"Yes—What? *No.*"

"I'm just messing with you." When the doorbell rings, I stand.

I don't care about Adam's stupid money. I'm buying dinner for my new roommates tonight. But before I answer it, I say, "You have my word. While I live here, I promise I won't make the first move."

She laughs. "What kind of promise is that?"

I wink at her. "A hint promise."

Chapter 22

Skyler

Everyone tears into the boxes like it's the first food they've seen in a week, and we settle in around the coffee table in our dinky living room rather than trying to cram in around our dinky kitchen table.

Beth and Titus spread out on the floor opposite Grey and me on the sofa. I give him a little more room this time, but he's still so damn large, it feels like he's *everywhere*. Or maybe I'm just so conscious of him. His beachy scent, the gravity of his body, so muscled and substantial. He's so big, I can't stop thinking of crawling onto his lap, being wrapped up in all that strength.

Mia hands Grey a generous slice of the pepperoni and pineapple, and we all wait for his verdict. He takes a bite that puts away half the slice and groans. Chewing, he gives Mia a thumbs-up and finally says, "Holy shit, this is good."

"Told you. Spicy and sweet, the perfect combo."

"Tell me about it," Beth says, and Titus gives her a dazed look, like cartoon birds should be circling his head. I can't believe he's her type. She usually skews older, more professional. Guys with ties and plans. Not stubbled blonds who look like they just climbed out of a van. But she clinks her beer bottle against his and gives him the famous Beth Pierce smile, bringing it in a big, big way.

"You need to have some of this," Grey says, handing me a piece on a paper plate. "And we might need to order another one. I'm going to house this whole pie in about five minutes. Trust me on this."

"I totally do trust you," I say, but I look down at my plate, at the beer on the table in front of me, and hear Kaitlin tell me to lay off bread and alcohol. Then I think about Garrett telling me that wheat is treated with pesticides, and that's why so many people have problems with it. He's gluten-free, too. But then, he's kind of *everything*-free.

"Aren't you eating?" Mia asks.

"Oh, yeah, definitely." I take a bite of the pizza, and try not to think about pesticides or bloating or ripping through the bottoms of my wardrobe like some kind of She-Hulk.

"Good, right?" asks Grey, and I have to laugh at how it's like he's the Magellan of pizza discovery, clearly unaware that I have had this exact pizza roughly a hundred times before. It's cute.

He's just . . . really cute.

And a kid. Worse: a musician without a steady job, who throws house-wrecking parties and gives off this simmering anger half the time. Remember that, I tell myself, working to drive the message into my psyche.

I say, "*So* good," and allow myself another bite. One piece isn't going to make a difference. A couple of sips of beer. I'm not going to starve myself, right? I don't want to be one of those girls who treat food like Kryptonite. I just have to be a little smart about it. That's all.

We make it through the meal without the need to order another pizza, though Grey gives the last slice a mournful look, like he's about to put it in a shoe box and bury it in the backyard.

"You guys should come check us out," Titus says. Though by "you guys," it's clear he means, "You, Beth, the only girl whose existence I seem capable of noting at present."

"That'd be great," says Beth. "What do you guys play?"

They've already agreed on favorite books—anything by Chuck Palahniuk, Caitlin Moran, or Andrew Smith, and movies—anything by Wes Anderson or Richard Linklater, so I'm dying to see how they sync up with music.

Titus looks at Grey. "I don't know. Kind of . . ."

"Like alt-rock," Grey provides. "But roughed up. A little dirty. Like if Imagine Dragons went through a concrete mixer."

He has a voice a little like Eddie Vedder's, I think, so I can totally hear that. It makes me wish I'd stayed in the car and listened to more of his music. More of that sexy rasp that I know is going to develop into something even more devastating with practice and time.

Beth and Titus launch into a discussion of AWOLNATION, which she loves, and OneRepublic, which he loves, pretty much diving so deep into one another that the rest of us exchange awkward smiles and decide, en masse, to find other places to be.

"I'm going to head out," says Mia. "I've got to do some storyboarding for the new Boomerang campaign."

We say our good nights, and then Grey helps me clean up the paper plates and pizza boxes. I give him a quick tour of the kitchen, show him the balcony with its prime view of the alleyway and billboard cluster, and push open the door of the bathroom, so he can have a peek inside.

"Hello Kitty?" he smirks. "Really?"

"First of all, she's awesome," I tell him. "And second of all, it's at least a better shower than the beach."

"Did you know she's not even a cat?"

"What do you mean? Of course she's a cat."

"Nope. Apparently, she's a weird little girl in a cat costume."

"She is so not a weird little girl in a cat costume. She is a cat. With a hair bow."

He shrugs. "Google it. Weird little girl."

"*You're* a weird little girl." I push him back out of the bathroom, up the short hall toward Mia's room.

He laughs. "I guess I better get some hair bows then."

"I guess you need some hair first."

"Working on it." He scrubs at the dark stubble on his scalp.

At Adam's house, I saw a couple of photos of Grey pre-head shave, and his dark hair softened his eyes but made his cheekbones look a little more chiseled, his jaw even more striking. I'm glad to see he's growing it out again, though I remind myself that my preferences don't count for much.

I open the door to Mia's bedroom and switch on the bedside lamp.

Grey sets his duffle on the upholstered chair near Mia's vanity and glances around the room, taking in the lavender walls, the white eyelet comforter, the silver lamp with butterflies painted on the shade.

"It's definitely . . . purple."

"I think it's better than the 1950s mold you have going on over at the garage."

"No kidding." He walks over to the bed and runs his hands over the delicate wrought-iron headboard. "You think this thing'll hold me?"

"Only one way to find out."

He sits, and the box spring lets out a horrific groan. Laughing, he shifts his weight, and the headboard slams up against the wall behind it.

"I'm guessing Mia and Ethan don't get it on in here."

"Oh, I've heard some wall banging in my day," I tell him. "But mostly they're at Ethan's."

"Smart."

I come and sit down next to him. "I forgot to tell you, you're required to lie perfectly still every night. House rules."

He sprawls out on the bed. "I might need you to climb on," he says, patting his stomach. "You know. Keep me pinned down."

My face heats. I try not to imagine myself moving up the bed to straddle his powerful thighs, run my hands over his broad chest.

"I'm afraid that's not a service I provide," I tell him. I'm pretty sure we'd break the bed. Or die trying.

"Too bad."

My text alert chimes, and I pull out my phone.

Brooks: Hey, you busy?

I feel a weird flush of guilt. Like I'm cheating on Brooks. Or cheating on Grey. I don't know, and that's nuts, anyway, because I don't have anything going on with either of them.

"Sorry," I say to Grey. "Just have to . . ." Part of me doesn't want to say it's Brooks, but that feels wrong, like I'm hiding something. Because I have some motive I can't possibly have.

"No problem." But I feel his eyes on me. He shifts up in the bed, bunching Mia's three hundred pillows behind his back and folding his hands across his chest.

Skyler: Not busy. What's up?
Brooks: Can you come over? I've got Leigh here. Want to talk through a few things with you.

If I go, I'll feel like I'm disappointing Grey. But if I don't go, I'll be letting down Brooks, Mia, Adam, and dozens of other people who are counting on my commitment to the film.

"Everything okay?" Grey asks.

"Yeah, sorry. Brooks wants me to come out and work on some stuff with the screenwriter."

"Can't it wait for tomorrow?"

I shake my head, texting Brooks that I'll be there in twenty minutes. "I guess not."

"All right," says Grey. "Guess I'll have to christen this mattress all by myself."

His tone is neutral, but then he slips off the other side of the bed and heads around it toward the door.

"Sorry to miss out." I follow him out to the living room, where Titus and Beth now sit on the sofa together, still talking and laughing, possibly unaware that we ever left the room or that we've returned.

Grey plops down in the armchair next to them. "What's going on out here?"

Titus turns to give him a shy smile. "Nothing, man. Just talking."

"Well, count me in," he says. "Skyler's going to head out, though."

"Yeah?" Beth asks, looking up at me. "What's up?"

"Brooks wants to talk about the screenplay. He's got the writer over at his place, and I'm going to head over there."

She nods. "You think you'll be long?"

I shrug. "No idea. Why?"

"You just look a little tired. And we've got an early call tomorrow."

I head over to give her a hug. "I don't think I'll be long. Thanks for caring."

"That's how I do."

"I know." I kiss the top of her head. "Night, guys."

Titus offers a wave, and Grey gives me a clipped, "Night." He doesn't look at me.

I hesitate at the door for a second, listening to Beth, Titus, and Grey debate whether to watch a movie or take a walk down to the pier. I'd so love to stay and join in—or just get a good night's sleep. Beth's right. I am tired.

But I'll be fine, I decide, and head out into a cool, dry night that carries the scent of hibiscus. I climb into the truck—Grey's truck— and I find he's got a stack of demo CDs in the glove compartment.

I slip one into the dashboard console and smile as Grey's voice washes over me, keeping me company all the way across town.

Chapter 23

Grey

Something happened between you and Skyler, Greyson. Don't deny it," Garrett says on Saturday night. The shoot's wrapped for the day. Usually we head out pretty fast, but tonight we're lingering around the table in his trailer. We have a whole day off tomorrow so the soundstages can be reset with new interiors. Garrett doesn't have dinner plans until nine. I'm going to drop him off, then meet the band at the garage.

"We're roommates," I say, pushing around a vitamin bottle.

"I know this already. And?"

"What is this?" I hold up the bottle.

"Something Kaitlin gave me for weight control. And don't change the subject."

The dude's persuasive as shit. He doesn't miss a damn thing when it comes to people. Must be what makes him so good on-screen.

He probably sees emotional fluctuations in color auras. Everything else, like money, traffic laws, politics, math, telling time, he's pretty useless.

"Fine, I'll tell you. The girl . . . she's amazing, right? A million kinds of hot. Smart. Nice. Funny. I mean . . . I was really thinking she might be something special. But I've been paying attention around the apartment and she only flosses every *other* day. Can you believe that shit? Total deal-breaker."

Garrett crosses his arms, and nods. "Ah, yes. Poor dental hygiene. I've had relationships end for the same reason. And here I was thinking this had something to do with Brooks Wright. My second theory is that your brooding silence these past days has something to do with the Blackwood Family Drama."

So he's noticed that, too. I've managed to go almost three days without talking to Adam, Skyler, or Mom. I've seen all three of them. But I have this new trick now. I got a headset from Mia, so I can just pretend I've been summoned on some urgent errand when I see them, which actually happens a lot anyway.

I shrug. "You're way off-base."

"Obviously."

There's a knock on the door. I stand to open it, but Adam lets himself in, hopping up the two steps. "You're still here," he says to Garrett. He glances at me. What I notice is his button-down shirt, which is a light blue/purple color. I don't recognize it. Why am I hung up on a goddamn shirt? But then I get a mental image of him, Ali, and Mom walking into his apartment with shopping bags and realize . . . I feel out of the loop. His life is going on. He's doing things without me. All of them are. I mean, it was my choice to leave . . . but it still sucks.

"We've got a little surprise for you," Adam continues, to Garrett. "Can you come down to my office?"

"Of course!" Garrett beams.

Of course he makes me go with him. When we get there, a small crowd is gathered around Adam's laptop. They're excited about what's on the screen, but my eyes go right to Brooks's hand. It's resting on Skyler's lower back. She's still in Emma Beautiful Emma wardrobe, and for some reason that pisses me off. Like . . . let the girl punch the hell out. I don't know what my problem is with clothes today.

Then I see my mom, who's toward the back, laughing at something Mia said. Everyone on the set loves her. She was an actress for a while, before she had Adam. Every day someone new comes up to me in the production and says how lucky Adam and I are to have her as a mom. Yesterday it was the director of photography.

When Mom sees me, the laugh dies in her throat, and her smile fades away.

Great. Hell of a reaction.

I do a one-eighty, but Garrett's hand clamps on to my wrist. He wedges his way into the mix, taking me with him. I end up bumping into Skyler a little hard, because I'm twice the size of the path Garrett is forging. Skyler edges aside and doesn't say anything. Maybe because I didn't say anything. We're both ignoring each other. Obviously. Brooks's arm settles on her shoulder, and it's a possessive gesture. I make myself look at the computer screen before I punch him.

Everyone's excited about some early media coverage on the film—but Brooks's hand on Skyler is all I see. Garrett reads the photo caption in a comical voice, making everyone laugh. Skyler laughs, too, and I don't understand how it's so easy for her to be near me. Every second is torture for me. So much worse now that I see her around the apartment. I can't close my eyes without seeing her face, or hearing her voice. I thought it would get easier if I ignored her for a few days around the studio, but it isn't, and I can't take it anymore. I shove my way out of the huddle and head out to the hallway.

"Grey," Mom says behind me.

I wheel toward her. *"What?"*

She startles at my tone of voice, her eyes flying wide open. I remember that shocked look. I saw it at our home in Newport last August, before I left. I probably saw it a thousand times before that. How many times did I get in trouble, or say something rude, and get that look from her?

"I don't want to do this anymore," she declares. "Why are you pushing me away?"

"Because I'm hard to love. Remember?"

Now the shock turns to hurt. "That's not what I said. I said *you* make it hard to love you."

"It's the same thing."

"No, it's not. You are easy to love. It's impossible *not* to love you, Grey. What I meant when I said that is that sometimes you act like you don't need to be loved. I shouldn't have even said that, but you were so angry, and I was upset, and . . . I'm human, Grey. I made a mistake. With you . . . I feel so often like I'm doing the wrong thing for you. I feel like I never get through—"

"You can stop talking. That's the right thing." The door swings open, and Adam steps out but I keep going. I keep going because our fight is starting to come back to me, and it's making me want to bash my head against the wall. "And stop trying to *get through*. You did your job. You fed me. You raised me. I'm nineteen now. You don't have to pretend anymore."

"Come on, Grey," Adam says. "That's bullshit, and you know it."

"Please, Grey. Just tell me." Madeleine takes a step closer. "What happened that day?"

The hallway feels like it's elongating behind her. I can't believe this is happening right now. Here, in the hallway outside Adam's office. "Nothing happened. I went to see Lois. I went to her apartment and saw her. That's it."

Adam's eyes lock on to me. "You went to see *Lois*?"

He says my birth mother's name like it's the name of an airborne pathogen. Anthrax. SARS. Lois. "Yes, Adam. I went to see my real mom because I was tired of my fake mom's shit. Is that a fucking crime?"

Adam's too stunned to respond, but Madeleine isn't. "I just wanted you to apply yourself a little more, Grey. You're so smart. You could make something of yourself, but you don't *care*. You act like . . . like . . ."

"Like a white trash piece of shit? Say it, Madeleine. You know you want to say it."

"I was *not* going to say that."

"I'm never going to be your perfect son. I'm not him. Stop trying to make me him."

"Grey—" Adam says. "Grey, wait—"

But images from that day in August are coming up, and I need space. Fresh air. Freedom. So I'm gone.

My cell phone buzzes when I reach the Mercedes outside. Adam. I stand there, staring at my phone, trying to make sense of what I just said, what just happened outside his office.

Am I *jealous* of him? I never thought I was. I don't want to be. I love my brother, even though I hate him right now.

I don't envy what he's accomplished. I'm proud of him. And I don't want the business and the studio and the car. What I want is his ease with people. I want his fearless goddamn heart. His first wife, Chloe, died, but he's found someone again. He has Ali now. He's put the past behind him. How the fuck did he do that?

I know I push people away before they can ditch me first. I know that's what I do. But knowing doesn't change anything. I'm still the five-year-old kid who was given up by his mom.

Anthrax . . . SARS . . .

Lois.

Titus calls when I'm almost home. "Game time, Grey. Rez got a call. We're filling in at the Amber tonight. Their headliner backed out an hour ago. Drummer broke his hand last night punching a wall. Can you be here in twenty?"

Adrenaline roars through me. I gun the Mercedes and get there in ten.

The Amber is a small club, the kind of club that's *the* place to be for about six months before it's busted for something and shut down. Tonight, it's packed to the rafters.

The opening act is already on and they're loud, so no one answers the stage door, even after I pound on it for a solid minute. I have to go around front and tell the bouncer who I am. As I weave through the crowd toward backstage, a few girls check me out—one even trails me for a little while. I must be in a really shitty mood because I keep going and don't give it a second thought.

I find the band backstage. Everyone's pumped, and not just because we're about to gig. Rez has an update from Vogelson. He's gotten us into a band showcase called the Ring of Fire, which is a big deal, a huge event in a few weeks that's by invitation only. We've been invited. Vogelson's hooked us up. He'll be there to watch us play. With our kind of music, whether we can fire up a crowd and perform is the difference-maker. We need to be able to blow up stadiums with our sound—and we can. We will. So it's official. We've got our big audition lined up.

Emilio and Shane are so amped, they can't stop tackling each other. Titus and Rez look more dazed, both of them wearing shit-eating grins. But the news gives me mood whiplash. And I can't quite pull myself out of rage-mode, so I go from being two hundred pounds of anger to two hundred pounds of focused, ass-kicking, let's-kill-this-gig front man.

I sing the *hell* out of our set. Completely slay it. My voice already bends toward anger and pain, and tonight they're all over our songs. I have an endless supply of both, and I let them out, all the grit, and grasp, and grunt, and growl. I am myself as I sing. Wounded and angry. And I feel the entire club tune in to that, and to us. Our music casts a spell.

But between songs, when I'm talking and introducing what's next, or the rest of the guys in the band, the audience laughs and shouts back at us, easy and comfortable. After hearing me sing, I think they're surprised I'm just a dumb kid, jamming with his buddies when I start talking. Or maybe they just laugh and yell because I'm funny.

We play "Runner" and Sky's song even though they're both new, but I feel them more than our other songs. It's during that one— "Surprised by the Sky"—that I become aware of what I'm doing instead of just doing it, and I realize I'm holding back. I'm doing the same thing to the audience that I do to everyone. I'm singing, I'm rockin' it, but I can't quite give them *all* of me. I can't take that last step and bare my soul. I feel it, just beyond my reach. As the song progresses, I stretch toward it, that eclipsing, all-consuming place where I hide nothing. I push for it, and push—but it only moves farther off. The way to that next level isn't by effort. I don't know *how* to reach it, and the set's over.

When I come fully out of the performing trance and step off-stage, my shirt's off. I'm dripping. I feel human again, whole again, my demons exorcised, and the roar of the crowd is ear-shattering. We don't have an encore song. We've played all our original music.

"We have to do another song," Rez says. "They're losing their minds!"

Nora and Beth, who's been hanging out a lot with Titus, come up. They've sold out completely of our CDs, and every one of our promo cards is gone.

"We have to play something else," Shane echoes.

The manager's standing behind us. When we checked in two hours ago, he looked like every other jaded club manager. Now he's all smiles and compliments. "You hear that? That doesn't happen every night," he says.

I look out to the bright lights onstage. Dust motes swirl around the mic stand. I think about what I felt while I was singing. I should go out there. I should do one more song and open up, give it everything. But I shake my head. "That's it for me tonight."

Chapter 24

Skyler

Sometimes, it feels like this movie is more real than my real life.

Or maybe it's that the movie feels like the life I wish I had—one where I feel witty, charming, and just perfectly delightful all day, every day. Of course, it helps to have someone else write your lines, tell you how to stand, where to be.

I watch the dailies every now and then, and I'm amazed. The lighting, the makeup, the clothing—all of it makes me look so different from how I see myself. Makeup makes my lips look full and glossy, inviting. My features contoured to perfection. My posture, mannerisms—all of it feels like some other girl. One with perfectly fitted clothes. With the right words for every moment.

And I have to admit, the yes-girl in me, the go-to girl, likes the attention, likes knowing I'm good at this, that I'm making people happy. I know music does that for me, too, but this is different. I feel like I'm carrying more here, like it's not just for me but for my mother and brother, for all the people gathered on set, and—eventually—for an audience much larger than any I've ever played to before.

Beth and I sit at a table in a fake coffee shop together, goofing around between takes while Kaitlin and Bernadette fuss over the jacket I'm wearing. It's pulling across my upper arms, which are not dainty LA arms, elegantly sculpted through a billion hours of yogalates, but super muscled from dragging my cellos around for years. And to make it all more frown-worthy, apparently my bow arm's a good inch larger, which makes me feel like some kind of freak. Half girl, half fiddler crab.

"On the plus side, we had to take in your skirt a little," Bernadette says, peeling the toffee-colored jacket, which I really loved, off me and handing it to Kaitlin.

"Is that going to be weird?" I ask. "I mean for continuity. If I keep losing weight?"

She laughs. "That would be an awesome problem to have, right? It'll be okay. I doubt you can make a drastic enough change in the next six weeks to really screw up the visuals. But it'll help everything lay better. And definitely help when we're on to the beach stuff."

Right. We're heading to Virgin Gorda in a few weeks to film the big finale. Which means bathing suits. Lots of skin.

"Just keep doing what you're doing," Bernadette adds.

"Girl's hardly eating," Beth mutters.

Bernadette heads off with Kaitlin to find me something different to wear.

"I'm eating." Just not as much. Or as often. "I just want to look good, Bets."

She doesn't have to worry about it, I think. She's model-tall and a perfect size four, top and bottom. *And* she's not the lead.

I take a couple more of Kaitlin's supplements, swallowing them down with black coffee, which is cold now and tastes like charred feet. My head feels a little buzzy, and my stomach growls to remind me I haven't actually had anything to eat yet today.

"Did you ever find out what's in those?"

I shrug. "Just, you know, herbs. Plant extracts. That kind of thing."

She arches a brow. "Hemlock's a plant."

"Ha ha."

"I am serious as the heart attack you're gonna have if you keep living on coffee and mystery pills."

"You see me eat all the time. Didn't we just destroy the buffet at Mayura?"

"Girl, you ate, like, a thimble-full of fish curry and two bites of tandoori chicken."

I laugh. "I had more than that, and you know it."

Didn't I? I mean, I passed up the fried bananas and the naan, which made me want to cry, but I ate plenty. I just don't feel as hungry lately.

Finally, they get everything reset, and we play out the scene. A short one where I clumsily attempt to set my best friend up on a date, and she rebuffs me because she's interested in another guy, though my character's also trying to set *that* guy up with a *different* girl, creating a hilarious chain reaction, which eventually leads to a set of scenes I can't wait to play. It's like an old-time farce or a Shakespearean comedy, with all the mismatched couples stuck together in a run-down resort in the Virgin Islands.

We get through it a few times, riffing a bit. Beth's an awesome improviser. I wish she had more scenes with Garrett, who I think would love to play against her. But they appear together just a handful of times and only interact directly once.

The scene ends, and Beth picks up the conversation like no time has passed at all.

"I'm making paella tonight. You going to be home?"

My stomach literally whines at the thought of Beth's paella, which is like the crack cocaine of foods. I can already taste the chorizo, the spices, the saffron rice that I imagine shoveling into my mouth by the spoonful until I expand into a giant Skyler ball, and they have to roll me to my room.

"Not sure. Brooks asked about getting together. What's the occasion?"

"No occasion. Grey's having the band over . . ."

"You mean he's having *Titus* over, don't you? Your *lover*?"

It's only been a week, so they haven't really gone there yet, but it's brewing. You can feel it between them like waves crashing up against a flimsy seawall. I do know they've made out like crazy, though, because every time I come across them, he's smeared with Beth's signature poppy lip stain and looks like he just saw God.

"Grey's having the *whole* band over," she tells me. "And Titus is . . ." I can swear the girl blushes a bit, and Beth *never* blushes. "He's just unexpected."

"You sure you want to make such a garlicky dish?" I tease her. "And all that food? I mean, you don't want to have a paella baby in you when you finally get down to business with Titus."

"Well, you can help me out by actually eating something. Like a normal human amount of food."

This again. I'm too tired and hungry to argue. "Fine. I'll eat a giant helping."

"Great." Beth sits back in her chair with a triumphant grin on her face. "I'll make extra."

I get home later than everyone, which means I walk into a party already in progress. The Bleachers are playing. The conversation is loud. And the balcony door's wide open, bringing in the smell of car exhaust and the smoke from our neighbor's grill.

Just as I step into the living room, my phone chirps. My mom. I shoot her a quick text that I'll call her back later. I haven't had a chance to talk to her all week, and I feel awful. Apparently, my dad didn't pay any of their utilities before he left. I've sent a check overnight to her and tried to cover things by credit card from here, where I could. But she's coming apart a little, and I need time to really sit and talk to her. Someplace private and quiet, though I have no idea where that place might be.

"There she is!" says Beth, whose eyes are already a little glassy from the prominent jug of punch she's got on the pass-through between the kitchen and living room.

Before I know what's hit me, she's taken my purse and laptop bag, stripped off my coat, thrust a big glass of punch in my hands, and pointed me toward the sofa, where a space materializes between one of Grey's band members—Emilio, maybe?—and Shane, who I think dates Nora.

"Where's Grey?" I ask, squeezing between them. He doesn't seem to be talking to me—not much at least—since the night he came to live with us, but he's not exactly avoiding me, either. He just always seems to be on his way to somewhere else. And when he's not at Garrett's beck and call, he's holed up in some corner, listening to music and mumbling lyrics under his breath.

"I sent him to the store for some saffron," Beth tells me.

"And some Dos Exes," Titus calls from the kitchen, where apparently Beth has put him to work on the mussels.

She giggles like a twelve-year-old girl. Good Lord, what's happening here?

In the space of five minutes, my mom texts back asking when, exactly, we can talk. Then Brooks texts to ask if we can get together after all. Even if it's late. He's pumped and wants to share ideas. That's followed by a text from my brand-new agent, Parker, asking about a get-together with Jane, my brand-new publicist. And then Grey walks through the door, carrying a lot of beer and one tiny bag, presumably, of saffron.

"Hey," he says to the general assemblage, including me more or less by default, but he doesn't look my way, just carries everything into the kitchen.

Parker texts more thoughts about meeting on set tomorrow. Better to get started early. Jane is rounding up "beaucoup opportunities" for me.

Then Brooks texts to reiterate that he is really okay with meeting late. Even 10 p.m., though he knows we have a super early call time so he understands if I can't make it.

Brooks: But I hope you'll make it.

My head starts to throb. I put my phone on silent. I just want a minute. I wish I could put my life on silent, too.

"We've got about thirty minutes," Beth says, and I want to cry because I'm so hungry.

The band and crew are loading up on beer and chips, but I go into the kitchen to grab an apple.

When I come back, Nora says, "I didn't know you play the cello."

"Well, we just met three minutes ago," I say, and it comes out about twenty notches bitchier than intended. I try a smile, but I feel how fake it is, like I'm some weird game show host, in the weirdest, most unfriendly game on earth. "But, yeah. Been playing since I was a kid."

"Electric cello, too," Beth calls from the kitchen. "Play something, Sky."

"No, that's okay." I just want to eat my apple and melt into a puddle on the couch. "You guys are—"

"Electric cello's totally rad," Titus says, coming into the room with more chips.

He tosses Grey a beer and then settles onto the arm of my dad's old club chair, one of the few things I hauled across country for sentimental reasons. My brother and I used to all pile onto it with him, when he was home, and he'd read us stories or sing songs. Then he went away for a long summer, and when he came home, it felt weird, somehow, like my brother and I had gotten way too big in just a few months.

"I'd love to hear you play," says Nora. She's a beautiful girl. Totally sporty, blond with an asymmetrical haircut, biker shorts, and a Plain White T's t-shirt, which is neither plain nor white.

"Just give us a quick mini concert while we wait," Beth says, coming into the room. She pushes Titus onto the club chair and then flops onto his lap. Even though she's probably his equal in height, she doesn't care. She's so comfortable with him, and with her own body. "Please? I'll pay you in chorizo."

I take another bite of my apple, which tastes dry and grainy, making me feel cheated. "Nah, I don't really feel like it."

"Come on," she says. "Grey, turn down the stereo."

He gets up to do it, looking at me for the first time but not speaking. I can read the interest in his eyes, though, the excitement he's trying not to show. He wants to hear me.

Maybe it will help, I think. A little musical therapy to fight off my pissy mood.

"Okay," I say, and everyone breaks into applause and cheers. I smile, a real one this time. Yeah, maybe a little concert's what I need. Just to connect to my music and let everything else drift away.

I get Christina from the room and plug my amp and speaker in by the balcony, turning it down low so the sound doesn't melt everyone's faces.

"What do you want to hear?"

"Do the Fall Out Boy one," Beth says. " 'Centuries'?"

"Well, I'm still working on that. I mean, I haven't really gotten it yet."

"It sounds amazing."

It would sound better with my looper. Also with a bass. Some drums. Patrick Stump. Maybe just the band and not my cello at all.

"I love that song," says Titus, giving me an open, encouraging smile. "We're all musicians. We don't care if it's perfect."

But I care. I don't know why, but I do.

I sit down and warm up a little bit. It feels like years since I've played, though it's only been about a week and a half. Still, that's a long time away from it—for me.

My fingers feel stiff as I start to play, the cello awkward in my arms.

On the coffee table, I see my cell phone light up then go dark. Light up then go dark again. My mother? Brooks? Parker? Or someone else completely? Someone else with ideas for my life, who wants to help me or who needs my help? Someone else who comes with a set of expectations about who I'm supposed to be, what I'm supposed to do?

The song's not working. I have to think too much, and I'm out of the pocket. The rhythm's wrong. It just sounds lousy.

I put down my bow. "Sorry."

"For what?" Beth asks. "You sounded—"

"Like crap. Let me do a different one."

"It didn't sound like crap," Grey says. Finally, a whole sentence just for me. And a fat frickin' lie at that.

"I can hear it," I say. "I mean, it only *sounds* like I've gone tone deaf."

"Not at all," says Reznick. "I liked it."

"Well, thanks, but let me do something else." Something I'm goddamned good at, I want to say. I feel this rush of anger in me, way out of proportion to anything that's going on in the room.

I go for "Bittersweet Symphony," because it's one I've played a thousand times before. One I can do in my sleep.

It's better, but it's not great. My fingers are just stupid stumps at the end of my hands. The amp is making a grating crackling sound. My belly roils, pushing acid up into my throat. Everything's wrong, and my phone won't stop going bright and dark. Bright and dark. Over and over.

I stop playing and get to my feet. A chilly calm settles over me, but my eyes burn with tears. I have to get out of here.

"I'm sorry, guys. I guess I'm out of practice. Maybe another time. Sorry."

I want to say it a hundred more times. Sorry. Sorry. Sorry.

Stopping just long enough to pull the plug on Christina, I flee to my room.

Chapter 25

Grey

*A*ren't you going to go talk to her?" I ask Beth, once Skyler's gone.

I've never seen her this way. Apologetic and skittish. Faded. That wasn't Skyler. I don't know who that was. Her ghost?

Beth looks toward Sky's closed door, thinking for a moment. She shakes head. "She's tired. Sleep's the best thing for her."

"You're her friend," I say, getting up. "But I'm going to have to go with my gut on this." I grab Skyler's cell phone from the coffee table and head to the kitchen. I find the knife drawer, then slam the butt of a butcher knife into the glass a few times, then I toss it in the trash.

From the living room, I hear hushed comments about my supposedly "legendary temper." But this isn't a temper tantrum. I feel completely calm. I have a mission. Eliminate anything that's bothering Skyler. The phone had to die.

When I come back into the living room, Beth and Titus force some conversation about what they're doing later. Maybe Netflix a movie or go out to a bar with the rest of the band. But I feel everyone watching me as I knock on Skyler's door.

"Hey . . . Sky? It's Grey." She doesn't answer. I turn the knob. The door's unlocked. "I'm coming in, Sky."

She's sitting at her desk. Her laptop sits in front of her, but it's closed. Light streams in from the street and her bedside lamp, but the room is dim, blue. "Need something?" she asks.

"Yeah. I do. I need to know what's going on."

"With me? Nothing." She rises and leans against the desk. Her face is a mask of composure. She's becoming a better actress. She's learning from Garrett. But her eyes give her away. They're puffy and red. Like she's on the brink of crying, or maybe was crying before I walked in. "And we don't need to be friends, just because we're roommates."

"What does that mean? We're friends. Aren't we?"

Her composure melts away. Her features harden with anger. She comes over and jabs her finger at my chest. "I don't need friends who ignore me for three days then think it's okay to barge into my room and pretend to be all concerned. What do you want, Grey? Why are you here? Why are you always so nice when you're not being an asshole? It's really confusing."

I don't know how this became about me. But now that she's close, I see that her shoulders are trembling. "Skyler, you're shaking."

"I'm fine." She steps back and wraps her arms around herself. "Don't change the subject. It's just cold in here." It's not. It's only slightly cool, but she's wearing a dress with thin straps that doesn't look very warm.

"For the record, you changed the subject first." I move to the window and close it. This is one of my jobs as roommate. Skyler's window always jams. I'm the only one who can close it. It makes me wonder what she did before I moved in.

The street noises die down. In the living room, faintly, Nora's laugh erupts.

"Look, Sky. I'm not trying to be confusing. It's just easier for me to steer clear of you."

"Because?"

"You know why."

She moves to her bed and sits, hugging her arms. Just like that, she looks small and vulnerable. I know she wonders why she was chosen for Emma, but every small emotion is clear on her face, her body. She's like a day with sunshine and hail and wind and big, rising clouds. You can't help watching her, to see what's next. To feel it with her.

She sighs softly. "I can't believe I'm going to ask you this, but . . . the night you moved in you asked me what you could do to help."

"I remember."

"Can you just . . . hug me for a minute?"

"Yeah—yes." I sit next to her and put my arms around her. She leans against me, burrowing her head against my chest, and wrapping her arms around my waist. I thought this might be awkward, but it's not. She fits perfectly under my shoulder. It puts the top of her head right below mine. I want to lean down and kiss her right on her shiny pink hair. "How's this?"

"Amazing. You're so warm and big. Like hugging a lawn chair that's been sitting out in the sun except with muscles instead of cushions."

"I get that a lot. Want to lie down on me and take a nap?"

"Yes."

"Yes as in yes?"

"Yes."

My heart's going bananas as we scoot back onto her pillows. Skyler curls up right next to me, her head on my chest. I'm having a hard time processing whether this is actually happening, or whether it's one of the many dreams I've had that start this way. I can't sit still, so I trace letters on the smooth skin on her shoulder. I write things like:

Us

Finally

Beautiful

"How you doing?" I ask.

"So good. What are you writing? I can't figure it out."

"Here's an easy one," I say, and trace the letters S-E-X on her shoulder.

"My name?"

I laugh. "Close."

For a little while, we just lie there, settling into each other. I force myself to stay relaxed, when what I really want to do is pull her beneath me. Touch her, taste her, feel her. Everything her.

"I think I got overwhelmed," she says, quietly, "with all the expectations put on me. Not just from the film, but from . . ."

"From who?" I prompt. If she says Brooks, I'm going to pound the shit out of him.

"My mom. It's complicated with my parents."

I ask her how. She peers up at me, and it's like she's weighing whether I'll understand. Then she tells me about her mom in Kentucky, who's not able to support herself. And her father, who's a musician and leaves for long stretches without giving any notice. A picture starts to emerge in my mind. Her father's irresponsible and selfish. Her mother's irresponsible and co-dependent.

"I've been sending her money, trying to help," she says, "but it's the emotional support that's hardest. She's just so needy sometimes, especially when my dad's gone. I just feel too young to be my mother's mother, you know?"

I don't want to disagree with her. But something about what she said strikes a chord. "You never know what made her the way she is. She could be trying. And I doubt she's trying to make your life harder." I get this feeling like I'm protecting someone in *my* life with those words. My birth mother? Madeleine? Me? "But it sucks that she's adding to your stress."

She's quiet for a long moment. Then she reaches over and shuts off the lamp. Darkness settles over us like a secret. It feels like we're really alone now, even though we have been. I don't want this moment to ever end, and I want to change it *now*. More. That's what I want. More of her.

"Grey? Do you think it's possible to be an artist . . . a true artist, who gets lost in your work, and still have a balanced life?"

"That's a damn good question." It's one I've thought about a lot, especially over the past few weeks. "There are times I feel like my music eclipses everything else. It's like being on a boat out in the middle of the ocean, no land in sight, and you're just focused. Connected to all the rises and falls of being alive. It's amazing, that lost and drifting feeling. I don't think there's anything wrong with it at all. But for me, it wouldn't mean much without being able to come back to someplace, or someone."

It's where I am right now, not talking to Adam and Mom. I'm adrift in my music. *Too* adrift, without being able to tell them about it. Somehow my family exile is spreading to Dad, too. He never gets involved in drama, but he called today. I saw the call come through and let it go to voicemail. I've never done that before. I don't fuck around with my relationship with him. But it's all such a mess, and I knew he was calling to talk about Mom.

Skyler is quiet but I feel her, alert and listening. Waiting for me to continue. So I do.

"I guess I see the lost part as a good thing. Being lost means you're searching. It means you're trying to get somewhere, understand something. I wrote a song about it recently. I wrote it the day I met you." Shut up, Grey. Shut up. That's off topic. "But, to answer your question, I don't think an artist needs a balanced life, as much as one that has meaning."

"How do you define meaning?" she asks.

"Family."

"Right . . . That puts me back where I started."

"Yeah. Like you said, it's fucking complicated."

She laughs, and when the sound fades away, there's a knock on the door. It's Beth. Everyone's going out and she wants to know if we're okay. I let Skyler answer. I'm obviously doing pretty damn great. She tells Beth we're fine here, and to have fun.

"I feel like we're on the boat right now," Skyler says, when the apartment falls quiet. "The two of us." Her hand slips under my t-shirt and moves up my stomach. I have a heart attack, and my entire body goes cement-hard.

Her cool fingers start tracing circles on my stomach. *What the—?*

I'm on *fire.*

Burning.

Chill, Grey. Just freakin' *relax.*

"Grey?"

"Um." There are no working brain cells in my head. "That's, um, me. Grey. That's me, right?"

She laughs and lifts her head. Her smile is soft, seductive. The end of me, basically.

"You said you wanted me to make the first move. Here I go." She leans down and kisses me, her soft lips sucking gently on mine.

I kiss her back slowly, and sweep my tongue against hers. Skyler sighs and shifts higher on the bed, more onto me. She's warm and tastes sweet. Her soft pink hair brushes my cheek as she leans over me.

I wrap my arms around her and pull her tight against me, and our mouths find a rhythm that's full of improvisation. We kiss hard and deep, and her eyes flutter closed, her fingers digging into my shoulders, then slow and soft; we stop to smile at each other, then start again. I've never kissed anyone this way. Fast, slow, hungry, gentle. It's like we want to do everything, try everything, be every way with each other *right now*.

I don't know where this is going. I know where I want it to go. My body *definitely* knows where it wants this to go. I want her so much, it's agony.

Then reason. Reason taps me on the shoulder.

Does she really want this? Or am I just the guy who's here right now?

Who *cares*?

I run my hands over Sky's body. She's curvy and so goddamn soft. She makes me insane. I want to crush her with my body. I want to make her mine. I want to take care of her. Want, want, want. She makes me into pure want and I'm having a hard time being gentle and slow now, kissing her, touching her. Skyler breaks our kiss and her hazel eyes come to mine. She likes what she sees. Me, out of breath. Drunk on her. Me, at her mercy.

Skyler shifts so she's straddling me, and her kisses move to my neck and my jaw. I tug the hem of her dress up and run my hand along her leg. Then I reach back and find the zipper. When the dress falls to her waist, she leans down, covering herself.

"Wait," I whisper. "Let me see you."

"Okay. Okay." She gives me a shy smile and straightens, and I memorize the way she looks, which is perfect. I've imagined her a million times. But she's a million times more beautiful than what I imagined. I lean up and taste her. Soft, warm, full. She wraps her arms around my head and I grab her hips. We need less clothes. But any second now, she's going to tell me to stop.

"Sky . . ." What are we doing here? Are we doing this?

She pulls my shirt off, and reaches for the button on my jeans. I grab her around the waist and pull her beneath me, swapping our positions on the bed.

Skyler tugs my jeans down, then my boxers. Her panties come off. Things are happening fast. I know I have some kind of concern. What the hell was it? I remember. *Fuck.* I remember and I don't want to remember, but . . . damn it. "Sky . . . You're upset."

"I'm not. Not anymore."

I can't think with her hands on me, her naked body beneath me. "It's okay, Grey. I want this."

I do, too. I want her.

Chapter 26

Skyler

I'm in bed with Grey.

I'm *in bed* with Grey.

I'm in bed with *Grey.*

I know he's my lifeline in this moment, my drug to help me forget everything else. I know it's wrong. Not smart. But I don't care. I want it. I want him.

We kiss and kiss, my tongue against his, tasting all of his sweetness, the taste of mint and spices. I'm not trembling now. I'm light and solid, all tongue and fingers and lips and teeth.

He kisses like he sings—raw and skilled and searching. I trace the cords of his muscled arms, feel the rippled breadth of his back. His weight tethers me in the best possible way.

We break off, and he stares down at me. His eyes, his beautiful light gray eyes, like sunshine glimmering through rain, they hold me here. See me. For who I am in this moment. Not who I'll be in another seven pounds. Or when we wrap the film. Or when I send a check.

"Sky . . ." he starts, but I don't want words. I just want him.

I pull him closer and feel the length of him, the *really* full length of him, against my belly. Pressing against me. So close. Nothing between us. He's so huge, all of him, not just his body, but his big beautiful heart, his energy, the power and goodness of him. I want it all inside me. Want to be filled with it. With him.

We kiss and kiss, and I graze my teeth and tongue along his jaw-line, nip his smooth shoulder.

He groans and presses hard against me, making me gasp.

"Shit," he says, shifting his weight. "I don't want to hurt you."

I pull him back against me, reaching down between our bodies. I'm ready for him. So ready. "Hurt me," I say. But it's not pain I want but *feeling*. Being in my body. Being here and now.

I shift my thighs apart, my need for him a sharp hot throb in every part of me. I'm scared and excited, but I want him so much. Even for just one night.

But Grey's stopped moving, gone still beneath my hands.

"Grey?"

He looks at me, and it's all wrong. There shouldn't be so much hurt there. Or fear.

"What's wrong? What did I do?"

"I don't want to hurt you," he repeats. But it's different now. Guarded. He eases off me, and I know somehow I've spoiled things.

"You're not. I promise. I want—" All of it. Everything. So much, I can't find words for it all.

He looks at me, and his jaw flexes. His lips press together.

"Grey, what just happened? Talk to me."

Shaking his head, he says, "I just . . . Shit. I can't believe I'm saying this, but it doesn't feel right." His eyes shift away from me, and his hand comes to settle on the sheets now bunched between us. Everything's wrong. "Like I said, I don't want you to get hurt."

"Stop saying that. That's not what this is about."

It's like a light's gone out, just blinked into nothing. How can that be? I can't make sense of it.

He still can't look at me. "You were crying. You just ... I shouldn't have taken advantage of that."

"You didn't," I tell him, fighting to keep from touching him, from pulling him back onto me, which felt so perfect and so right. "I made the first move, remember? Just like you wanted."

"Yeah." All the warmth's gone from his eyes. He's somewhere else, and I can't follow him there.

"You won't hurt me," I tell him, gently. "And even if you do, I'm not a child. I can handle it. I won't shrivel up and die."

"But I will," he says. "I mean, I won't die. But I couldn't take it if I hurt you. I'm sorry."

He slides up on the bed and tugs his wadded-up jeans out from under my legs. Getting to his feet, he pulls them on then picks up his briefs and his t-shirt and just stands there, looking down at me.

I feel more naked than ever now. And wrong in every possible way.

It's not me he's worried about at all. I see that now. He's the one who can't stand to be hurt. Who can't trust. He's just going to keep picking at that wound inside himself, over and over. Until he grows the hell up.

"Can you give me my dress?" I hate the sound of my voice, dead in this quiet room. I need to get out of here. Talk to my mother. Answer calls. Go see Brooks.

He does, and I slip it on, zip it up without asking for help. I find my underwear and step into them.

Grey hovers by the doorway, watching. I feel how much he wants to leave, to get the hell away from me. And how much he wants to stay, to keep an eye on me. To protect me, like *I'm* the one who needs protecting.

I move past him into the living room, which is still littered with beer bottles, empty bags of chips. Great. I push aside the debris in search of my cell phone.

"Sky, we're cool, right? You understand?"

I nod, barely listening. Where did I put my phone? "We're fine."

After consolidating some of the junk, I take everything into the kitchen and find, in the trash, my cell phone, smashed to pieces.

"What happened?" I pick it up. The screen isn't just cracked; it's pulverized. I try to switch it on, but it's dead. "Did it fall? How did it get like this?"

Grey rubs his jaw, and the look on his face tells me everything.

"Did you do this?" I ask. But I already know. "*Why* would you do this?"

"Because it fucking stressed you out every time you got a call." His tone is angrier than it should be. Especially for a person who just ruined hundreds of dollars of technology that *I* have to replace.

"You think it won't stress me out to have to get a new one? To not be able to get calls when I have to be somewhere every minute? When my mom's having a crisis thousands of miles away?"

"I'm sorry. I didn't think about it. I just . . . did it."

"Well, no shit." I dump the pieces of the phone back into the trash. "But if your solution to every problem is to smash it, then I'm glad things didn't go any further back there."

"I don't smash every problem," he says. "Christ, Skyler. You make it sound like I'm the Hulk. I was just trying to give you a break."

"No, you don't smash everything. Mostly you just avoid it. Like your mom. Like me for the last few days." I'm going to cry again, and I don't want him to see me do it. He's not what I need. I've been right about that all along.

I push past him, find my shoes, purse, and car keys, though I don't know yet where I'm going. Just that I need to go. It occurs to me that I could go to the bar and meet up with the others. But I don't want to be around Grey's band or around Titus and Beth and whatever it is they have going.

Brooks, I think. I need to go see him, like I promised. Work on the film. I can't call him to say I'm coming over, but I know it'll be okay. He said he'd be home all night, so I know that's where I'll find him. He'll be where he's supposed to be.

And that's where I need to be now, too. Somewhere safe and sane. I'm sure I can call my mom from there, and then we'll just get to work. It'll be such a relief, I think. To be with someone who just, plainly, wants me. Someone straightforward, stable, and easy. I don't know why I haven't let myself have that. It looks so good to me right now.

I say good night to Grey, who barely answers, then I head out, closing and locking the door behind me.

Chapter 27

Grey

Garrett, mind if I take off for an hour?" I ask him. He's in a tuxedo, and he looks sharp. We're filming a Christmas party scene for the movie.

I've spent the day watching him and Skyler pretend to flirt in front of six film cameras and two dozen people. I don't mind them flirting, obviously. What I don't like is how Brooks pulls Sky aside whenever there's a break in the shoot schedule. What I don't like is the way his goddamn hands touch her back or her arm or her hands, like he can't freakin' speak unless he's touching her. I feel possessive of her. Insanely. And I've pushed her right into Brooks's arms by acting like a total tool last night.

Skyler didn't sleep at the apartment. I know she slept at Brooks's place, even though I'm pretty sure they didn't hook up. I don't think. I don't know why I think that. Maybe it's just what I want to believe.

"Sure, Greyson. I'll survive without you for an hour, most likely." Garrett looks from me, to Brooks and Skyler, to Adam and Mom, who are standing together holding lattes. So alike. Stylish and lean. Polished. Garrett takes my face in his hands. "Try and come back without that frown you've been wearing all day." He winks and lets me go.

I glance at Skyler as I leave the soundstage. She's under the bright lights, surrounded by tables and props that make this warehouse look like an upscale restaurant. Skyler is sitting at a table, and Mia has plopped into the chair Garrett was occupying during the scene. They look like they're in a deep conversation, and I wonder if it's about me.

What choice did I have last night? If we'd slept together, she'd have regretted it. Does she have any idea that stopping us was one of the toughest things I've ever done? It destroyed me. Mentally, it was the right call. Physically, I'll never forgive myself. It *hurts me* to imagine what I passed up—and I've been imagining it all damn day.

I close my eyes and hear her voice. "If your solution to every problem is to smash it, then I'm glad things didn't go any further back there."

Even last night, she was already relieved. Smash or avoid. That's what she thinks of me. That's how she thinks I deal with problems. She's right. I left home last August, when the shit hit the fan with Mom. And I left Adam's place last week, when the same thing happened. Avoid and avoid. And I did smash her phone last night. I really am the Hulk.

I walk to the parking lot, feeling better with a little fresh air, and hop in the Mercedes. Twenty minutes later, I'm talking to a salesman at an electronics store. I buy an unlocked model of the newest iPhone and drive back to the studio. It's dark, but all the cars are still here. They're still filming. I open the box and take out the new phone and power it up. Then I find the record voice memos option, and click it.

"Sky . . . It's Grey. I have a few things I want to say. First thing. Sorry about your phone. Hope this one's an okay replacement. The guy at the store said this is a better model than the one you had. Newer. Anyway, I hope you like it. Second thing . . . I've been think-ing you're right about some of the things you said about me. How I smash or avoid, and . . . I'm going to do better. You probably don't give a shit what I do but . . . I'm going to change that stuff about me. I'm standing by what I said, though. I mean, by what I did, by not hooking up with you. Skyler . . . I can't risk messing up with you. I couldn't use you, and I couldn't let you use me, and I think that's what last night would've been. You're too good for that.

"Anyway, I'm not going to avoid you or make it awkward be-tween us. I don't want to do that again. It's going to majorly suck, because I think you're kind of with Brooks, but whatever. I'll deal. So, if you're up for it, we should be friends. I want to be your friend. That sounds really lame. Shit. I actually had a plan going into this. All right, I'm going to wrap it up. Sky, this is me, making the first move: let's be buds?" I'm laughing at my idiot self as I stop the re-cording. Let's be buds? Seriously? But I leave it the way it is. That message burned all my courage.

I put the phone back in the box. Then I sit in the car for a little while, just watching the parking lot. I already feel better. I know she'll accept my offer. When we talk, when there's none of the at-traction bullshit going on between us, it's so good. We connect. I know she feels that, too. That's what I don't want to lose. That's what I'm fighting to keep.

I use my truck's spare key and unlock it, and leave the new phone on the driver's seat. I notice, as I lock back up, that my truck smells like her now.

I don't see her the rest of the night. We miss each other at the studio. When I leave, I go straight to band practice since it's late. The guys give it extra gas as we move through our songs. I feel us improving, fueled by the upcoming showcase. We sound awesome. The girls are quiet, watching us, Nora and Beth. Evie and Renee. In their expressions, I see something that's close to wonder. I see us becoming something unique, whole. But at the same time I'm conscious of the barrier I noticed at our Amber performance. How I hold back the last small part of myself and don't give over completely. I push for it when we play "Runner." I push for honesty. I push to let out the pain, the rejection, the fear. I edge right up to it, but I can't break down the barrier.

We shut it down around midnight, and I head back to the apartment. Now that Beth and Titus are together, they've been going to his place a lot. Titus lives in a studio apartment, and privacy is a big plus for them right now. They can't keep their hands off each other.

I'm disappointed when I get home. Skyler's still out. I grab my guitar and sit on the couch and mess around with it for a little while, telling myself I'm not waiting up for her. At two, I shower and get in bed. At two thirty, I hear her come in. I hear the shower go on, and then I hear her get out, and the door to her room shuts.

Damn it. She's still mad at me.

My phone lights up on the bedside table.

Skyler: Are you awake?

I grab it and text back, typing so fast I confuse the hell out of autocorrect my first few tries.

Grey: Yep. I'm up.
Skyler: I like my new phone. Thank you.

I'm smiling so big, I want to punch myself.

Grey: Welcome.

It's quiet for a long pause, then another text pops up.

Skyler: Good night, buddy.
Grey: Night, Sky.

In the morning, I'm brushing my teeth when Skyler pushes the bathroom door open. She's working some serious pink bedhead. She gives me a sleepy smile, and I scoot aside. She loads up her toothbrush, and we stand at the sink for about five minutes, scrubbing the hell out of our teeth, like it's some kind of competition.

I hand her a towel after she rinses.

"Don't you love having clean teeth?" she says, wiping her mouth.

"Who doesn't?"

We're both smiling. I'm not noticing the soft t-shirt that barely reaches her thighs. She's not noticing that I'm only wearing flannel boxers. It's cool. We decide to drive to the studio together, since we're both going there, and we talk music the entire time. Skyler has an idea for changing the arrangement in "Runner." She describes it to me, and I spend the entire morning playing it in my head. It's going to make that song unforgettable, and I can't wait to get to the garage tonight to tell the guys.

With her schedule today, I don't expect to see her again the rest of the day, but she steps into the trailer around one, holding a plastic salad container. I set my half-eaten sandwich down and wipe my face with a napkin.

"Garrett's not here," I say.

"I know. I saw the shooting schedule." She lifts the salad. "I saw you leaving the lunch spread and thought maybe we could eat together."

"Sure. Have a seat."

She slides into the bench seat opposite me. I take down my sandwich in about thirty seconds, and Sky pushes her organic greens around. As we eat, we laugh at some of the takes from the morning. Garrett was in rare form. My eyes keep moving to Skyler's bare shoulders. She's wearing wardrobe again, a cocktail dress that's silver and shimmery. I notice she's looking smaller. I think she's dropping weight since the shoot started. The way she picks at her salad's a pretty good indication why.

"Want me to get you something else?" I ask.

She pushes her salad away. "No. I'm fine." She sighs and melts against the booth seat, closing her eyes.

"That dress, Sky," I say.

She peers at me, quirking an eyebrow. "You like?"

"Hell yeah." Then I change the subject, because it feels like we might be violating the buddy code of conduct. "So, how's it going with Brooks?"

Skyler gives me an upside-down smile. "He's nice." She sits up. "We're going out tomorrow."

I nod. I can't say anything to that.

"Grey, we don't have to talk about Brooks."

"It's okay. We should be able to talk about other people with each other."

"You're right. We should."

I want to tell her Brooks never wants anything serious with girls. I feel like Skyler should know that. It was something he and Adam had in common before Ali came into the picture. Brooks is really only looking for someone to have fun with for a little while. But as much as Brooks is getting on my nerves lately, he's a friend. And maybe that's all Skyler wants, too. Shit. I'm thinking too much.

"Brooks is a good guy," I say, at the end of all that. Skyler is smart. She'll do what's right for her. Which is me. Hah.

"I think so, too." Skyler frowns. "Grey . . . Are *you* seeing anyone?"

"No. Nora's been trying to set me up with someone. But, no."

"Who's she setting you up with?"

"She hasn't yet. She's friends with some girl who just got back to LA after working in Paris for a year and a half. Nora's trying to introduce her around. She just texted to see if Juliette could come to band practice tonight."

I shake my head. It's all true, but why the hell did I say it? Why the hell do I feel weird that I said it?

Skyler picks up her fork, then sets it back down. "Is she? Coming to band practice?"

"I said it was fine with me."

"Cool. I hope she's cool."

I shrug. "Me too." Shane's met Juliette and says she's a Kate Upton look-alike. I guess I should be pumped about that, but I can't even picture a casual hookup. All I picture is Skyler. Who, if I didn't know better, is showing hints of jealousy.

I don't think we're just buds. What the hell are we?

Mia knocks on the door and steps inside. "There you are," she says to Sky. "We need you."

"Okay," Sky says. "I'll be right there." Mia's a little surprised Sky doesn't jump up to leave, but she shuts the trailer door. Skyler looks back at me. "I don't want to go back."

"Stay."

"I wish. See you at home later?"

"Yeah. Hey, Skyler. Brooks is persuasive. I mean, he's a good guy. But he's good at getting what he wants, too."

She studies me for a second. "Thanks, Grey. Let me know how 'Runner' goes, okay?"

"It's going to be epic."

Skyler gives me a huge smile. "Yeah," she says. "It is."

Chapter 28

Skyler

I open the front door to find Brooks standing there with a huge smile on his face and an African violet in his hands.

"This is for you," he tells me, handing me the plant, which is gorgeous, with budding purple blossoms. "The lady at the flower shop assured me it wouldn't be a pain in the ass to take care of, so I hope it's okay. I didn't want to buy you something that was going to die in two days."

"It's beautiful." I rub a velvety petal between my thumb and finger, feeling suddenly shy around someone who's already seen me in various states of dress and emotional upheaval.

But this—Brooks at my front door, with flowers—makes it official. It's not just hanging out; it's a *date*.

"Good," he says. "Now, pack an overnight bag, because I'm kidnapping you."

"Oh, really?"

"Yep. I decided we both needed a break and that neither of us would take one unless we physically removed ourselves from the city and anything to do with the film."

That makes me feel a little panicky. Not just at the idea of being somewhere overnight with Brooks but at the idea of being *away*. I don't know why. I get this weird feeling, like I'll come unglued and spin off into space if I leave LA. But that's stupid and probably a perfect reason to *go*.

"So, um, not to put a damper on things, but wherever we're going, separate rooms, right?" After my debacle with Grey, I'm not ready to hook up, or attempt to hook up, anytime soon.

He smiles. "Separate but adjoining, just in case."

I must get a look on my face because he adds, "Don't worry. It's going to be great. And I'll have you back by late tomorrow, so you can still do your Sunday brunch thing the next day, and I can prep for the week. Also, not to hurry you, but we have to get to LAX in forty-five minutes, so chop-chop."

"Where are we going?"

He smiles again. "You'll see."

Three hours and seventeen minutes later, I'm standing in the lobby of the Hotel Monaco in downtown San Francisco. It feels like a dream—or like a movie. I'm the leading lady, swept away by the leading man. Only, this leading man isn't gay and allergic to every substance on earth.

"Wow, it's beautiful," I say.

And it is, in a really funky way. Kind of Tim Burton meets Art Deco, with plush-looking furniture, an ornate gilded staircase, and super high ceilings painted with clouds and striped balloons. It's magical and inviting, and when Brooks actually checks us into two rooms, I feel like I can truly exhale again.

In my room, Brooks drops his bag on the carpet and relieves me of mine, setting it on a black glass coffee table. Then he moves in close, taking my face in his hands and looking down at me. I like his rough, wide features, his warm brown eyes that crinkle at the corners.

He gives me a surprisingly gentle kiss, pulling me in close to his body.

When we break off, he says, "I needed to do that sooner rather than later. Now we can go have a night on the town with a minimum of weirdness."

I laugh. "I don't think I do much of anything with a minimum of weirdness."

"Yeah, me neither. Let's go be weird." He plants himself on the striped settee near the coffee table and picks up a copy of *SF Weekly*. "I made reservations for dinner at Michael Mina and then thought we could go find some music. Sound good?"

"Sounds great." I feel myself being swept along, like a leaf on a current. But it's comforting, like being cared for and regarded, not just moved around like a prop.

I sit down beside him, and he hands me the paper. "Find us something great. I'm going to shower and make a couple of calls."

"I thought we weren't doing movie stuff," I tease.

He grins, guiltily. "Just one shower and three phone calls. And then I'm all yours."

Somehow, it's a relief not to be his central focus, to let whatever's unfolding between us happen in a way that feels casual and fluid.

After he leaves, I get up to drift around the room, which is bright and colorful, with mismatched Moroccan-style side tables and a vase with real flowers placed bedside. I love hotels. I always have. Maybe it's my dad's blood in me. I like discovering new things. And I like to think about the person who picked all the elements, who spent time designing a place so it would feel a certain way.

After a shower, I take a lot of time with my makeup, making my lips a perfect glossy red and rimming my eyes with black liner, which I haven't gotten to do in forever because that's not how Emma wears her makeup. She's subtle. I want to be dramatic. I straighten my pink hair and slip into a black shift dress with long lace-paneled sleeves and a sexy scoop back. It's looser on me now, but that's kind of the look, so it's okay.

While I wait for Brooks, I pick up the newspaper again to look through the entertainment listings. Not surprisingly, we have a ton of options, including a family jug band and a thirty-piece Bedouin ensemble from Mali.

And then I see it. The Forevers. My dad's band. Here, in San Francisco. Tonight.

How is that even possible? Isn't he supposed to be in Europe?

For a second, I feel that same spark of excitement I felt as a kid, when I'd get to go to some dank, smoky club to listen to him play. I'd sit cross-legged in a chair, either way in the back of the space, out of sight of the patrons, or in the wings beside the stage, where I'd feel the heat of the lights on me and get to see for myself the way people reacted to my dad. To music.

It feels risky, for some reason, to take Brooks to see my father play, but how often am I in the same city as my dad? And maybe I can shake some money out of him if I can get him alone for a second. It's an opportunity I can't let pass.

At dinner, Brooks sits beside me in a cozy booth, his warm firm hand tracing the bare skin of my back.

"Have I told you how much I love this dress?"

I smile. "Once or twice."

"I'm restraining myself from untying these laces." He trails his fingers over the bow holding the dress together in the back. "But it's a tough battle."

"I appreciate the effort."

"Believe me, you should."

We eat and talk about the movie, and then we talk about how we're not going to talk about the movie. Every now and then I see him glancing down to the side, at what I'm sure is his cell phone. But I don't call him on it.

The food is so good—especially the white truffle pasta, which I could eat with a trowel, though I remind myself to go easy, limiting myself to six bites and filling up on pear and endive salad instead. My cocktail, something called a Lou Reed, goes down gently but packs a major wallop.

I lean against Brooks, and his arm tightens around me in the booth. "Sorry I'm making you eat with one hand."

He laughs. "That's okay. I'm good with just one hand."

I feel myself blush. He feels good. Just really sturdy and present. I try not to think about the fact that I was in bed with Grey just a few nights ago. That I'd come really close to making a big mistake.

By the time we leave the restaurant and grab a cab the few miles to the Independent, where my dad's playing, I'm sufficiently floaty enough to unload a bit about my father, something I've really only talked about with Mia and Beth. And Grey, I realize.

"I want to see him," I say. "But I don't know how I feel about seeing him. You'll see. He'll charm the pants off you. But . . ."

"But he's left you a lot to deal with."

I nod. "And he always has. It's like he got to opt out of being a grown-up just because he plays music."

"You play music, too," Brooks says. "And you don't get to do that. I direct films. And I can't do that."

"I don't even believe you're tempted to do that."

He shrugs. "No, not really. I was one of those intense, overly mature kids who couldn't wait to get out of the gate. I think that's why Adam and I are buddies. We've both always just been good at putting our eyes on something and making it real."

I like that about him. Really, I like so much about him.

We make our way into the club, which is crowded, dark, and hazy, and I go to look for the manager, so I can have him let my dad know I'm here. They haven't come out to play yet, but the front of the stage is packed, as are most of the VIP tables. It's going to be a good night for him. Again, I think that maybe I can get him to send some money home.

I spot a merch table over by the bar and wander over to take a look. They've got CDs for sale. T-shirts. It's all looking a lot more high-end than it used to look. Or maybe I've just been in a lot more clubs and seen a lot more merch.

They've got postcards with their tour schedule on them, so I pick one up, thinking it'll be good to know where to find him for a change. I find myself looking forward to hearing him again. I realize it's been a while—a few years—since I've heard my dad play. And longer than that since he's heard me play.

I can't find anyone to find my dad for me, so I buy a CD and take the postcard with me back to the table Brooks found us. I'm almost to him when I see it: my dad's next club date.

Los Angeles. Tomorrow night.

I'm stunned as I sink into my chair.

"What's wrong?" Brooks asks.

"My dad's coming to Los Angeles."

"Really? That's great."

I shake my head. "Tomorrow. He's coming tomorrow, for two nights. And he didn't even tell me." My six bites of pasta sit in my stomach like cement. I can't make sense of it. It's one thing for him to be away all the time. To never be around when my mom needs him. It's another not to even think of me when he's in my city. When he's playing at a venue seven miles from my apartment.

I get up again, suddenly unable to sit still, feeling like I could shatter into a million pieces if I stay there. "You know what?" I tell Brooks. "Let's just go."

"Sky—"

"No, really. I'm okay. It was a dumb idea to come. Let's just go back to the hotel and get drunk in the bar. What do you think?"

He gives me a look, measuring my level of crazy. But I'm not crazy at all. I just know what I want. To get out of here. To go back to our charming hotel and have a few drinks, engage in some flirting, maybe more touching and kissing. Maybe a lot of touching and kissing.

I put my hand on the door at the exact moment they introduce my father's band. But I don't look back. I don't stop. I push the door open and lead Brooks out into the night.

Chapter 29

Grey

*F*riday night, we're all at the garage hanging out and waiting for Shane to show up for rehearsal. Nora, is coming, too. She's bringing her friend Juliette to meet me. For reasons I can't understand, the idea of meeting Kate Upton's look-alike has put me in a foul mood.

It's just that I need to focus on my music right now. Yeah. That's it.

Shane's almost an hour late when Titus gets a text. He takes his arm from around Beth's shoulder, where it lives now, and takes the phone from his back pocket.

"Aw, shit. Shane's not coming," he says. "He's been puking all day. He has some kind of stomach bug."

Rez, our slave driver, says, "Tell him to get his ass here. I'll put a bucket by the drum set."

With only a couple of weeks left until the showcase, every practice session counts. We still have a few songs to dial in, one of which is "Runner." I keep thinking of the ideas Sky gave me. I also keep thinking about Sky, who's on a date with Brooks. I missed her at the apartment earlier tonight, but I noticed all her toothbrush and bathroom stuff was cleared out. Which means Brooks took her out of town for the weekend. It's kind of his M.O. to come in fast and hard in the early stages then slowly back off.

Thinking about them together makes me sick. It makes me feel like I have the stomach flu, too.

Titus looks up from his phone. "Shane says he thinks he can practice tomorrow afternoon. He'll text in the morning."

With no other choice, we do our best to practice without him. But without a drummer, our up-tempo songs sound spineless, and our ballads sound like they're missing a pulse, so we wrap early. Everyone's hungry, and after some discussion, they decide to go to Fatburger, but I make an excuse about running an errand for Garrett.

That brings out all the usual comments about me being Garrett's bitch, but whatever. I'm not up for hanging out. We're close to big things as a band, and it's like I can physically feel my life leaning in, preparing to take a big turn. I'm too amped to sit around and chill.

I head to the apartment without a plan, but fired up to do *something*. I wonder if this is how Adam felt when he started Boomerang. It's just after ten when I get there and grab the keys to the truck, which is here, since Brooks picked Skyler up for their date. Inside, my truck feels familiar, but not. It smells like Skyler. A few of her things are on the center console. I study them for a little while—a red hair rubber band, a parking receipt, a tube of lipstick—without really knowing why or what I'm looking for. Then I turn the engine, and our demo CD starts playing through the speakers.

Was she listening to us? To me? It's kind of a shitty/awesome feeling to think that she drives around listening to our music. Like winning second place at something. Good, but not enough.

Before I realize what I'm doing, I'm heading to Adam's house.

It's only been a few weeks since I left, but this stretch of PCH already feels foreign to me. The streets of Venice Beach feel more familiar, but still not like what I think home should feel like. Maybe with the millions I'll make in music I'll buy some property in Washington with a cabin where I can chop my own firewood or something. I run with the fantasy for a while as I drive, thinking about Skyler walking around in my log cabin, wearing one of my flannels, *only* one of my flannels. Then I'm at Adam's house, pulling up to the driveway and I *still* don't know what I'm doing or why I came here.

I let myself in. The living room and kitchen are dark, but the lights on the back patio are on. Adam, Ali, and Mom are sitting at the table out there. Mom is wrapped in a fluffy white throw blanket that's usually on the couch. On her, it looks like some expensive fur poncho. There's a bottle of red wine on the table, three stemless wineglasses. As Ali listens to Mom, she absently picks hers up and swirls it, making a small whirlpool of the red wine inside the goblet. Beyond their cozy little scene, the ocean breakers are a glowing blue line against the darkness. A storm swell is coming in, and the surf is bigger than normal, roaring ferociously in the near distance. But Ali, Adam, and Mom seem oblivious to it. Untouchable. Immune to the dangers of such ordinary, pedestrian things as the elements.

It's all so fucking civilized and privileged. I grew up with this sort of thing playing out over and over in front of me, since I was five. But I've always hated it. And without my dad here to curse and tell off-color restaurant stories and generally dirty things up, I feel more than ever like an alien in this family. I'm the bastard son. A mistake. Just like me coming here was.

They didn't hear me come in, and since I'm in the darkened living room, they don't see me, either. I turn for the door but then I think of what Skyler said, about how I avoid and smash. Here again is an example of Avoidance Grey. I'm doing it right now. I'm never going to escape this thing until I confront it. And I miss my god-damn brother and my mom.

I turn back and head their way. Then Mom says my name, and I stop.

"I spoke to your father, and he's going to be able to make it," she says. "He'll come in the day before the showcase and stay until Monday. He's so excited about it. You'd think he was the one who's performing."

Showcase? What the actual fuck? How do *they* know about it?

"That's great," Adam says. "The shoot should be wrapped in the Virgin Islands by then, too, barring any problems, so Ali and I will be there." He smiles at Ali. Ali smiles at him. Adam looks back at Mom, who's smiling at both of them. "Can you imagine dad watching Grey sing?"

"Actually, yes." Mom laughs. "Your father and Grey have always had rock star swagger."

Again, what the fuck? Why is she making it sound like she *likes* that about me? Why have I always heard, "You're so much like your father, Grey," like it was a *bad* thing? My God. I don't understand *any* of this.

I should get the hell out of here. My instincts are screaming *leave, leave, leave.* But I creep forward like a fucking ninja.

Mom takes a sip of wine, and stares at the glass for a moment. "Do you think he'll be speaking with me by then?"

"I don't know, Mom. Whatever you said to him in August—"

"Adam, it wasn't me." Mom pauses. As the moments pass, I know she's struggling with whether or not to say more. To finally break silence. She sighs, her decision made. "You know he went to see Lois."

"Which should never have happened."

"He kept asking me, Adam. And she gave birth to him. Don't you think he had the right to know? To go see her?"

Adam has no answer for this.

She continues. "Your brother and I weren't getting along. He was letting his grades slip. He was going out all night. He stopped playing basketball, he stopped showing up for dinner. It scared me. You know how I can't stand apathy."

"Mom, Grey's not lazy. He just hated school. I did, too."

"But you had *plans,* Adam. You were already dreaming. You were already *acting* on your dreams."

"He's nineteen, Mom! And I was a freak! Not everyone is like me."

"You're not a freak, honey. If you are, then I am. Then your father is."

"Then we all are. Overachievers, every one of us. Passion and drive is not lacking in this family. Grey has that, too. He just took a little longer to find it. You should see him around the studio, Mom. He's figuring things out. And you've heard him sing. That's what he's supposed to do. He's . . . he's amazing."

How has she heard me sing?

How in the *hell* has she heard me sing?

Did he give her one of my demos?

My entire body's numb. There's no gravity anymore. I'm about to come off the floor and start floating.

Mom sets the wineglass down and adjusts the blanket around her shoulders. "I know, Adam. I was wrong. I see that now. But you know how your brother pushes me. He kept telling me he wanted to go to Lois. And I broke. I got tired of hearing him tell me how much better his life would be with his real mom. I know I shouldn't have done it, but I gave him her address."

"And the joke was on me, wasn't it?" I say, stepping onto the patio. I can't listen to this shit anymore. I'm done hearing about slow, lame-ass Grey who needs to be handled with special care. Screw that.

They all look at me, and the waves are crashing on the beach and in my head. They're crashing through my veins in cold, forceful swells.

"How do you know about my singing?" I ask my mom. A sick feeling creeps into my throat. "Who told you?"

Adam folds his hands together, knuckles going white. Beside him, Alison looks like she's trying to become invisible. "I found a copy of your demo in your room and gave it to her. There are copies getting around the set, too. The word's getting out, Grey. That's what you want, isn't it?"

He's manipulating the conversation. Changing the thrust.

"You got a copy and gave it to her," I say, because that's the point here. He betrayed me. He did something he knew I'd object to, and I want him to know I didn't miss that. "What about the showcase?" There's no way people on set could know about that. Only Garrett knows, and Skyler, and I want to know which one of *them* betrayed me. Looks like I'm going to have a list of traitors.

Mom and Adam look at each other.

"How did you hear about the showcase?" I repeat, my voice going gritty with anger.

"Grey," Mom says, "you don't let me be close to you. You've pushed me so far out of your life for the past nine months—"

"Eight—"

"Nine, Grey. It was nine months ago that you left."

"What does that have to do with the showcase?"

"I heard your music, and I got so excited."

Oh, no. It starts to sink in. No. No way. "Did you . . . Did you fucking set up a music producer for me? Are you fucking kidding me?"

She's shaking her head now, her eyes going glossy. "You're so good. I was so proud, and you haven't let me help you for almost a year, and—"

"Shut up."

"All I did was make a phone call. We'd worked with Vogelson's record label in New York on some fund-raisers. He *loved* your demo. He went on and on about it. He said your band was exactly what—"

"Stop, Mom. *Stop.* Don't say anything else."

I leave. I drive for a while. North. Then south. Then east. West is the Pacific, or I'd have driven that way, too. It's almost 3 a.m. when I get to the apartment. I shower and make some coffee and pace around my room for a while. I can't think. I can't hold a single thought in my head. It's like when I hit the basketball court freshman year and had a concussion. I have about a fifteen-second focus window, then I white out again and . . . nothing.

Beth must have slept at Titus's house, so I open Skyler's door and step inside. I lie down on her bed for a while and think about her. I find I can focus on Skyler for much longer stretches than anything else. The urge to send her a text is colossal, a clawing thing inside me. I just want to see if she'd answer it.

By sunrise, I'm on my surfboard, shredding the huge waves at the tail end of the storm. Carving isn't exactly what I do. I slash. I brawl with the water. When I finally drag myself out around ten, my arms are so spent, they're already getting sore.

But I know what I need to do.

I grab my phone and sit on the warm sand. There are a dozen texts and voicemails from Adam, Ali, my mom, and my dad. I clear them and send my own messages to the guys in the band, asking everyone to come down to the garage. Shane's still sick so today is out, and with Rez tied up at a recital for his students all day tomorrow, the earliest we can all meet up is Monday night.

We set it up. Eight o'clock at the garage.

I slip my phone into my pocket and think about how I'm going to tell them.

I go through all of it. How singing was mine and now it doesn't feel like it's mine anymore. How we didn't earn this chance; my family connections made it happen. How I'm not someone whose good graces can be *bought*. I think and think about how to explain it, but decide on being direct. Direct is best. I'll just say it.

We can't do the showcase.

Chapter 30

Skyler

*A*t the Seventy7 Lounge, Mia, Beth, and I sit in the corner of a brown leather banquette, crammed in between people who are little more than shadows in the dim light coming from old-timey glass chandeliers. I've never been here before, but if I wasn't so hell-bent on the mission at hand I'd probably enjoy the speakeasy feel of the place, the fact that they actually have an absinthe fountain, which makes me wish I could shrink myself to Green Fairy size and plunge in for a swim.

"So, what's the plan?" Mia asks, from her position half in my lap.

Usually, I don't mind that my best friends consider personal space a wholly optional concept, but tonight my body is one big ball of skittish energy, so I push away, just a bit, and gulp down half of my drink, called a Persephone's Dream, which makes me think about Persephone spending six months of every year in the

Underworld, and how that might be okay because it's probably quieter there, maybe dark and sultry like this club.

"The plan," I tell the inside of my glass, "is to throw a chair at him in the middle of his set."

Gently, Beth pushes the glass away from my face, and I set it back on the table. "Nuh-uh," she says. "The real plan. You wanna wait 'til after he plays? Try to get in there before he goes on?"

"I guess after. Is that okay? Are you all right with hanging out?"

"Of course," Mia says. "But I don't get why you didn't say something when you saw him in San Francisco."

"And how *was* San Francisco?" Beth adds. "You get whisked away for some super dream date, and you hardly talk about it? That's not the Sky we know."

A server walks by with a giant charcuterie board for a table near us, and my stomach immediately starts growling again, like this constant annoying serenade. Tonight, however, I'm opting for liquid calories.

"First, I didn't see my dad in San Francisco. I chickened out."

"How come, you think?" asks Mia.

I shrug. "Bad timing."

"Meaning, you didn't want to throw a fit in front of Brooks," says Beth.

"I don't think it's throwing a fit to be pissed off at my dad for coming to my goddamn town without saying a word. Or for leaving me to pick up the pieces with my mother like I'm in charge of their lives. Jesus, Beth."

"Whoa," says Beth. "I didn't mean it that way."

"Sorry."

I don't look at her, but I can feel her exchanging looks with Mia, like I'm not sitting at the table with them. A pizza goes by, and I feel my soul leave my body to float along behind it on a vapor trail of warm, oregano-scented goodness. Then I add pizza to the long list of foods I'm going to totally binge out on when this film wraps.

"Let's order something," Mia says.

"I'm not hungry," I say, though it doesn't sound even slightly convincing.

"Well, I am." She flags down a server, and we order some food. "Really, though, Sky. How *was* San Francisco? Other than the thing with your dad? How's Brooks?"

"Well, it's not like you don't know him." I don't know what's wrong with me. I sound like an asshole, and to my two best friends. "I mean, it was great. Or would have been great. He's pretty . . . great."

Mia laughs and tucks her arm through mine, leaning against my shoulder and looking up at me with her lively green eyes, her face inches from mine. She flutters her eyelashes. "So, was it *great*?"

I laugh and feel myself unknot a bit. She's such a goof. I love her. I love both these girls, and it's not their fault my dad's the way he is. Or that I feel stuck between two guys that I wish I could combine into one perfect person. Even though I'm not a perfect person myself. "Yeah. No. He's awesome. Really. He's like . . . an actual man, you know?"

"As compared to what?" asks Beth. "A unicorn?"

I roll my eyes. "Yes, as compared to a unicorn."

"Okay," says Mia. "So far, we've got that he's a man and not a unicorn. What else?"

"I don't know. He's just, he's got this great feeling of, I guess maybe I'd call it purposefulness. Like he knows what he wants, and then he goes and gets it. He's ambitious and smart."

"And hella sexy," adds Beth.

I nod. "And hella sexy for sure."

Mia moves away so she can fix me with one of her I'm-digging-through-the-contents-of-your-soul-now looks. "And the chemistry's good?"

"Really good." My mind brings me back to the hotel after we left the club, to Brooks holding my face in his hands, kissing me, sweet and warm, like settling into a bath on a chilly night. Not pushing but direct. Simple. He'd pressed his lean graceful body against mine, urgent but not desperate, until I mustered the will to usher him back to his room.

"So what *is* the plan?" Beth asks.

But at that moment, the lounge lights dim, and my dad walks onstage and gets behind the elaborate drum kit.

How does he have money for what's now—I count—a sixteen frickin' piece drum set but can't pay the damn bills?

My pulse spikes. I can't see him well in the dim light, behind all the equipment, but from here he looks younger. His hair's doing something different. It's longer maybe. And he looks leaner and a little wolfish.

Usually, he gets pasty and more and more bloated on the road— all the beer and fried foods—but now he looks like he's running marathons. For some reason that pisses me off, too. That he's not just on the road now but healthy, thriving, while my mom worries herself sick in their crappy little farmhouse in the middle of a bunch of land she doesn't know how to manage.

Maybe slinging a chair's not such a bad idea after all.

The rest of the band comes on, mostly the guys I remember, in- cluding Frank, their smarmy lead singer who used to hit on me when I was like fifteen years old.

Our server brings the food, and I order another round of drinks for the table, but mostly for me, as the Forevers launch into their first number. They're tighter than they used to be. Or more sober, I think. All of these guys look leaner, a little more upright and well-scrubbed.

I remember going shopping with my dad before he left on a tour when I was sixteen or seventeen. He stood in front of a three-way mirror, trying on leather jackets, and said, "You don't have to fall apart or fade away, kid. You can just get better."

That's what they've done. They're better. They look better, and they sound even better, though they were always good. My dad even sings a couple of songs from back behind the drum, something he never used to do. His voice is a little thin but true. Clean. It's all so clean that I get angrier as they charge through one song and the next—covering a ton of classic rock, a few modern hits, and a couple of originals.

My dad's finally gotten his shit together—but not for his family. Just for his music.

They finish, and I'm up and out of my seat, practically crawling over Beth, before they've even left the stage. I head down a dark side hallway, past the bathrooms, to a holding area in the back crammed with stage equipment. So many of these clubs are alike. These back rooms stacked with bottled water, club gear, plastic-wrapped pallets of bar mix.

A door opens, and I'm face-to-face with my father.

He gives me a curious, interested look and then his expression reforms to one of mild panic. He didn't know me, I realize. For a couple of seconds, my own father didn't recognize me.

"Holy shit, kid, you're a surprise!" He draws me in for a big hug while the other guys pour into the room around him. I feel myself stiffen in his arms.

"Frank, guys, look who's here," he says. "Skyler."

"Jesus, you're a knockout," says Frank, giving me a once-over that makes me feel like I've got ants crawling over me. "Finally legal, too, huh?"

"Cut the shit, Frank," says my dad. "He's just kidding," he tells me.

Right.

"You do look great, though, sweetheart," says Ted, their bass player. He gives me a kiss, leaning down like a giraffe looking for low-hanging leaves. He's about seven feet tall and stick-skinny. It's possible he's my godfather, though I wouldn't trust any of these guys to handle my moral education. "I like the pink hair."

"Yeah, it's real cute," says my dad. He's got this trapped thing going on, like he'd pay these guys a hundred bucks each to stay in the room with me. But after I say hi and make small talk with the others, including a few new players, they leave us alone.

The room goes quiet, feels suddenly hollow like someone's clamped a lid over us.

My dad cracks open the other door, which leads out into an alleyway. A cold draft swoops into the space, stirring a stack of newspapers and knocking down a broom that stood against some metal shelves.

"It's good to see you," he tells me.

He takes out a pack of cigarettes, packs them against the heel of his hand, and looks out into the night. It's all very Rock Star 101.

I don't know where to start. "It's good to see you, too."

It sounds weak because it is. Still, a part of me, maybe the molecular part, the part that comes from him and is just, simply, his family, brightens around him, makes me feel this rush of warmth and good memories. Like some kind of protective instinct made to anaesthetize all the other crap.

More silence. Awkward and brittle. Then I just come out with it. "How come you didn't tell me you were coming to LA? I thought you were off to Europe?"

He lights his cigarette, and the smell wraps around me. "It was kind of a last-minute thing," he says. "I mean, we just got booked here."

I feel a weird sting in my chest, like someone's snapped a rubber band beneath my ribs. He's lying. Why would he lie to me?

Pulling my purse around in front of me, I dig through it to the postcard with their schedule. The type looks filmy, and I realize it's because I'm tearing up. Damn it, that's the last thing I want to do.

"I guess last minute means you've known for—" I check the earliest dates on the card. "Three weeks. At least. Want to try again?"

"Skyler . . ."

"Don't *Skyler* me. Mom's losing it back home. Scotty is barely keeping it together with three kids to handle on his own. And you're just out here, floating around. Doing whatever the hell you want. As always."

"That's not fair. It's for your mom, too. For the farm."

"Really? For the farm? You left mom with nothing. They cut off the lights."

"I didn't know—"

"And I had to pay three months' back mortgage for you. For the farm you're supposedly supporting."

"You? How could you afford that?"

He doesn't even know about the film. Mom didn't tell him. It boggles my mind how they can be so separate but still keep coming back together, picking up like everything's fine. I don't understand either of them. I just know I want *my* life to be different.

"It doesn't matter how. It just matters that I did it. That somehow, someone always steps up for you and makes it okay. Uncle Dave or Grandma K. Someone's always filling in the missing pieces for you."

"This is why I didn't tell you I was coming," he says. "I knew this is exactly how it would go. That you'd give me a hard time over some damn thing."

That feels so unjust I don't know what to do with it. "So, you'd rather just not see me at all? Your daughter? Because I might give you a hard time?"

"Not *might*, Skyler. You and your mom. Your brother. You're all riding me all the time. Giving me shit if I so much as breathe the wrong way."

"You make it sound like you're the victim. Like we're all just waiting to jump on you over any imagined issue."

He shrugs, and for a second, I can't find words, I'm so angry.

"I'm not *imagining* that Mom's miserable and can't keep the lights turned on," I say, finally. "Don't make it sound like we're all just being unreasonable."

"Well, don't make it sound like I don't do anything," my dad says. "I'm working hard out here. My last tour bought us a brand-new roof. You know that?"

"*After* you got home. After you walked in the door with a wad of cash. After Mom and I spent two months on *food stamps,* not even knowing for sure if you'd come home or not." I'd worked so many after-school jobs I'd lost count of them all.

"What are you talking about? I always come home."

"Eventually."

"When the tour ends."

"If you don't add a month or two. Or a *European* leg. Or decide to stay out and play the goddamn county fair circuit. Or get on a cruise ship for three weeks."

"That was *one time.*"

"When I was *graduating.* When you *promised* you'd be there."

"I couldn't pass up the opportunity. And it's not just up to me. I have a band."

"You have a family, too."

"Stop talking to me like I'm a kid," he says. He flicks his cigarette out into the night and tugs the door shut behind him. "This is what I am, Skyler. I'm sorry you've got a problem with it. But this is who I am and what I do."

A million words crowd my mouth, all of them wanting to come out at once. I don't know what I expected. Pretty much this, I guess.

Suddenly, I feel like my bones are too tired to support my body. I just want to go home, climb into bed, and sleep for a decade.

"Is Evan still your manager?" I ask.

"Yeah, why?"

"Give me his number."

"Why?"

"Because I want him to send money home to Mom."

"I'll take care of it."

"Give me his number, Dad," I say and it comes out choked but dead serious.

Reluctantly, he gives me the number. "Let me talk to him first. I don't need him to think my kid's running my life."

As if.

I enter the number into my phone and then drop my new cell back into my purse. "Thanks," I say.

He shrugs. "Now you're here, you want to go get some food? I'm starving." Like we're buddies now.

"Sorry," I tell him. "I ate already. And I'm with my friends. I should get back to them."

Nodding, he says, "Well, how about tomorrow afternoon? I've got some time. You could come by. Have some three-star hotel food with me."

He's trying to charm me, but I feel beyond the reaches of charm. His, anyway.

"I have to get ready for a trip," I tell him. In another life, I'd rush to tell him about the movie, about leaving for the islands, where I'll spend the next couple of weeks. In another life, I'd probably say and do a lot of things.

But in this one, I just go and give him a kiss on the cheek, because I don't want it all to be bad. He is who he is. And whether he can't or won't help it, he's the father I've got.

Back in the lounge, I collect the girls, who know enough to save their questions. I feel their curiosity gathering like a storm, but I need to process. To find a safe place to come apart.

That place is down at the beach, where we talk through it all and where I finally really cry, with Mia rubbing my back and Beth's sweet, steady voice soothing me. Not for the first time, I think about the difference between the family you get and the family you choose. Sometimes, like for Mia and Ethan, it's the best of all worlds. You're born into something wonderful. And sometimes, like for Beth and me, maybe Grey—I can't tell—it's the chosen family, like Grey's band, that keeps you going.

Back at our place, Beth offers to come up and hang with me instead of heading over to Titus's house, but I tell her it's okay.

"You know where to find us," she says.

"Yep." I give them both kisses and hugs. I do know where to find them. And somehow, they always find me when I need them.

They drive off in Mia's car, and I head up to our apartment, dragging myself up the two flights of stairs like I'm hoisting myself up the Matterhorn. I really do just want to crawl under the blankets and sleep off this crap night.

But then I open the door and find Grey sitting on the couch, his head in his hands and four beer bottles clustered on the table in front of him.

He looks up when I close the door behind me. "Hey," he says, and tries something that's meant to be a smile. But it fails completely.

"Hey. Everything all right?"

Shrugging, he says. "Not even a little."

I go over and sit down next to him. As rough as it is between us, it feels good to be near him. It's like my body feeds off his warmth and strength, like a plant feeds off light.

I tilt my head to look up at him, at his solemn, beautiful face. "How about I tell you about my shitty night, and you can tell me about yours?"

Smiling, just a little, he picks up a beer bottle from the table and hands it to me. Then he taps his against mine. "Deal."

Chapter 31

Grey

*W*hen my night started, I didn't expect this. Skyler, curled up beside me on the couch.

I'm definitely missing something. Because didn't she *just* get back from San Francisco with Brooks? Maybe what I'm missing is that she ruled me out. Brooks got the boyfriend role. I got the roommate/friend role. I glance down at her, and my throat goes raw. But I can't lose this moment with her just because it's not everything I want it to be.

"Ladies first," I say.

Her long eyelashes flutter. She looks like she's going to fall asleep. "I'll be brief, otherwise I might start to cry again."

"You can cry."

She peers up and smiles. For a second, I think she's going to say something. Then I make the mistake of looking at her mouth, and it's pretty obvious to both of us that I want to kiss her. She looks away quickly, taking a sip of her beer, and I want to apologize *and* swear, because what did I do wrong? She's curled up so close to me. Of course I'm going to want to kiss her. And more. Doesn't mean I will.

"Thanks," she says, "but I'd rather not get going again. Okay, here it is. I saw my dad tonight. He's in a band. I think I told you that before. They're here in Los Angeles, and I had no idea. I found out by chance, and that's kind of how it is with him. It's like he doesn't think about us. His *family*. We're an afterthought. *I* am."

Jesus. What an asshole. I'd thought so already, based on what she's told me. But I didn't realize it was this bad. "Is his band any good?"

Skyler gasps. *"What?"* She play-punches me. *"That's* what you want to know?"

"It's my trade."

"Yes. They're pretty good."

She leans against my arm for a second, but I drop it on the back of the couch, removing that option. Replacing it with a better one. She scoots closer and snuggles against me. Win.

"Don't get fresh with me, okay?"

I laugh. "I'm not getting fresh with you. Anyway, you started it. Hey, speaking of which. How was the big date with Brooks? Awesome."

"You didn't let me answer."

"I actually don't want an answer. I just figured I should ask. Back to your dad. Want me to rough him up?"

"My *dad*?"

"Just keep it in your back pocket. I'm good with that kind of stuff."

"Liar. You're just a big softy."

"Based on the evidence I presented a few nights ago in your room, I think we both know that's not true."

She laughs. "Pig."

"Definitely." It hits me that cheering her up is cheering *me* up, but I don't want to make light of what she's going through. "Seriously, Sky. I'm sorry about your dad. If there's anything I can do, let me know."

"You're doing a lot by listening. By being here." Skyler reaches for her beer, then sets it back down, and stifles a yawn. "What about you? What happened tonight?"

"Tomorrow," I say. "You need to go to bed."

She's leaving with the traveling production crew in a few days for their location shoot in the Virgin Islands. The next few weeks are going to be even more tiring for her. She won't be coming *home* at the end of the day. And the hours are even longer on location. I'm supposed to go, too, but I'm not sure I will.

"Yeah, I do. Come with me." She peers up, and her brown eyes are sincere, warm. "I want to keep talking. I want to know what happened."

This idea sounds potentially risky, but I'm sure as hell not going to say no, so we go through a routine that feels new but familiar, of brushing our teeth, getting into pajamas for her, and sweatpants and a t-shirt for me. Separately, unfortunately. Skyler dead-bolts the front door. I hit the lights in the kitchen. Then we deviate from the norm and climb into her bed *together*.

"So you know. I'm going to burn up in about five minutes. I usually only sleep in shorts."

"I know. Why are you in sweatpants?"

"Safety measure. I triple-knotted the drawstring. Actually I tried to do a Double Carrick Bend knot, but it's been a long time since Boy Scouts."

I can't see her smiling, but I know she is. "I trust you."

"You shouldn't."

"I do."

We fall quiet for a moment, and I'm trying not to be turned on, but she smells amazing and she's snuggled up right next to me, and we're on a bed. It's a hell of a lot to ask, to ignore all of that.

Then Skyler says, "Is what happened tonight related to your mom?" And that completely kills the mood.

"Yeah . . . I learned some things today I didn't like. You know the showcase that's coming up? I guess she was the one who set that up. My parents are kind of . . . connected."

"Okay," Skyler says, carefully. "And you didn't want her help?"

"No." I want to succeed on my own merit. I feel like the success won't be worth it if it's just another thing lined up for me because I'm a Blackwood. I mean, how many freakin' things are going to come to me, just because my parents made some arrangements? How fucking spoiled is that? How could I ever feel like I achieved anything if I didn't earn it outright? I want to shape my own life. "I don't want any charity from her."

I'm getting angry, and Skyler must sense it. She sits up. Her expression is all concern, all worry. "Grey, it's your *family*. It's not charity. I *wish* my family helped me more."

"She's not my family. Not really. And she's just trying to make up for always trying to make me be like her real son." Aw, shit. My voice is starting to crack, and the world's going a little blurry. I reach over and shut the bedside lamp off.

Skyler doesn't move. She stays still, sitting beside me. Staring down at me like she can see in the dark.

I can't take it. I sit up and rub my face. I hear myself swearing. I want to leave, sprint out of this room. But I can't get past Skyler. I don't want to get past her.

"Grey," she asks, softly. "What's this really about?"

"Everything."

"Okay." Her cool hand takes mine. "Tell me everything."

I don't even think about it. I just start in. But there's so much to

say, and I've never said any of it before, so I make a mess of it. I tell
her about how Adam and I have the same dad. How Dad came and
got me from my birth mom when I was five and took me home to
a big house, a huge house, close to the ocean. I had a Spider-Man
lunchbox. It was my proudest possession. Really. The *only* thing I
was proud of. But then I got something a million times better. A
brother. I'd never had one before. I loved him instantly. Adam looked
out for me. He was . . . he was the best. Older. Just . . . like, my hero.

"I got a dad that day, too. He was busy a lot. But when he was
around, he didn't push. He let me come to him. And he was just so
damn sure of himself. So cocky and funny. You gotta meet my dad
someday, Sky. There's no one like him.

"Madeleine, though. I don't know what the hell happened.
She . . . she came on stronger. She wanted to be my mother. Except,
I had a mother. I had a mother who smoked and drank and partied.
Who forgot to feed me half the time. I'm not going to get into that
right now. She didn't beat me. A few of her boyfriends did. I'm not
going to get into that, either. What I'll say is this: I had a mother.
And didn't really want another one—not like the one I had.

"That's all I saw when I looked at Madeleine. For a long time,
that's all I saw. So we didn't get off to a good start. But then I started
to see that she was different than my birth mom. Madeleine had
expectations of me. She demanded manners, respect. She had standards for everything, how to dress and keep my room. What kinds
of grades I should get. She wanted top effort in all things. For a kid
who'd lived in and out of cars, in and out of crowded apartments, for
a kid who'd been yelled at and thrashed a few times, for a kid who'd
seen his mom drunk too many times, whose mom dated a new man
every other month—for that kid, Madeleine, with all her expectations, with her perfect house with its polished wood floors and high
ceilings; Madeleine, with her planned-out days and gourmet meals,
and her perfect son who did everything right; Madeleine, with her

charity functions for kids like me, who were *just like me,* well . . .
she was terrifying."

"Terrifying how?" Skyler asks.

"I don't know."

"Grey . . . you do know. How?"

"Maybe I thought she wouldn't care unless I measured up.
Maybe . . . Maybe I thought she looked at me like I was just some
mistake of my dad's that she'd inherited. A piece of trash that had
been dragged into her life. White trash."

I can't even believe what I'm saying. I haven't even admitted this
stuff to *myself.* Is this what I really think? I don't know anymore. I
don't know. But it's definitely what I *thought.* For a long, long time.
I see that now.

"Has she ever said anything to make you believe that's true?"
Sky asks.

"She's, um . . . told me I'm difficult. She's said that a couple of
times over the years. I was. And the night we fought, the night I left
home, she told me I make it hard for her to love me. It's the truth.
I've been such a fucking nightmare. I've given her so much grief. I
haven't made it easy. And that night everything blew up, it was the
culmination of—Jesus, where is my filter?"

"You don't need a filter. We're trading family misery stories."

"Yeah, but you did a lot less talking than I'm doing."

"I unloaded on Beth and Mia earlier tonight. Besides, who cares?
Stop keeping score, Grey. Talk to me."

"I feel like we left the living room so we could lie down, but
we're sitting again."

"Stop changing the subject."

"I think I'm done, Skyler."

She reaches out, and next thing I know, her arms are wrapped
around my neck. "Pretend it's a secret," she whispers, "and tell me."

I take a second to absorb how she feels. So soft and good. "No,

Skyler. It's fucking embarrassing. I'm not proud of it, and you're the last person I want to—"

"Shh," she says into my ear. The hair on my forearms lifts. "It's okay. I won't think less of you. I know who you are."

The words hit me like a brick to the chest. "Do you?"

"Yes."

"You've only known me a few weeks."

"Doesn't matter. I know you, Grey. Here. I'll start for you. The night I left home . . . Now, you."

"You're going to pay for this, Sky. But, okay." I make myself jump in, quickly. If I build up enough momentum in the beginning, maybe I'll be able to get through it. "The night I left home was about nine months ago. Madeleine and I were fighting, as usual. I'd just barely graduated high school. I mean . . . don't think I'm an idiot. I'm not. I just hated school and didn't try. I knew I didn't want to go to college, so what did it matter? But the paths available to me, as a Blackwood, were either go to an Ivy League, start a number of successful nightclubs and restaurants, or launch an online dating business and movie studio. Same as most families, right? Not knowing what you want to do—that wasn't okay. And that's where I was. I didn't know I wanted to sing yet and I guess I was lost-ish. Okay, I was lost. So I started partying a lot, and getting in trouble. Madeleine was going crazy with me. The night I left, the fight was over some career counselor she had paid for me to see. I'd gone surfing instead. So she cornered me in the kitchen and made me feel like a loser piece of shit who had no ambition. Again.

"I couldn't take it anymore. Being a disappointment." Shit. My momentum is washing out as I remember that night. This was a bad idea. I have to force myself to keep going. "So that night, we were fighting in the kitchen. And all these things started coming out of my mouth, like how I wanted to find my real mom, who wouldn't hassle me all the time like she did. I told Madeleine it was torture living under her roof, that I was sick of being a project. I asked for my birth mother's address, and she gave it to me. That was new. That was something I'd asked for before during fights, but she'd never actually given me the address. And it surprised me. I felt like she was done with me. I didn't stop to think. I took off. I took my dad's Cobra, the one he and wonderboy Adam had built from a kit, because it was blocking my truck in our driveway.

"An hour and a half later, I pulled into a dumpy apartment complex in New Haven and went up to the second floor and knocked on the door. Lois answered."

I stop, reliving the scene. Not wanting to talk about it.

"Keep going, Grey," Sky tells me.

"She was frail and sick-looking, my real mom. I didn't realize it until then, but for the past decade, I'd made up this story about her in my mind. In the story, she had cleaned herself up. She'd gotten sober and stopped dating drug dealers. This was all because she wanted to be a perfect mom for me, by the way. This makeover. That's part of the story I told myself. She hadn't wanted to see me yet, because she wanted everything to be perfect when she did. I imagined that she'd have a job, a nice house, and maybe even kids. Smart, funny kids who I could call my siblings. I'd actually made her into a version of Madeleine. But that wasn't the case. It wasn't who I saw that day.

"She looked like a woman in a cancer commercial . . . sunken and ashy. Bad. Just . . . not healthy. I wanted to die when I saw her. When I thought that was the woman who'd given birth to me, I almost left. I probably should've. But I stayed. And I told her I wanted to move in with her. I said this while I looked at a coffee table littered with beer bottles and cigarettes. At the stack of bills sitting under an empty bottle of Absolut on the wooden bureau next to the television, which was playing some kind of daytime game show. Which just about fucking killed me. I don't know why. Maybe because it seemed like such a denial of real life, that you can win money by spinning a wheel. It went against what I believed. It went against the Blackwood way.

"But then it got worse. It got worse because she told me my dad only sent enough money to cover the one-bedroom she lived in, plus just enough for her to eat. 'But maybe he'll kick in for more, if you live here,' she said, and went into this huge tangent about the apartment upstairs, which was a two-bedroom. And how much it cost, and how it was coming vacant in the next month and how she'd had her eye on it for a while because it had a balcony, and how perfect it was that I'd shown up, because now if my dad sent enough money, for both of us to live, she'd get to move into the apartment of her dreams."

"Oh, God," Skyler says. "What did you do?"

"I told her I had to think about it some more. Then I left. I got in the Cobra and drove home, but I couldn't actually go home. It was around midnight, I think, when I pulled off the road onto a private beach a few miles from home and did some donuts in the sand. Then I realized I liked it even better when I did donuts in the shallow surf, so I did that for a while. I whipped that car in circles, trying to flip it. Trying to destroy it. I worked my way deeper and deeper until finally the sand was too soft, the waves too high, and I was stuck. I could feel the car rocking with the waves, but I just sat there. And all I could think about was that I wished I'd taken Madeleine's car. I wished it was *her* car getting swallowed up by the Atlantic."

I guess that was the smash. I was just crazy. Crazy with how much I hurt. The avoid came later.

"Eventually, I left the Cobra, walked home, got in my truck, and drove across the country to Adam's house in Malibu. So, that's the story of how I left home. Now you're caught up on the saga of Grey Blackwood's riveting family issues."

I can feel the intensity of Skyler's stare. I thought I'd want to disappear after I told her all of this. I only sort of do.

"Grey, I'm so sorry you went through that. But I have to say this . . . I think you're worthy of being loved. I don't think it's hard to love you." She laughs. "I mean, it's not like *I* do. I'm just projecting . . . in order to shed light on the situation."

I laugh. "You love me? Wow, Sky. I'm a little surprised, but—"

"I was trying to explain that I think Madeleine loves you and that, difficult or easy, the result is what matters."

"I feel like I should say it back, but it might not seem genuine—"

She pushes me. I was expecting it, so I grab her wrists and pull and she lands on top of me. She laughs and digs a hand into my side. That leads to play wrestling in which I act like I'm trying to match her while being careful not to accidentally hurt her. In about ten seconds, I'm not thinking about wrestling anymore. I pull her next to me and picture dead puppies and influenza and banana slugs, trying to undo the effects of our bodies rubbing up against each other. Doesn't work.

Skyler yawns and nestles in beside me. Her small hand rests on my chest, and I wonder if she feels how fast my heartbeat's going. "You know what I think?"

"What?"

"I think life's tough," she says. "Everyone needs help along the way. But when you let someone lift you up, it can really be a beautiful thing."

"Are you trying to tell me I should accept Madeleine's help and do the showcase?"

Skyler laughs. "I do think you should do both of those, but no." She peers up at me and smiles. "I was trying to say thank you."

Chapter 32

Skyler

I wake to find that Grey's gotten up but that his side of the bed is still warm and the sheets still smell like him. I know I'm dating someone else—starting to, anyway—but I can't resist hugging the pillow he used, breathing in his scent, which is like smoke and surf all in one.

It's still dark out, but a thread of orange gleams on the horizon. I have to get going to the set, but I still have a little time, which is the best feeling ever.

Smiling, I think about last night, about us dozing together, waking up here and there to talk some more, safe in the darkness, the open window carrying in the rush of passing cars, conversations on Abbot Kinney. Every now and then, Grey would tell me he should get up and go to his room, and I'd agree, but he'd just stay there, or I'd keep his hand in mine, and we'd fall back to sleep just to wake an hour or two later and do it all again.

I hear a clatter in the kitchen and start to get up to investigate, but Grey calls to me: "Stay where you are."

So, I stay where I am and pick up Grey's pillow again because I'm a big dork and he's delicious, and I'm going to miss him when he doesn't live here anymore.

After a couple of minutes, Grey appears in the doorway, and I burst out laughing. He's shirtless, wearing only his sweats, but he's got on Beth's Wonder Woman apron, which fits him more or less like an oversized bib.

"Cute."

He grins. "I know. Hey, how do you like your coffee?"

"What are you up to?"

"You'll see. Coffee? How?"

"Actually, I like tea. There's some lemon verbena."

"Tea." He nods. "Got it." Then he disappears again.

"Seriously, what are you doing?" I call. "We have to get going soon."

"We have forty-three minutes until we have to leave for the studio. But if you feel stressed, we can always save time by showering together."

"Funny."

"It's a good plan," he calls. "I mean, just for the sake of efficiency. Not because I want to see you naked."

"Of course not."

Because you already have, I think, and that night comes back to me again, the feel of him against me, his powerful, warm body over mine. Skin against skin. We'd been so close. I don't know what would have happened if we'd gone through with it.

Grey returns, distracting me from my unproductive thoughts. He's carrying a breakfast tray, which he sets down on my nightstand. On it is a mug of tea with a bottle of honey and two plates holding some kind of towering breakfast sandwiches. What he lacks in presentation skills, he more than makes up for in quantity and the world's most adorable grin.

"What are these?"

"They're my famous hangover-busting ham, egg, and cheese sandwiches."

"But I'm not hungover."

"No, but they're really good." He picks up one of the plates for himself and then nods at me. "Dig in."

It smells amazing. No one has ever brought me breakfast in bed before—except my mom, once or twice when I was sick. He's so sweet. So different than he appears. Than he *lets* himself appear.

But all I can think about is the fact that I'll be in a bathing suit in three days. In front of a crew of thirty—and Brooks.

I pick up the sandwich, trying to shake this weird superstitious feeling, like every bite I take is going to show up as a pocket of fat on my body. I'll just skip lunch, I tell myself.

Grey watches me, a smile on his face, waiting for my verdict. I take a bite, and it's salty and buttery and crunchy and perfect. I groan.

"Oh my God, this is the best thing I've had in my mouth in months."

His eyebrows shoot up, and I hear what I've said and start to laugh so hard that I inhale English muffin and choke. I cough and take a sip of my tea, while Grey rubs my back. I'm a mess, but I'm okay with being a mess in front of him.

After I take another couple of bites, I remember my supplements and lean down from the bed to grab my purse from the floor.

"What're you doing?"

"Getting my vitamins." I dig them out of my bag and then pop a couple out of the pack.

"What are those, anyway?"

Seriously, I wish I had a dollar for every time someone asked me what's in these things. I'd be able to bail out the farm *and* buy a new car. Shrugging, I say, "I don't know. Just helps with weight loss."

He gives me a skeptical look. "You think you need to lose weight? That's nuts."

"Well, I mean, just a little. Because of the cameras."

"Who told you that?"

"Everyone."

"No way. Mia told you that? Beth?"

"No, I mean everyone who's not my best friend."

He scowls. "Brooks?"

"Well, no, not Brooks." Though he's given me a lot of compliments lately on how things fit now, how great I look on-camera. Garrett has. Bernadette. Everyone tells me I'm looking good and to keep going. "Anyway, it's just for the movie."

Grey takes a bite and points at my sandwich. "Isn't the idea that you're going to do a lot of movies? Isn't this a start of your whole big career?"

For some reason, that thought panics me, but I tamp it down and take another bite—a smaller one.

"Well, yeah." I don't think I can make it through a quarter of this meal, but I don't want to hurt him. The supplements shrink my appetite. Also, we're leaving in less than forty-eight hours, and they're talking about a bikini. The thought of my hips and thighs displayed on a sixty-foot-wide movie screen, in high-def, pretty much crushes my soul.

"So, doesn't that mean you're going to have to take those things indefinitely? And eat like a bird all the time?"

"Well, I guess I figured I'd lose fifteen or twenty pounds and then—"

"From where? Jesus, Sky. You're gorgeous. Every bit of you." He looks so earnest, so personally offended on my behalf, that I want to launch myself into his arms and kiss him for a week.

"You're sweet."

Another scowl but with a hint of a smile. "I'm not sweet. And I will seriously beat the shit out of anyone who makes you feel crappy about yourself."

"I promise, no one is making me feel crappy." And I realize they're not. No one's said there's anything wrong with me. It's more this feeling that things could be more *right*.

I take another couple of bites, though I'm not really hungry anymore. Then I wrap the rest in a napkin and tell him I'll take it with me for the road. "Unless you want it?"

"Nah," he says and slides off the bed. "You have it. I'll have a second breakfast on the set."

I laugh and get up, too. "Fair enough."

Picking up my plate, he asks, "So, how about that shower?"

"Sure. Let's do it."

Grey's eyes widen. "Really?"

"No, not really, you goof. You go. I'll clean up."

"You suck, Skyler Canby. For real."

I give him a little push, which feels exactly like I imagine it would feel to push a tree. "I know. I'm a terrible human being."

He looks down at me, his expression sad and sweet and penetrating. "Yeah," he says, softly. "You're the worst."

Chapter 33

Grey

*M*ust have been some night, Greyson," Garrett says to me.

"What?" I snap out of a daze. Have I really been driving to the studio with a smile on my face like a complete asshole? Yep. I have. "It was nothing. Skyler and I hung out. That's all. We're roommates."

Garrett nods slowly. "Huh. Are you now?" He's looking a little perplexed by me, a little worried, and I can just imagine what's going through his mind. He knows Sky went to San Francisco with Brooks on Friday night. I probably look like an even bigger asshole now that he knows I've been thinking about some other guy's girl. Time for a subject change.

"Garrett, there's something I want to talk to you about."

"Uh-oh." He lifts the Salted Caramel Latte I picked up for him on the way to his place. "I knew this drink was a harbinger of doom."

"Naw. You've been drinking black coffee for weeks. A little

sugar splurge now and then won't kill you." The film business puts some effed-up expectations on actors. I don't like it. I mean, I stand behind keeping Garrett from binging on sugar drinks every day, but there's no reason to get military about his diet. It should be a balance. A lot of things should be about balance. Fuck yeah, balance.

Garrett beams at me. "Thank you, Greyson. Now give me your bad news before I go into hysterics. You know I don't have the patience to be patient."

"I'm not going to the Virgin Islands."

Garrett's smile fades. "What? You—well, goat shit! Double goat shit! Triple, quadruple goat shit!"

"That's a lot of goat shit."

"It is, Grey. It is! Why? What happened? Explain!"

There are a few reasons I've decided not to go. My music, for one. I've decided I'm going through with the showcase. So what if my mom greased the wheels and helped things along with Vogelson? It doesn't mean we aren't deserving. And the guy's got a great reputation. He wouldn't sign a band on as a favor. Then there's my relationship with Adam and my family. Much stuff to sort out there. And finally, there's Skyler. I want to be with her in the Virgin Islands. I want it *too* much. I'm falling for her in a big way, and nothing good will come from me watching her flirt with Brooks for three weeks. As much as I want to be with her, I can't put myself through that.

"Don't answer, Grey. It's okay. I think I know," Garrett says. "But just for the record? She thinks about you when I kiss her."

"What? What the hell is that—" I brake sharply at a red light, which only makes Garrett laugh harder. "You're an asshole." He's killing himself. Dude has a weird sense of humor.

"Actually when I kiss her, I think about kissing you, too!" he yells, and loses it all over again.

"Aw. Come on, man. "

"It's only true some of the time." He wipes tears away. "Your face right now, Grey. Your *face*!" He sinks against the leather seats, shaking his head. "God, I'm going to miss you. I hate that you're not coming. Hate it. But wow, I love sugar. This drink is so good. I don't remember it being this good. I can't believe you kept me away from these for weeks. It's true what they say. Absence really does make the heart grow fonder."

All I can think is, it better not. I'm banking on the opposite effect. I could definitely use some *un*fonder feelings for Sky.

Sometime around mid-morning while they're shooting a scene where Emma Beautiful Emma runs into Knightley at a florist, as young would-be lovers often do, I find a chair in a dark corner of the studio and pull my phone out of my pocket.

I scroll up to my last group message to the band from this weekend, when I was thinking of calling off the showcase. I told them we needed to talk. Usually we all say gig or practice. We never *talk*. I know they picked up on it because their replies as we worked out scheduling logistics were pretty short.

I'm smiling as I type out a new message. It takes me a few tries since my big ole fingers aren't made for quick texting, but I get it and hit send.

> **Grey:** Are you idiots ready to burn it up tonight or what?
> 8 p.m. Last one there pays for the beer.

Immediately my phone lights up with replies.

> **Reznick:** Fuck yeah, motherfucker!!!
> **Titus:** WTF, Grey!! I thought you were breaking up with us! Thanks for the ulcer, you dick!
> **Shane:** Told you dumbasses nothing was wrong. Tight-ass, you owe me $40!!!

Titus: Hold on, your sister's right here. Lemme see if I can borrow.

Titus: Wait she can't talk she's busy.

Shane: Does Beth read your texts?

Titus: No, Dude. That was a joke.

Emilio: Some people R trying 2 sleep, U shitheads

Reznick: Loser, it's noon. And stop texting like a little girl. KK? LOL? TTYS! ILYSM!

And so on.

"No cell phones in the studio while we're shooting."

I look up. Adam's standing above me. I slip my phone into my pocket. "Sorry."

In the pool of stage lights, Garrett and Skyler are talking between takes. Skyler squints into the darkness, searching, and I wonder if she's looking for Mia, Brooks, or me. Probably not me.

"I was kidding, Grey," Adam says, with a small grimace. "You got a sec?"

"Sure."

I follow him out into the bright sunshine. The day is unseasonably warm, but we walk for a few minutes. I'm not sure where we're going or if there's even a destination. I haven't been alone with my brother in almost a month and a half, I think. Maybe longer. And it feels like the walking we're doing is just to let the two of us expend a little pent-up aggression.

Finally, Adam stops around the corner from some commotion. Bernadette and Kaitlin are stressed about shipping out wardrobe to the BVIs, which should have left two days ago. Adam and I stand there for a minute, listening to them hassle the shipping company rep. I would not want to get on Kaitlin's bad side. Girl's tough.

"I'm not going," I say, finally, because I'm sick of waiting for him to talk.

"I heard."

Garrett. The traitor.

Adam slips an envelope from his back pocket and hands it to me.

It's my paycheck. But I've already done the calculations. I hand it back. "That should cover the rest of the cleaning fees for your place."

Adam shakes his head. "I want you to keep it. You're going to have expenses for the showcase, and the point was that you understood. Your actions have consequences."

"That wasn't the point, Adam. The point was that . . . that I understood I was disrespecting you by trashing your house. I get it now. And I'm sorry. It was stupid of me. I think . . . things are different now. It's like I didn't have anything that was making me think ahead or to . . . I don't know . . . to get excited about. I don't think I was seeing clearly what mattered. What matters."

"And now you do?"

"The band. My music." My family, I add silently. Then my mind supplies an image of Skyler's smile, as an addition to that list.

He nods. "Okay." A shaky smile appears. "Okay, Grey."

"I'm not done yet. The Cobra you built with Dad?"

Adam lifts his hand. "No need. Mom finally broke silence and told me. Don't get mad at her. She's been—"

"I'm not mad." She should be able to talk to Adam about what I did. And I know she was only trying to protect me by keeping quiet about what happened. "I'm going to replace the Cobra, too, when I can."

"Talk to Dad. See if he still wants that car."

"You don't?"

Adam lifts his shoulders, the gesture tight and tense. "I don't care about a fucking car. But I do want my brother back. How do we put all this shit behind us, little bro? I want you to come home. I want to hear you sing. Ali misses you. Mom's beside herself. You've even got Dad worried. Jesus, Grey. We're all just waiting for you to come back. You know that, right?"

I wrap him up in a hug, quick and fierce. Then I push him away and press my thumbs into my eyes. "You're an asshole for trying to make me cry."

"You're crying?"

"Not what I said." And like he's not in the same boat. Adam's grinning, but I know he's welling up.

We hear Bernadette and Kaitlin coming before they round the corner. Kaitlin breaks off in mid-sentence and starts in like she's going to deliver a status report to Adam, but they both pick up pretty quickly that this isn't a good time. "Sorry," they say in unison, and keep going.

"So Dad's even worried?" I ask.

"He's flying out here."

"I heard. For the showcase."

"Not for the showcase, dumbass. For *you*. God." Adam runs a hand over his face. "I feel so *relieved*."

"Like you just took an epic dump? Me too."

"You're really not coming to the Virgin Islands?"

"Can't. I don't qualify. And I don't think you do, either."

"Can you be serious for a second here? Garrett's all flustered about it. He says you're his good-luck charm. And I want you there, Grey. If it makes a difference, Mom won't be there. She's been working on a fund-raiser with Ali's mom. Some big dinner at the LA Country Club. It's next Saturday afternoon, so she's staying behind."

Adam shifts his weight. I feel his sharp eyes home in on me. I think he knows what I'm going to say before I do because a calm, satisfied expression settles over his face.

"It makes a difference," I tell him, more sure than ever about my decision. "I'm staying. There are a few things I need to work out."

Chapter 34

Skyler

*M*ia bounces around our apartment like Garrett on sugar. She stayed over so we could have a last hurrah with Beth before taking off for Virgin Gorda. And Grey was out all night with his band. He better get here soon to get his stuff together, or the plane's going to leave without him.

It's barely sunrise, again, and I'm trying to pack the last of my suitcases for the big trip. Figuring out what to bring for three weeks, when you'll be in someone else's wardrobe for eighteen hours a day, is tougher than you think. In the end, I still have two jam-packed suitcases, a carry-on, and my biggest purse, stuffed so full, I can barely zipper it. I know I'm going overboard. I've just never been away for so long, unless you count college, and it's possible I'm packing more for *this* than I did for *that*.

Finally, I drag everything to the front door and turn to Beth, who's curled up on the sofa, wrapped in a blanket and nursing a cup of tea.

"I wish you were coming."

She shrugs. "They don't need me."

"*I* need you," I say, and plop down beside her. "What am I going to do for two and a half weeks without you?"

"You're going to be so busy, you won't have time to think." She blows across the surface of the tea, making a tiny ripple. Then she takes a sip. "Besides, you've got your steamy love triangle to keep you hopping."

"Gosh, you're funny," I say and mentally run through every item in my bedroom, trying to determine one last time if I've left anything behind and if it's possible to sneak a cello onto the plane. I haven't played in weeks, and going away without Beyonce or Christina feels like leaving a limb behind. "How did you get so funny?"

"Just born with it, I guess."

"Too bad there's no triangle." I tell her. "Or much steam for that matter."

"Now, that's a shame."

"Well, we all can't be you and Titus."

She tries to take another sip of her tea, though the ridiculously big grin on her face makes it difficult. "True that."

"I guess I don't have to worry about you being bored while I'm gone."

"No," she tells me. "I've actually got a call back on a TV pilot and some other stuff going on."

"I meant because of Titus, but that's awesome, too." A wave of relief spreads through me—that she's finding all these opportunities, that her small part in the movie is helping her get offers, too. I didn't realize how much I've been nursing this guilt still, about taking something from her, until now.

"Yeah, it's all good. You don't have to worry."

"I wasn't—"

"Sky, please. I know you. But, seriously, things happen the way they're meant to happen. In no way am I right for the part. Not with Garrett. But you two are magic. And I got you into it in the first place. I can hardly be mad about that."

"I know, but I just kind of wandered in, and you've been studying and working at it forever."

She shrugs. "It happens. And maybe I need to study less and loosen up more. Anyway, you didn't just get plucked out of obscurity like some street urchin. You earned it."

Grinning, I pull a corner of her blanket onto me. "Do they still have street urchins?"

"Yeah, I think they keep them in a big warehouse," offers Mia, who can't seem to stop wandering by and looking out the window every four minutes. "With the newsies and chimney sweeps."

"What are you looking for?" I ask.

"The limo." She looks at her phone. "It should be here in a few."

"Really? What about Grey? Should I phone him? Or is he getting another ride?"

Beth and Mia look at each other.

"What?"

"Grey's not going," Beth says. "How did you not know that?"

"Of course, he's going." I look at Mia. "He's going, right?"

She shakes her head. "No, he's staying behind to prep for the showcase."

This incredible feeling of sadness plummets through me, so outsized, like a sinkhole caving in my chest. How could everyone else know he's not coming but me? Why wouldn't he tell me? I feel like crying, and then I feel like kicking myself in the ass for feeling that way. It's just eighteen days. Jesus.

"I guess everyone assumed you knew," Mia says.

I shake my head. "Somehow, I didn't get the update."

Or maybe I did. I've been feeling a little light-headed and out of it lately. Maybe Brooks told me while I was drooling over his lunch.

It's good for Grey to stay back, to work on his music for the showcase. It occurs to me that maybe I had a hand in that—maybe the talk we had the other night swayed him a bit. Which is great and crappy all at once. Because, I realize, it's going to be so different without him there. Without his dumb jokes and his hilarious, endless appetite and his sweet, thoughtful heart.

If he's taking this opportunity to get it together, I should be happy for him. The same way Beth's happy for me. That's how friendships work, right?

"And you still have Brooks, right?" asks Beth. "I mean, that's still a thing, yeah?"

"Yeah," I say. "Of course."

We were just in San Francisco a few days ago. Of course, it's a thing. Or the start of a thing. A better, smarter thing than whatever the thing it is I have with Grey. Which, I remind myself, is a friendship thing, and that's it.

Still, I pull out my phone to shoot him a text but just stare at the screen. Everything I want to say sounds petulant.

Finally, I settle on something.

> **Sky:** About to head off to the airport. Will miss you. Kick
> some musical ass while I'm gone.

I don't expect an answer right away. If he doesn't have to be up at this hour, I doubt he will be. But I see the little ellipses that tell me he's typing a reply and sit there, half holding my breath, waiting for it.

Grey: Will do. Just had to stay and take care of things.

Sky: I know. Have a good few weeks.

Grey: Shit. That's a long time.

No kidding, I think. Then another text comes through.

Grey: Hang on. Sending you something.

An audio file comes through. His song, "Surprised by the Sky." I've heard it a hundred times already on his CD.

Grey: Working on a new arrangement and new lyrics. Let me know what you think.

I smile, touched that he wants my opinion and knowing music is his way to keep us connected, even while I'm gone.

Sky: Can't wait to listen.

Grey: Text me from the set. And send pics.

Sky: Okay.

Grey: Especially if there's a nude beach.

I laugh and find myself wanting to hug the phone.

Sky: I really will miss you.

Grey: I know. I'll miss you, too, Sky.

"Limo's here," Mia says.

I look at my phone for a second, feeling like there's something else to say, but I can't imagine what that is. And it really is only three weeks. It's not like I'm taking a century ship to Mars.

Beth, Mia, and I manage to get the approximately three hundred suitcases and carry-ons down the stairs to the street, at which point the limo driver decides to get out and help us haul them the last six inches to the trunk.

We hug Beth goodbye, and I make her promise to call us every day and water my African violet a couple of times. And give us progress reports on the band. And break a leg at her auditions.

She laughs. "Anything else, Mom?"

"Just . . ." I feel like saying so many things. I don't know why it feels like I'm never coming home again. "Just that I love you, Bets. You're good people."

She gives me another fierce, tight hug. "You too, Sky. I'm so proud of you, girl. I hope you know."

"I do."

We smile at each other. Then Mia comes in for another hug. And we do a three-way hug. Then the limo driver lays on the horn, and we break apart, laughing.

"Guess we need to go," I say.

"I know. Go. Kill it, Sky." She looks at Mia. "You too, okay?"

"You too. At your callback."

"Oh, I will," she tells us, and I don't, for one second, doubt it's true.

Chapter 35

Grey

*T*hursday afternoon, my phone lights up with a text. Beth, who's in the studio control room with me and looking pretty swag in cordless red BEATS, grabs it off the sill, where I left it earlier.

"Grey, it's Skyler," she says, tossing it to me. "By the way, it's not right that she's texting you more than me."

"It's so right, Beth. So right."

She probably can't hear me, but she rolls her eyes anyway, and turns back to Titus, who's in the sound booth playing the guitar solo in "Runner."

I read Skyler's text.

> **Skyler:** Cali status?

This is how it starts now between us, a few times a day. Either from my end or hers. I send back a reply.

Grey: Titus is tearing it up. Strings are red hot.

Without the long days on the film set, without Garrett to drive around and babysit, I thought I'd have a billion free hours in the day, but I'm busier than ever. To prep for the showcase, we're in the studio every day, taking every one of our songs apart and putting it back together to make sure we're happy with every note, every run, every instrumental solo, every harmony, every everything. It's costing us a mint in studio fees, but we're all in. We want to create something Vogelson won't be able to deny. We're spending money to make money. No. We're spending money to go after our dreams. If that's not a worthy investment, what the hell is?

Skyler: Is Beth there?

I snap a quick photo of Beth, who has a goofy, love-struck smile on her face as she watches Titus, and hit Send.

Skyler: OMG. Ew. What's wrong with her?
Grey: Lots of action. Island status?

She doesn't answer for a few moments.

Skyler: Okay. A little rainy. Jetlag is my nemesis.

She's not telling me something. I don't know what it is. I've got a nagging feeling, though. I start to type my reply, when Emilio, Shane, and Rez walk in with a late lunch. Or early dinner. Whatever meal you have at four.

"How's Blue Skies and Fairytales?" Emilio asks as soon as he sees the phone in my hand. For whatever reason, that's what he calls Skyler. He sets down a bag of sandwiches and Shane hands out drinks. Food isn't allowed in the control room but the studio owner is a guy Rez knows, and he's not only giving us dirt-cheap rates, but letting us cut some corners on studio rules. It amazes me how many people are helping us out. One of Shane's buddies who's a graphic designer is doing an overhaul of our band logo for us for free. And before they left, Kaitlin and Bernadette kicked down a bunch of great gear from past jobs they've done. Boots, jackets, jeans. We didn't think we'd use any of it. Everyone thought it was hilarious that we were getting designer movie crap. Poser-ish. But when we were going through it at my place, we kept everything. Even the belts and cuffs, all of it. I gotta admit, we look sharper now. Dialed in. It's like Kaitlin and Bernadette knew what we wanted to look like as a band, and they took us there.

My phone buzzes with another text.

Skyler: I have to go. Send me a picture of you, too, okay?

"That's adorable, Grey," says Emilio, who's reading over my shoulder. He snatches the phone out of my hand. "Hey, guys! Skyler wants a picture of our young Grey here."

"Dude, give me th—" Someone grabs me around the shoulders from behind and suddenly I can't see.

"Pull his shirt off!" Shane yells.

They try, but I stop them. We come to a standstill with my t-shirt halfway off, over my head, and me trapping the arm of whoever has me in an arm lock. I'm swearing and laughing as I struggle, my rolling chair pushing around as I blindly fight four guys. We sort of settle down, and I hear Beth say, "Smile, you guys! Everyone say, 'Hi, Skyler!'"

They take the group shot then back away quickly, releasing me, because they all know I'm not above delivering instant payback.

Beth hands me my phone with a fake-mean look. "Don't ever take pictures of me without my consent again, Blackwood," she jokes.

"Noted." I leave the control room so I can do some damage control in private. I head outside and hop in my truck, which is my ride again now. No more Mercedes. It's weird that my truck reminds me of Skyler now. It still smells like her. Or maybe I just remember her smell when I'm in it.

I pull up the photo and laugh. My band is piled around me, making faces and obscene gestures. Titus is out of the frame except for his white-blond starter dreadlocks. I'm right in the center. A triangular, red t-shirt shape. I'm basically just a torso. A struggling torso.

Awesome. This is what she's going to see, halfway around the world. I type a quick message.

Grey: Pretty great, right? They really captured my best side.
Skyler: Love it.

A pause, then:

Skyler: I want to be there.

I push the Call button without giving it a thought. It rings once, and she answers.

"Sky, I know you need to go—"

"It's okay. I have a second." She does? I hear people in the background calling her name. Then it gets quiet, like she's shut a door. "Hi." I can tell she's smiling.

"Hey."

We sit on the phone for a few seconds saying nothing. Still, it feels different than the texting we've been doing. More revealing. Like we just took our clothes off or something. Finally, I make myself say what I called to say. "You doing all right?"

"Um . . . yeah. I'm just tired. But it looks like you guys are having a blast."

"We are. We're working hard. But it's been fun."

"I think I'm just working hard."

Her voice breaks a little. I knew it. Something isn't right. I want to teleport to the Virgin Islands. "You're almost done, Sky."

"I know." Someone else is in the background, talking to her. I recognize the voice. Brooks. "I should go," she says.

"Okay. See you, Sky."

"I wish."

"Me too," I say, but she's already gone.

I think about our conversation for the rest of the day. I'm still thinking about it when I get back to the apartment at ten, drop onto the couch, and kick my designer grunge boots off. We spent fourteen hours in the studio today. Insane. I loved every second.

Usually, Skyler and I text at night, but I guess not today. Maybe I scared her off with the phone call? Shit. I don't know. What am I even doing? She could be with Brooks right now. I thought being away was going to help me stop thinking about her, but only a few days in and it's gone the other way.

It occurs to me that I have a roundabout way of checking up on Skyler. I send Adam a quick message, asking him how the production is going. If anything major is going on, he'll tell me. Then I drop my head back and close my eyes. Beth is with Titus again and the apartment is quiet. I smile, remembering earlier when I caught them stepping out of the studio bathroom together. Things seem to be going well for them.

I'm tired, but I'm restless. Nowhere close to being ready to sleep yet. Adam's response comes through. The production is going well.

They're hustling, because there are some hurricanes developing that might affect the tail end of the shoot, but everything is fine. Garrett's right next to him, he says, and sends his love.

I read his message a few times. It just feels so good to be reconciled with him. Then it hits me, and I know what I have to do. Why I feel restless. I'm not done mending bridges yet.

I send my mom a text.

Grey: Can I take you to lunch tomorrow? I have a lot to say.

She replies instantly. Like she's been sitting by her phone, staring at it.

Mom: Yes. I'm free all day.

I tell her I'll meet her at Geoffrey's in Malibu at noon. Five minutes don't go by that I get two more texts, one on top of the other.

Adam: Good job, little bro.
Dad: Shit, son! Took you long enough! See you soon, rock star.

I laugh, a little choked up. I guess good news travels fast.

Still not tired, I get up and grab my guitar. I'm still learning. I'm nowhere near where Titus or Sky is on the strings, but I can do all the major chords, some of the minor ones. My fingers are getting faster, surer. My favorite thing is finger picking. I like the classic vibe. For the past few nights I've been messing around trying to figure out one of Skyler's original songs, on the cello. Today at the studio I got Titus and Beth to help me nail down the rest. I butcher it, compared to the way she does it, but I like playing the song she wrote. And that's what I do until sleep finally seems possible.

Chapter 36

Skyler

I'm in paradise with my feet burrowed into the warmest, softest sand I've ever felt, looking out at an ocean so clear I can see schools of fish darting everywhere, and I'm currently having my thighs oiled by two women I barely know.

Bernadette and Kaitlin have each taken a leg. While in the process of basting me like a turkey, they discuss my body with a weird dispassion. I feel detached, like my head's a balloon, barely tethered to the rest of me, just hovering there, watching the lacy white surf curl against the sand, while they tune me up, or polish me, or do whatever it is they're doing with the rest of me.

"Okay, she's a little smudgy over here," Kaitlin says. She's crouched in the sand behind me, and I feel her tap a spot just above the back of my knee. "But they did a pretty good job with the tanner."

"Yeah, not bad," Bernadette says. "Feet are a little darker than the rest, but no one will see that." She moves around in front of me. "Do me a favor, and bend forward."

I'm already eighty percent out of this bikini top, but I bend so Bernadette can make some adjustments. I straighten and look down at myself. Make that ninety percent. I'd estimate that about one millimeter of hot pink Spandex is keeping my nipple from public display.

Crew walks by, dragging equipment and then brooming over the tracks they've made in the sand. Brooks stands with Mia, who looks over to give me a sympathetic smile every now and then. Her wild curly hair blows everywhere in the breeze stirring off the ocean, and in her white flowing sundress, she looks like a tiny goddess, risen from the sea to capture men's souls with the lens of her camera. I, on the other hand, feel like a hot, sticky blob.

"Okay," says Kaitlin, tugging down the bottom of my bikini just a bit and then adjusting the strings at my hips. "Just stay exactly like that. Don't move."

I stand there, feet apart, feeling a little bit unsteady. Probably, I should have had more than a piece of toast and half a grapefruit this morning. Plus, two cups of black coffee that I'm beginning to regret.

The two women step back and consider me.

"It's good," says Bernadette, but something in her expression says the opposite. I try to stand up straighter, suck in a little.

"No, no, honey, you're fine," says Kaitlin. "Just be normal. You look great."

I wish I could see for myself. But then maybe not.

Not for the first time, I wish Grey had come after all. To joke me out of my insecurity, to look at me with that hungry expression that tells me that he, at least, likes what he sees. I smile, remembering our conversation about my diet. "You're gorgeous," he'd said, and with him, it feels true.

Mostly, I've felt that way about myself my whole life. Maybe not that I'm gorgeous. But that I'm pretty. That I look fine. That, more importantly, my body did the things I wanted it to do—work out, run around, haul my cello. I felt good, and I don't feel good now, but I know I'll get used to this. It's all an adjustment. And I tell myself that a temporary bout of insecurity's a small price to pay to support my family. Support myself. Make everyone happy.

Speaking of which, I ask Bernadette and Kaitlin if I can get my phone, but they both tell me not to move.

"I'll get it for you," Bernadette tells me. "Just stay put another few minutes. You're doing great."

She gets my phone for me, and I punch in my mom's number, watching the crew set up light panels and boom mics with long escalating necks. Garrett sits under a huge white awning with some of the other actors, chatting up one of the local crew, and sipping cucumber water with a straw. The crew guy leans in and whispers something. Garrett laughs and slaps the guy's arm, keeping it there long enough to send sex vibes sparking in every direction.

Ladies and gentlemen: my leading man.

The call connects.

"I hear you spoke to your father."

"Why hello, Mother. How are you?"

"Skyler."

"Mom."

"I'm fine." Her sigh sounds like static in my ear. "Are you doing okay?"

"Yes," I say, though I don't know if I'm telling the truth. Mostly, I'm okay. This place is gorgeous. Everyone's nice. I just don't feel exactly . . . right.

"So, I heard you talked to your father," she says again.

"Yeah. He was playing in LA. Did you know that?"

"I don't follow his schedule anymore. What's the point? Anyway, he called me with his head on fire. Thinks I sicced you on him."

"Well, you didn't sic me on him."

"I know, but—"

"And anyway, what difference does it make? He needs to send you money."

"It's okay. With what you've sent, I'm doing all right."

I turn my attention out to the water, looking to be soothed. But watching the waves spill onto the sand gives me a weird tilting feeling, so I look away again, back at Brooks, who's watching me through the camera. I wonder what he sees. What he *thinks* of what he sees.

He straightens and gives me a little smile, but it's distant, distracted. I don't know if he's just busy—a definite possibility—or bummed that I sent him back to his room last night with just a quick kiss. I'm just so tired, and the days are so long.

". . . coming out there," I hear my mom say and realize I've tuned out of the conversation for God knows how long.

"I'm sorry, Mom, what did you say?"

Another sigh, more static.

"I said I'm thinking about giving your brother the farm and coming out there to live. What do you think?"

"What do you mean, give Scotty the farm? How can you do that?"

"I just mean to run. We've been talking about it a lot lately. They're not giving him promotions at work. With the kids, he can't shine like all the other guys there. He's late. He has to leave when they're sick. You know how it is."

"I know it's tough for him. I just don't get how giving him the farm to run is going to solve the problem. Why can't he just find someone to watch the girls? Why can't *you* watch the girls?" I ask for the hundredth time.

"Honey, I just don't have the energy. They're so high-spirited."

"They're just normal kids."

"Anyway, I thought he could give it a go on the farm. And I could come out there."

So, does that mean helping to support the farm in Kentucky *and* my mom here in LA? My mind does furious calculations, and I wish I could sit the hell down already. Aren't they supposed to cater to the leading lady? How come Garrett gets a tent and cucumber water and a cute crew guy to flirt with, and I get *this*?

Kaitlin trudges back across the sand toward me, a spray bottle in one hand and a long swatch of fabric in the other. "It's go time," she whispers.

"Mom, I have to go. I'll talk to you later." I can't think about this now. I wish I hadn't called her.

"Honey, just tell me what you think of the idea."

"I don't know yet. Let's talk more about it when I'm back in LA."

"Okay, but Scotty's lease is up this month, so—"

"Sorry, Mom, really. I have to go. Love you."

I press End and see I have a text message from Grey, but Kaitlin takes my phone and hands it off to someone before I can read it. "We're going to roll in just a few. You're doing great."

"I'm just standing here."

"Well, you're awesome at standing."

"Can I get some water?"

"Yes, sorry, of course!" She calls for some water, and then says, "We're going with a sarong."

"A sarong?"

"Yeah, we think it'll look a little sexier. More dramatic when you come out of the surf. I think Emma would wear a sarong, don't you?"

I really don't know. All I can think is that they're trying to cover me up. That I haven't lost enough weight yet to look the way they want me to look on camera.

On the plus side, I won't have to worry about thigh jiggle at a billion pixels per square inch. "I think a sarong's an awesome idea."

She gets busy tying it around my hips, tugging it lower, than raising it up a bit. Knotting and re-knotting it. Smoothing and then re-smoothing. Then she uses the water bottle to spritz my entire body, wet my hair, and slick it back from my face.

"Very pretty," she says, and gives my chin a little squeeze. "The camera's going to love you."

"Good for the camera," I mutter. And I think about how that's not me. I've always been pretty sunny, light. But I feel weighed down now, heavier with each pound I lose. I lick my chapped lips, which I know will necessitate another five minutes of makeup touch-up, but I don't care. The sound of the surf pounds in my ear. It's so beautiful here. The clouds are wisps in a startling blue sky. The palm trees stir, and two white-sailed catamarans crisscross out near the horizon. I try to breathe and enjoy it, to remind myself how lucky I am. To remind myself that we'll be wrapped soon, and then I'm going to eat a cheeseburger the size of my face.

"Okay, clear the set," Mia calls, and everyone hustles.

Finally. I close my eyes to let it all go, to pull Emma back into me. To be the sweet hopeful girl who's come here to make amends with a man she now thinks loves someone else.

Garrett lounges in the cabana where I'll join him. I just have to walk a few feet across the sand. Just have to walk, in my sarong, looking luscious for the camera. That's my job. Just to walk.

Brooks yells "Action." I put a smile on my face, the smile meant for Garrett's character. My Mr. Knightley.

And I walk.

Chapter 37

Grey

$\mathcal{I}$ arrive at Geoffrey's half an hour early, which gives me time to request a table with a better view of the Pacific, order wine for my mom, cancel the wine, then reorder it, second-guess the bouquet of peonies I brought, all as I'm grinding my teeth down to the bone.

Meeting her in a public place was a bad idea, but it seemed important that I make a bold gesture. That's how I went off the tracks nine months ago, when I stormed out of the house, then mired the Cobra in the ocean, so that's how I should get us back *on* track. I adjust the collar of my button-down and check my phone to see if Skyler sent a message. She knows I'm having lunch with Mom. No message, but I know she has a jam-packed shoot schedule today. I read through some of our old conversations. She hasn't mentioned Brooks. Not once. Not that she would mention him to me, but I am starting to wonder what's going on—or not going on between them.

I glance up and see Mom walking into the restaurant. She tends to draw the eye normally but today, wearing a yellow dress that's as bright as an egg yolk, smiling as she searches for me, it's like the sun just walked in. She reaches our table, and then we're hugging, tight and for a long time. I try to relax. I try to ride out the waves of emotion that rock through me.

Just like surfing. Don't fight it. Go with it. Lean into it. Feel it.

I know this is what I needed after so much time apart. Just to feel that she's real, and wants to be close to me.

When we sit down, we're both smiling twitchy smiles. She lifts the bouquet of peonies. "My favorite," she says. "Thank you."

"Is it weird I got them for you? Like date-y?"

"No. It's great-y."

I laugh, because I didn't expect that. And she laughs, because I don't know why.

And there's too much going on in her eyes right now, so I mumble something about the wine and focus on repeating the Pinot Grigio's merits as given to me by our server. Crisp, zingy, with some delightful persimmon undertones and a wonderful, steely finish.

Mom laughs. "Really? All that?" She knows I couldn't care less about wine. She takes a sip, agrees with all the merits of the Pinot Grigio, and there's nothing else to do or say. We grow quiet; the restaurant becomes noisier, dishes clanging, people laughing, corks popping. It's not awkward between us. It's something tougher. It's painful. I've done this. I mean, she was a party in it. But it's, like, ninety percent on me. It's my move.

I pick a starting point—the night I left home—and start talking. My nervousness drops away almost immediately, and it's all flow now. Like singing, I'm just hooked into the way I feel, and the words come. They come pouring out.

I tell her how I always felt like I was letting her down because I wasn't racing off to college, like Adam. Because I was tougher on her than he was, rougher in general, directionless when it came to school, when it came to most everything. I tell her how I felt like she expected me to be something I could never be, a perfect kid with college plans and post-graduate plans. Taking a track that was measurable in semesters and degrees and startup companies, and how it felt like that was the only way I could make her happy. How I never felt like I was what she wanted—and that's when she interrupts me.

"Maybe that's how it came across, Grey. And I'm so sorry if it did. I never meant to push you to be something you didn't want to be. I just wanted you to have every opportunity you could in life. I wanted to give you everything you deserve."

"It felt like you wanted to change me."

"No, Grey. Never. I only want you to be happy."

"And you didn't think I was?"

She hesitates. "It's not that I thought you were unhappy." She sips her wine. "It's more that when anything happened, anything intense—happiness, fear, whatever—you'd retreat. I suppose there were times I wondered if you weren't holding yourself back from being as happy—as comfortable and easy—as you could be."

I nod. I swallow. I breathe in and out and have to do all of it once more. "I never thought anything that mattered was supposed to last."

"The things that last *are* the things that matter."

"I didn't know, Mom."

"But now do you?"

"Yes." Jesus, I've missed her. "Now I know."

We have to stop when the waiter comes and drones on about daily specials. Mom dabs at her eyes with a napkin, and we manage to get our orders in.

When we're alone again, she jumps right back in and says, "I should have never given you Lois's address."

I shake my head. "It's okay." I grab a roll from the breadbasket and butter it, then set it back down. "I guess I've always known she didn't want me."

This is the hardest thing for me to say and, I see, for Mom to hear. We both need a few seconds to wrestle that one down. I finish my water. The busboy refills it. I'm still trying to get my breath.

It's the truth. There's no denying it. It's the ugly truth of how I came to be. My dad never loved my birth mother. She was just a pretty girl he knocked up while he and Madeleine were taking a break. I came into the world completely by accident. I was a burden to Lois before I was even born. It's possible I've felt that way with other people. With everyone. That I'm something you grow tired of and pawn off, like an unwanted pet.

I've never actually asked how much my dad bought me for. Monthly rent, it sounds like. I'm pretty sure, based on my conversation with Lois the night I saw her. But maybe it was more than that? I'd like to think he paid Lois a little more for me than that. Then my curiosity gets the better of me and I just freakin' ask the question.

"How much was I worth?"

Mom refolds her napkin. It takes her so long to look up, I'm wondering if she's going to hedge. But then she answers. "It was a set payment for some time. The first few years. But she . . . she was irresponsible with the money. So your father started paying the landlord and main utilities directly."

"That was smart of him."

"It was my idea. My suggestion."

"That was nice of you."

"She gave birth to you, Grey."

"Yeah. She did. Wow. This is a lot."

"I'm sorry, Grey. She doesn't know what she's missing. But it's my gain. *You* are my gain. And your father's and Adam's. I love you. You were a surprise, and you haven't always been easy, and I haven't always been a perfect mother, but I love you. From the bottom of my soul, I do. I have from the start. From the very first day I learned about you. Before we even had you, I did."

"Even though I'm not yours."

"You *are* mine. I've always felt so."

Eventually, I find the word I want. "Same."

She smiles. "That's good to hear."

And because she means it, and deserves more, I rally some courage and tell her that I love her, too, using the actual words.

For a little while, we laugh just from the sheer *lift* we're both feeling.

"I think I need another glass of this zingy, persimmony wine," she says, and right then our food shows up, which is perfect. I can't take anymore. I don't think she can, either. We fall into easy conversation about how much she's enjoying spending time with Ali's mother, who's going through a divorce. They're planning a trip to Scotland together. Apparently, there's some obscure castle they both have always wanted to see.

She's so social, I think, as I listen. This love connection between her and Ali's mom isn't common—I can tell it's something special— but I feel like I've been in the position of hearing about a new friend of hers a thousand times before. She and Adam are so alike, always seeing the best in everyone. It's like there's a party going on in their hearts all the time with wall-to-wall people in there, everyone smiling and getting along.

I'm not like that. I don't think I have the bandwidth for it. My heart's probably just a small gathering-type deal. Maybe a dozen people or so. Just my band, my family. A few others. But it's a rockin' party. Today especially.

Mom and I order dessert even though we're stuffed. Neither one of us wants lunch to be over.

"Will you move back into Adam's?" she asks me as she takes a spoonful of crème brûlée. "I know you've been staying in Venice."

"No." I've been thinking about my living situation a lot over the past week. Adam, Beth, and Skyler have all been great, but I'm tired of living at other people's places. It's time for me to get my own spot. Something that's mine. I'm banking on us getting a contract after the showcase, but if it doesn't happen, I've already decided I'll break open the trust fund I've been sitting on since I turned eighteen. It's money I've never touched. It's never really felt like it was mine. Plus, you don't play around with big money like that.

But the thing is, there are things I want. Things that are worthwhile. And I'm done feeling like I don't deserve my fair share of what it means to be a Blackwood. I've had a few shitty breaks in my life, but it doesn't mean I have to feel guilty for the good ones.

I tell my mom about a house up in the Hollywood Hills. "It's just a little bungalow I saw online, but it used to belong to a guy who mixed sound on films, so it has a full studio in the basement. It'd be a great place for the band to practice. And the house also has a detached garage with enough space for a person to build a Cobra from a kit."

Mom smiles. "Is someone going to build a Cobra from a kit?"

"If someone's dad wants his Cobra replaced, and his brother agrees to help him, since someone doesn't know the first thing about building cars, then yes." I still have to talk to Dad about it, but it's the right thing to do.

"I'd love to see this place," Mom says.

That's exactly what I wanted to hear. No one sees potential like she does.

I pay the bill. As we walk out into the sunshine, we make plans to meet at the house in the morning. We hug and say goodbye, and when I'm finally in my truck, the lightness inside me is so intense, it feels like my seat belt is the only thing tethering me to this planet.

Chapter 38

Skyler

How many actors does it take to change a lightbulb?" Garrett asks me.

It's 10 p.m. We're on take eleven of some complicated nighttime scene where the camera tracks around us as we dance under white lights strung from the beams of a waterfront bar.

I have to admit, the set looks absolutely magical. Votives flicker at every table; the water has this incredible phosphorescent glimmer; and all around us, extras act like they're having the most romantic night of their lives. I'm freezing and exhausted but trying so hard to be game.

"How many?" I ask.

We're going again, so Garrett repositions his arms around me. "Ten. One to change the lightbulb and nine others to bitch that *they* could have done it better."

I laugh and rest my cheek against Garrett's chest for a moment. The breeze stirs against my silk dress, and I shiver.

Rubbing his arms over my back, he asks, "You okay?"

I nod against his pale blue linen shirt. "Fine."

Garrett pushes me away, just a bit, so he can fix those laser-blue eyes on me. "You don't look so hot there, beautiful. What do you need? Should we ask for a break?"

I shake my head. "No, I'm fine. Really."

"Want some water? A handful of almonds or something?" He signals for the runner, Laurel, to come over, but I wave her off.

"I'm fine," I insist. The thought of eating or drinking anything nauseates me. "Let's just keep going."

"I know you want to make everyone happy, sweetness, but you have to take care of yourself, too."

"I know." It's just that some days making other people happy is the only thing that makes *me* happy.

"Five more minutes, guys," Mia calls. She wanders over. "You need anything?"

"*This one* needs to get off her feet," Garrett tells her, nodding in my direction. "And I wouldn't mind calling it a night soon, myself. What're the odds?"

"They're good," Mia tells us. "I promise. We're just losing the light in part of the shot and want to make some adjustments."

The ocean roars in my ear, and for a second, I feel that weird shifting feeling I felt earlier, like the whole world just tilted about forty degrees and then righted itself. I clutch on to Garrett, steadying myself.

"What's wrong?"

I shake my head and swallow. "Just got a little light-headed for a second."

Brooks comes over, and I want to cry, because if everyone is talking to us, no one is getting things rolling, and I'm going to have to keep standing here, shivering and weak-limbed, for another God-knows-how-long.

"Everything okay?" he asks, smiling down at me. "What do you need?"

"Just to shoot the scene already," Garrett says. His tone is honey, light as air, but there's a whole lot of steel in it. "I'm freezing my giblets off out here, and my darling Skyler has to get off her feet."

Brooks looks at me, and it kills me to feel like I'm letting him down. Like I need to be pampered in any way.

"I'm okay," I protest. "Just a little tired, but it's no problem."

"Okay, we'll be ready to go again in five."

A groan escapes me, but it's swept up by the stirring of the tide.

Brooks and Mia head off, and Garrett wraps his arms around me to rub my back briskly, trying to work his own plentiful body heat into me. He's like some kind of self-contained sun. Always warm, radiating this perfect assuredness.

"I'm worried about you," he tells me. "And young Greyson will kick my ass six ways to Sunday if I don't take care of you down here."

Just the sound of Grey's name makes me miss him more.

"I promise, I'm okay. I just need some sleep."

Again, I feel that weird shifting, and for just a second, my eyesight goes red, like someone slammed a shutter in front of my face. As quick as it came, it recedes, but I feel a little flare of panic, not knowing when it will return, if I should, actually, be worried.

"Okay," Garrett says. "I'll stop being a father hen. But you tell me what you need, okay?"

I nod. Everyone keeps asking that, but the answers feel way too big to put into words. "I will. I just don't want to be a problem."

"Honey, you have no idea what a problem is." He grins. "I could tell you some stories."

"Really?"

"God, yes. Get me a few virgin Mai Tais at the wrap party, and I will talk your ear off."

"I'm looking forward to that." Not just the party, I realize, but the wrap. The downtime again, even though Parker has me primed for a ton of auditions the second I get back, and Jane has me doing some feature about "Hip New Hollywood" for *Entertainment Weekly*.

We're about to get going again, but this time Garrett stops everything and asks for some touch-ups. While his forehead is being powdered, he gets a big grin on his face and asks again, "How many actors does it take to screw in a lightbulb?"

"How many?"

"Just one. He stands there, and the world revolves around him."

It's 1 a.m. by the time I drag back to my room, and I have to hold on to the corridor walls to keep from toppling over. My stomach feels like it's trying to chew its way out of my body, I've got a headache, and I'm truly not sure how much longer my limbs are going to hold my body upright.

In my room, I topple into the bed and feel that crazy dizziness again, and this weird pressure in my ears, like I'm plugging them with my fingers. I want to get up and get myself some water; I feel like I could drink for days. But I'm too tired. I need to sleep and sleep and sleep. Except I have to be on set again at 8 a.m., which means makeup at 6:30.

I pick up my phone and find about twenty messages from Grey, Beth, and my mom. I ignore my mother's but thumb through Beth's. It's looking good for that pilot. And she met Shane and Nora's cat, Thor, and now wants a kitten.

She and Titus also seem to be going strong, judging from the endless number of band shots she's sent, including one of Grey asleep in a chair in the studio, head back, mouth open, and one hand resting in the V of his t-shirt. He looks like a kid, though he dwarfs the chair, and his long, long legs sprawl completely out of frame. Somehow, it looks like his hair has grown an inch in the couple of weeks I've been gone. It's sticking up a little on top, a bit punky, but still short on the sides. He looks good. Really good.

I zoom in on the hand inside his shirt, resting against his heart, and think of the night we spent lying together in my bed and talking, my ear up pressed against his chest, listening to the slow steady drum of his heartbeat.

Before I know it, I'm calling him, pushing away my worry that it's already late, that he's working so hard and might be asleep. I just want to hear his voice, even just his voicemail message.

He picks up right away. "Wow, I was just thinking about you."

Immediately, I start to cry. It's like a tornado, blowing up out of nowhere, shocking me. It's his voice, so warm and right here but not here at all. And I know I'm tired. My feelings are all over the place and can't seem to settle anywhere.

For a second, I can't say anything. I even think about disconnecting. I don't want him to hear me like this. Being weak.

"Hey," I manage, finally. "I was just thinking about . . . everyone there."

I can't bring myself to say that I'm thinking about him, that I've been thinking about him so much, missing him. It sounds so pathetic, and I'm with someone. Grey's nineteen and a musician who just wants to eat and breathe and live music. I just can't have that in my life. Can't sign up for the path my mom took, even though I know I'm not her. Even though I know Grey's not my dad.

"What's going on?" he asks. "It's late there, right?"

"Yeah, we had a long day."

"You're just finishing? Jesus." I hear the telltale groan of springs and know he's climbing onto Mia's bed.

"Is it okay? Were you going to sleep?"

"Nah," he says. "I just got back myself. We finished the album today. I'm totally wired."

"You did?"

Again, tears come. I feel like I'm missing everything. Which is ridiculous. I'm in this paradise, making an actual feature film. I'm so lucky, and I know it. I just didn't expect to miss him so much. To miss Beth. And home. The people at Maxi's. All of it. My life. My old life.

"Yeah, we did. Sky, it's so good. I can't wait for you to hear it."

"I can't wait, too."

He's sent me a few songs, and they've been amazing. The arrangements are so much tighter, the lyrics punched up. And Grey's voice: it's just perfect.

Again, the sound of bedsprings and then I hear his heavy footsteps on the wood floor, the sound of the window sliding open. I smile, thinking about how many times he's had to pry open my own bedroom window for me.

He won't be there for much longer, I realize. He's found a place to buy—not so far away but still. He's made up with his mother. Things are coming together for him, and while he tells me all about the band's last few days of recording, I can feel the difference it's all made in him. This buoyancy seeps through the phone to wrap around me. I feel his happiness, and for a second, it feels like I've got no place in it, and that makes me start crying again, hard, and this time I know he hears me.

"What's wrong?" he asks. And when I don't answer, he says quietly, so sweetly, "Talk to me, Sky. What's going on there?"

I wish I knew. But I don't, exactly. It's like something in my peripheral vision. I know it's there, but every time I try to turn and look at it, it slips away. I'm just tired, I tell myself. And I don't feel well. I'm running on coffee and adrenaline, and I know it's not great for me, but I can't make myself stop.

"I'm okay," I say, finally. "Just a little worn out. It'll be good to be back."

"It'll be great to have you back," he says. "Just one more week, right?"

"Right."

"Seriously, though. You need to tell me if something's wrong. Did Brooks—"

"No." I drag myself back out of the bed, though it feels like pushing through quicksand. I go into the bathroom and find some tissues to dab at my eyes and nose. I've got this sharp pain in my throat, like a sob's caught there. It's making it hard to speak or breathe. "Brooks is great. It's all good down here. Just working really hard. It's okay."

"You sure?"

"Yeah, I'm sure."

"When you get home, I'm making sure you take the whole week off, and I will personally punch Parker and Jane in their throats if they schedule anything for you."

"Fair enough." I get some water and take it back to my bed. Even out of the cold water tap, it's lukewarm, but I drink it down so fast, it adds to the knot in my esophagus. "I guess I should let you go. I just wanted to say hi and hear how things are going."

"I'm glad you called." He's quiet for a long time, and I can hear the sound of cars driving by his open window. "Everyone misses you."

"I miss everyone, too," I say. My eyes burn with tears again, and it's starting to feel like they're just going to keep coming, popping up over and over at the most ridiculous, inappropriate times. "Give Beth a big hug for me, okay? And say hi to the guys." I wish I knew them better, I think. They seem great, and though we've hung out a few times, it feels like I've missed out on them, too.

"I will." We should wrap up, but neither of us says goodbye. Instead, we're quiet for a moment, so quiet I can hear his breath. Or maybe my own.

"Okay, well, I guess I better get some sleep."

"Hang on a second," he tells me. "I've been working on something. I was going to save it for when you got back, but I want to do it now."

"What is it?"

"A new song," he says. "I hope it's okay, but I used one of your compositions. Just added lyrics. They're still rough, so don't judge."

"Really? One of my songs?" I try to imagine which one that could be. I don't write a lot of original music, but every now and then there's something I can't find, something that doesn't exist that I need to work out on my cello.

I hear him picking at his guitar and then start playing in earnest. He's gotten so much better, so quickly, it's astonishing.

"It's called 'The Long Way Around,'" he tells me. "Which is kind of how I do things."

"Me too."

"Yeah. Okay. Seriously, it's not great, but I—"

"Play it." I lie back against my pillows. Moonlight slants in from way up high, casting stretched-out shadows on the wall next to me. "I want to hear you sing."

"Okay," he says. "Sure. Here goes."

He plays, and it's my song but so much better. Grey's slowed the tempo, reworked it in a minor key, so it's more somber. And the lyrics are beautiful. It's about finding your way toward a place you know is home. Aiming for the light in the window, even when you seem to walk for miles and miles and get no closer.

"I'm still working on this next part," he says. "But what do you think of this?" He sings the next bit:

> *And I don't know if life's a map*
> *With all the directions gone,*
> *Or if it's a lantern that you*
> *Have to keep switched on. . . .*

"I love it."

"I'm still hacking at the chorus. Any thoughts?"

"No," I tell him. "It's really, really good."

And it is. But more than that I don't want to offer any other opinions. He'll find his way through the rest. It's already so good, better than anything I could ever hope to write. He's brought my music to life in a way I couldn't have imagined. Given it purpose.

"Play it for me again," I tell him. "From the beginning without stopping. The whole thing."

"Really? You want to hear it all again?"

"Yes, please."

I pull the sheets up around me, smooth them over my body. I feel myself fading, and I know I run the very real risk of falling asleep while he sings. But with Grey, it doesn't matter. He doesn't have a list of expectations for me. He just wants to play his music, share the thing that brings him to life.

And right now, I just want to lie here and listen, to drift off with the moon pouring silver light over my body, and Grey's voice—beautiful, sharp-edged, and warm—carrying me into my dreams.

Chapter 39

Grey

$\mathcal{I}$t needs work," Mom says as she steps into the kitchen of the cottage in the Hollywood Hills. "The kitchen and bathrooms need updating, but you could do that in a few years. The floors need to be refinished, and the whole thing needs a fresh coat of paint, but it has great bones, great light, and the location is terrific." Her eyes move over the outdated appliances, the cracked white tile countertops, to me. "That's what I think, but what's important is what you think."

"What you think is important. You know more about this stuff than I do."

"True," Mom says. "Let me ask you this: how does this house make you feel?"

I lean against the old fridge and cross my arms, trying to imagine myself living in this small, Spanish-style two-bedroom. It's not as big as the other sleek, modern homes around here—not by a long shot. But it's got potential. Room to expand if I ever feel like doing that, and it's got personality. More importantly, the moment I drove up, I felt something. A kind of rightness. That feeling's only getting stronger by the second.

Through the window, I see my Realtor wandering around in the backyard, checking her phone so Mom and I can talk. The yard is just a modest grass square framed by overflowing bougainvillea. More space than I need. It's not like I have a dog. Buy maybe I could get a dog? The prospect makes me smile. I can't believe I could do that if I wanted to. Suddenly, I see all of it. A couch, a table. My guitar on a stand in the corner of the living room. My mutt asleep at my feet. Sand, from the beach, dusting the floorboards by the front door.

Yep. I can see it. I run a hand over my head. "I think living here will bring me closer to who I want to be."

Mom's smile goes wider. "I can't think of a better reason to buy a home."

My Realtor seems to be able to smell money in the air. She's back in less than a minute. "So? Any decision?" she asks.

"Let's write an offer."

She hugs me, even though I only just met her a few days ago. And then we start tossing around numbers that give me a stomachache. I've already gone through them with my dad, but it's a lot of greenbacks. I'm not crazy about spending a truckload of money without having income on the way. But this area is only appreciating in value. All signs point to this being a good investment. I guess I've come a long way from throwing parties that trash my brother's place.

My cell phone buzzes in my pocket. It's Adam, speak of the devil, probably calling to find out if I'm making an offer. I excuse myself.

"I'm buying it," I say, as I step into my future bedroom. I move to the window, studying the hills that I'll be able to see from my bed one day. One day soon. It's incredible to consider. With the band showcase only two days away, this is becoming a historic week for me.

"What?" Adam says. "Oh, the house. Grey, we need to talk. Something happened over here. Are you listening?"

His voice is reedy and thin. He sounds shaken up. Adam never sounds that way.

"What happened? Is it Skyler? Is she okay?"

"She fainted on set about an hour ago, but she's fine now. She's under a doctor's care, getting some fluids through an IV at the island hospital. We don't know exactly what's going on yet, but it looks like a combination of stress and dehydration shocked her system."

"Adam, is she okay?" My body goes hot with adrenaline. My hands ball into fists. "It's those fucking weight-loss pills. And she's been losing too much weight."

"We're considering everything. Grey, she's going to be all right."

He's telling me this because he knows there are a dozen alarm bells going off inside me right now. Fear. Fear is what's filling me up. So much it feels like rage. Randomly, Mom's words come to mind. *The things that last* are *the things that matter.*

In the background I hear Garrett's voice pleading with Adam to hand over the phone. I hear Mia, too. Adam concedes, telling me he's passing me off for a moment.

"Grey, it's Garrett—"

"And Mia."

"We wanted you to know what's going on, because she asked to talk to you earlier—"

"She's resting in her room now, but she's still not herself. And we didn't want you to worry—"

"What do you mean, 'she's still not herself'? Is she okay or isn't she?"

Silence. Then it's only Mia on the line. She's stepped away, somewhere private.

"I've never seen her like this. She's pale, and when I look into her eyes, I don't see *her,* you know? It's like she's slipped into some tunnel and all I'm getting is this distant echo. I know she's going to be okay. The doctor is confident about that. But I'm worried about her."

"I'm coming."

"No—wait. What did you say?"

"I'll get on a plane today. Tell her I'm on my way. I'll call as soon as I can."

"You don't have to. We're on the other side of the continent, and there are a dozen people taking care of her."

"She's asking for me. That's why you called, isn't it?"

There's a soft sigh, then Mia says, "I asked her what I could do to help. She told me, 'Get Grey.' "

It's a heartbreaking thing to hear. I don't know what it means. What the hell are we to each other? But nothing is going to keep me away from her. Nothing.

I make some quick calculations. It'll take me a day to get to the Virgin Islands. Even if I'm only there for a day, and turn around and come back, I won't make it back to Los Angeles in time for the showcase. I feel a slow chill spread through me. It's not my dream I care about passing on. It's the guys, the band. This decision affects them, too. But I can only hope they'll understand. I need to go to her.

"I'm coming, Mia. I'll call you when I have my flights booked. Tell Sky I'm on my way."

Chapter 40

Skyler

Waking is like slowly unwrapping layers of gauze. It takes forever, the light behind my closed eyes growing brighter a second at a time. I'm drowsy and floating, and it feels so good, like backstroking through a warm sea, but I know I can't remain in this dreamy place.

Finally, I open my eyes. For a second, I think I'm still dreaming because Grey is next to me, sitting in a chair pulled up to the bed, his expression serious and intense.

"Grey?" It comes out as a whisper.

He gives me a smile that's so big and openhearted I want to cry. He's here. I can't believe he's here.

"There you are," he says. "Welcome back."

"What—" I try to say something more, but my throat feels like it's been sandpapered. I reach out for him and see a bandage on my hand and a tube extending down to an IV pole and a bag of clear fluids. Panic rushes through me. What's wrong with me? What happened?

"I'll get you some water," another voice says, and I turn my head to find Mia sitting in a chair on the side of the bed opposite Grey. Her tawny skin is sallow, her eyes red-rimmed and shadowed.

She rises and pours some water from a pitcher.

"Let me help you." Grey pops out of his chair so fast, it topples over. He fishes around behind my pillow, and his warm scent—soap and sea—washes over me. I still can't put it together that he's here. That I'm here in a hospital.

He finds the bed's remote control and raises the mattress. His huge warm hand settles for just a second on my collarbone, strokes the skin there. His touch anchors me and buoys me at the same time. I want him to climb into bed with me. Want to wrap myself in his strength.

Mia brings me the cup, and I sip. Then drink and ask for more.

"The doctor said to go easy," she tells me. "You don't want to get sick. But here's a little more."

I drink another half a cup and try to speak again. "What happened? Why am I here?"

Random memories flare in my mind. Running down a hotel corridor toward the camera. Then needing to stop, the walls closing in on me, the breath leaving my lungs. People crouched over me. Worried faces. A nurse wrapping a blood pressure cuff around me in the middle of the night. But not much else.

"You passed out, Sky," Mia tells me. She brushes my hair away from my face. "You . . . just went down." She starts to tear. "You really scared us."

"I'm sorry."

"No, *I'm* sorry. I should have paid more attention. I didn't realize you were getting sick."

"What's wrong with me?"

"Exhaustion and dehydration," she says. "Also, you're a little anemic, and your blood pressure was super low. That's what made you pass out."

"But you'll be okay," Grey says. "You just have to take care of yourself. Eat. And rest." Again, he gives me this sweet, fierce look that makes me want to give him anything he wants.

"I will. I'm so sorry."

"Seriously, don't apologize," he says. "Whoever gave you those fucking pills and worked you eighteen hours a day should apologize."

"It's not their fault. No one forced me to do anything. I could have said no. Or said it was all too much."

"Well, I guess your body said it for you," Mia says, with a sad smile. "But you'll be all right." She refills my cup and hands it back to me. "I'll let everyone know you're awake and doing better. And I'll go track down your doctor for you."

"Can you, um, give us a few minutes?" Grey asks. "I want to talk to Sky for a second."

Mia looks at me, and I nod. I want to talk to him, too, though I don't know what I want to say. It just means so much that he's here.

"Okay," she says. "I'll go find some coffee in the hospital café. Will let people know you're awake when I come back up. That'll buy you a few minutes."

"Thanks," says Grey.

She goes. And for a second, Grey and I just look at each other.

Finally, he sits back down and closes his hand over my wrist. He squeezes, gently, and I can feel the intersection of our two pulses. "Do you remember asking for me?"

"I asked for you?"

"That's what they said. That you wanted to see me."

I try to remember, and it comes back as a feeling more than a literal memory. I can remember lying back against the pillows, crying and so weak I could barely move a muscle. Even my eyes. And I remember wanting Grey with me more than anything. Missing him so much I could barely breathe.

"I'm so glad you came," I tell him. "I can't believe you flew like a million hours to see me."

"I would have flown a *trillion* hours to see you. You know that."

"You're such a good person, Grey. I hope *you* know *that*."

With a shrug he says, "I'm working on it. But I didn't come here because I'm a good person. I came here because I had to. Whether you asked for me or not."

I can't pretend not to know what it all means. That I wanted him more than anyone else. That he wanted to be here more than anything else. It doesn't matter if he's younger than me or a musician or still figuring things out. It doesn't matter that we're wrong on paper, that Brooks and I make more sense. He's here. And I want him here.

I just want him. Plain and simple. I want him.

"Grey." I put my hand over his, hold on tight. "Will you stay?"

"Of course. I'm not going anywhere."

"No. I mean, will you be with me? Like *with* me?"

He doesn't move for a long moment. Just stares at me with those steady, slate-colored eyes, like he's absorbing what I said. The muscles in his neck roll as he swallows. "What about Brooks?" he says finally, his voice deep and hoarse.

"I'll talk to Brooks. He'll be fine. What matters is this." I squeeze his hand between my two. "It's just . . . it's everything. You're . . . everything to me, Grey. I don't know how else to say it."

"That was perfect." He lifts my hand to his lips and kisses my palm, bandage, tubes, and all. "It's the best thing I've heard in months. Or . . . ever."

Being this close, saying these things, I can feel my strength building, feel myself knitting back together. It's not that he makes me strong or whole. It's that with him, I remember how strong and whole I am.

"I want to kiss you so fucking much," I tell him, "but my mouth tastes like a nuclear waste dump right now."

He laughs, making the bed shake. "I guess we're going to have to wrestle over who's most romantic." Rising again, he says, "Let me see what we've got."

I hear some rustling around, and he comes back with two sticks of gum from my purse. "This'll have to do."

We unwrap the gum like we're getting undressed, giggling, our eyes locked together.

"Cheers," he says, and taps his stick against mine.

"Cheers."

Grey pops a piece in his mouth, and I do the same.

"This is the sexiest gum I've ever chewed," he tells me.

"No kidding." I pat the bed next to me. "I think you need to climb on up here."

"I'm scared I'll break it. Or rip out your IV."

"I'm scared you won't get your ass on this bed."

"You win." He comes around to the other side, and he lowers the rail like he's done it a hundred times. Then he slides half onto the bed, careful not to crush me or dislodge anything. "Okay." We get our arms and various tubes and pillows sorted, and then we take out our gum, and it's the least romantic thing ever but romantic for just that reason. Because with him it doesn't matter if I'm in a hospital gown. If I'm not perfect. With him, it all falls away. The bed, the sounds and scents of the hospital. It's just Grey, his firm, full lips on my own, his mint-scented tongue sweeping over mine. I pull him against me, as close as he can get, my hands bracing against the broad expanse of his muscular back.

It's awkward and messy but as real and truthful as it gets. Just

Grey and me, holding each other, squeezed together in this tiny bed, pulling tubes and remotes out from under us, laughing and touching and kissing—lightly, so lightly. He's still gentle with me, and I need that now. But I can't wait to get my strength back again. The things I plan to do to this boy.

A knock on the door interrupts us, and we break apart, laughing.

"Shit," Grey mutters, scrubbing at his short punky hair. "We might have gotten a little carried away."

"Just a little."

Mia enters the room just as he sits back in the chair, but it's evident from the look on her face that we're completely busted. "Sorry to interrupt," she says, "But the doctor's going to come by in just a few. Also, Brooks asked to see you."

Grey looks at me. "Want me to stay here while you talk to him?"

I shake my head. "No. I'll take care of it. I promise."

He nods. "Okay. Do you need anything? Real food? Change of clothes? What can I do?"

You can bar the door and climb back in this bed, I want to say. But I feel the toll those last few moments took on me. It's scary to think how much harm I've done to myself while believing I was making perfectly sound choices.

"I don't need anything," I tell him. "Except maybe more gum."

He laughs and heads for the door. "I'll dig up a twelve-pack."

My face hurts from smiling, and when I turn back, Mia's beaming at me, her green eyes positively shining.

"So, that's a thing now, huh?"

"Yeah," I tell her. "I'm pretty sure it's been a thing all along."

"I'm pretty sure it has, too," she says. "I'm glad, Sky. He's crazy about you. And I like how he always asks about you. How he wants to care for you. I think you need that since you care for everyone else."

I nod. But I know I have to do less of that anyway. Maybe I don't have to be the yes-girl, after all. Maybe I can be the sometimes girl. The not-now girl.

"Hey, Mia," I say.

"Yeah?"

"Tell Brooks I'll see him now. And maybe give us a few."

Her eyebrows pinch together. "You sure you want to tackle that right now, Sky? You're still pretty worn out."

I nod. "I know, but I'll feel better if I just take care of it."

"Okay," she says. "I'll go get him."

She heads back to the hospital room door, and I straighten up in bed, smooth my gown and blankets over me. I take another sip of water and then fold my hands in my lap and wait for Brooks.

Chapter 41

Grey

*L*et me get this straight. You're on your way to becoming a homeowner, you're shedding your irresponsible, jackass persona, and settling down with a girl, but you've forgone your dream in the process?" Adam takes a sip of his beer and shakes his head. "I have to say, I'm not sure it's a good trade."

We're walking on the beach on the hotel property. Skyler's been released from the small island hospital and transferred back here. She's up in her room sleeping right now. The rest of the crew left this morning. Only Mia, Garrett, Adam, and Alison, who came in a few days ago, are still on the island.

I take a sip of my beer, which is warm, as warm as the tropical air that's tugging at my t-shirt and rustling through the palm trees, paving the way for a storm that'll hit sometime tonight. "Yes to the homeowner and girl comments. As far as giving up my jackass persona, sorry to disappoint. And forgoing my dream? Postponing, more like."

I knew what I was doing by coming here. Rez has sent Vogelson a few messages letting him know the situation, but the guy won't even reply. Not surprising. We probably look irresponsible and like a terrible investment if we can't even show up for the audition.

I've talked to each of the guys in the band. They've all been cool on the phone, but I know they're probably hugely disappointed. In a way, it's like we're back to square one. But it doesn't quite *feel* like square one. We've come together as a band over the past weeks. We've gained something. It has nothing to do with the showcase.

Earlier on the phone, Shane told me we're an organism, with a heart and a mind and lungs and limbs. We need each other. We fail and succeed as one. I'd asked him, jokingly, if I was the organism's asshole. Shane laughed and said, "Heart, dude. Heart, all the way."

"Postponing," Adam says. "Did Vogelson get back to Reznick?"

I smile. It still feels good to have my brother be "in" on my life again. "No. We haven't heard anything." I shrug. "I just meant we'll figure out something else."

Adam's gaze moves across the water. I notice the tension in his jaw, the way he's pursing his lips.

"Don't tell me you feel responsible," I say.

"Of course I do. I should've seen that we were asking too much of Skyler. You've been working toward the showcase your entire life."

I laugh. "Wow. Drama. I think you've been hanging out with too many actors."

Adam gives me a sidelong glance. I'm not telling him what he wants to hear. And I know he's going to drive at me until I do.

"Okay. I'll say it. It sucks, all right? I wanted that showcase. I thought it was going to be our break. But . . . I'm okay. I mean, I will be. We'll find something else. Vogelson's not the only producer out there. We'll figure it out. And I had to be here for Sky. That was nonnegotiable."

It's hard to look him in the eye when I say that. It's so new, this Skyler thing. It just feels like it's all over my face, this blaring, over-the-top awesome feeling. "Besides," I say, "if Vogelson backs out, then he's an idiot because we are fucking *great*."

Adam laughs. "And that, little bro, is exactly why I know it's going to work out. There's some serious confidence buzzing around you. It's cool."

"Thanks. Can we stop now? I can't handle any more feelings."

He laughs again. "Okay." The skyline is black with clouds, except for the occasional flash of lightning. I've gotten used to Southern California. Weather—real weather—seems so flashy and dramatic. "Actually, there's one more thing before we shut the feelings down. I'm going to ask Ali to marry me tonight."

He reaches into his pocket and takes out a small velvet box, showing it to me.

"I had this whole thing planned. A private boat. Scuba. Dinner. I wanted to be out on the water with her when I asked, but . . ." He lifts his shoulders. "Storm. Anyway, I can't wait any longer. I'm just going to drop to a knee and beg. Tell her anything she wants to hear, and hope she agrees to make me an honest man."

This is the second-best thing I've heard in a long time. Second only to what Skyler said earlier. There were a lot of years I wondered if he'd ever marry again, after losing Chloe. But I knew it would lead to this with Ali. I think I knew right from the beginning. He was different with her from the start.

"So, assuming she says yes, will you be my best man?" he says.

"You're not going to drop down on a knee and beg *me*?" I pull him into a hug. But there's so much going on inside me, I have to rough him up a little and push him around, mess up his hair and try to trip him. He's quick and manages to slip away.

As we make our way along the lighted path to the hotel, it's like we're in a horse race, the two of us almost breaking into a jog. I can't stop smiling.

"What?" Adam says.

"I was just thinking . . . between Skyler and being your best man, I'm winning over Brooks. Hugely winning. I think I knocked him out of the game."

"Jackass."

"As advertised, bro. Always."

I slip into Skyler's hotel room quietly, stepping into the suite's small sitting room. Mia is curled up like a cat on a chair, reading.

"How's it going in here?" I was only outside with Adam for an hour, but I feel like I missed out. Like I was gone too long.

"Still asleep," Mia says. She closes her book and stands. "It's almost eight. I was going to order some food. Garrett said he wants to join, too."

"Mia, why don't you and Garrett go grab a bite at the restaurant? You haven't left her side in days. And, no offense, but it's probably about time for you to rest up, shower, call Ethan . . . whatever it is Mia Galliano does with her spare time."

She smiles. "Mia Galliano could definitely use a little break. And I know you'll take good care of our girl." She grabs her purse off the couch and casts a quick look toward the bedroom. "Sky's got water and Gatorade in there, but when she wakes up, she'll probably want some tea. Then probably something light to eat."

"I'm on it. Look, text me if you're worried. But don't be worried. I've got it."

"Okay. Thanks, Grey. You know, you're really good for her."

"So are you."

We do a fist-bump and laugh. Team Skyler.

After she leaves, I let myself into the bedroom. I'm surprised to find the bed empty. The bathroom door is slightly ajar, and a shaft of light pours into the darkened bedroom. The shower turns on.

I step toward the door. "Skyler?" I knock, lightly. "You all right?"

"Grey?"

"Yeah. Just . . . just checking on you. Everything okay?"

"No."

My heart stops.

"I mean, it would be, if you were in here with me."

That blows my mind for a few seconds. Maybe it's minutes. Or maybe time stops. Who knows?

I get it together and push the door open and there she is, a little hunched, because she's still weak, standing under the spray of water, smiling. I've seen her naked before, but never in water, never standing, never waiting for me. Never like this. She's beautiful. Crushingly, painfully beautiful.

Knowing what's been going on, what she's been through, I notice she's thinned out. She's less curvy. But she's no less gorgeous than she was. I don't think I could ever look at her and not find her beautiful. What I don't like is the fragile slant of her shoulders. The wavering strength I see in her eyes.

I realize I'm standing here. But I don't want to move. All I want to do is stare at her. Except that's definitely, *definitely* not all I want to do.

I tug my shirt off. "Sky, are you sure?"

We've messed around before. We've texted a thousand times every day. I've written a song for her. Two, technically. I'm pretty sure she's my best friend and that I'm gone for her. But it still feels like this . . . where we're going . . . what's about to happen . . . it still feels like something that's too good to be true.

She nods. "I think I've been sure for a long time. Maybe since our first audition, when you told me I'm good at fake kissing."

I step out of the rest of my clothes. "Why the hell did you wait so long to tell me?"

"I don't know. Maybe I wanted you captive when I did it?"

I step into the shower and wrap my arms around her. Try not to pass out at how good she feels against me. *Insanely* good. Or to laugh at how obvious it is that I am ready to go. "You've got me, Skyler, beautiful Skyler. Now what? Should we talk music?"

"I think we can save the talking for later." She rolls up on her toes, wrapping her arms around my neck. "You are *very* tall."

I lean closer. "You're short."

She blinks, slow and sultry, her gaze warm, like she can see into my soul. "Your eyes, Grey."

"Your everything, Sky."

Then I bend a little lower and kiss her.

Chapter 42

Skyler

*T*his is an even better kiss than the one in the hospital, all sweetness and heat, the steam from the water enveloping us, his firm, towering body pressed against me. His hands brace my back and neck, and it feels like I could fall into them, trust him to buoy me. His lips and mine—it's like music, the perfect tempo, the perfect balance of give and take, high notes and low.

His tongue traces my lips, sweeping over me, light, almost tickling, building this yearning to take him into me, his tongue, his fingers—all of him. I move my hands up to his neck, the spray from the shower going everywhere, and I deepen the kiss, wanting to dive in and taste every bit of him, touch every inch of his slick, beautiful body.

"Sky, I may not survive this shower," he murmurs against my lips. He kisses the side of my face, then, hands firm on my back, he runs his hot darting tongue along the hollow of my throat, his teeth grazing my collarbone, tasting me. His mouth on my skin is perfection, and he's so hard, pressed against me, it literally makes me breathless, creates a caving ripple inside, a need like nothing I've ever felt before. I want him so much, but I can barely hold on to his broad shoulders and massive triceps, so slick from water, and my legs start to tremble.

"Grey?"

"Hmm . . ." He bends me back, and his tongue is everywhere now—on my throat, my lips, the delicate skin beneath my ear. His breath is hot against me; the warm water swirls around us, and it's all so electric, so pure and good, I don't know what to do with myself.

My knee buckles a little, reminding me that I don't want to go down in a heap in a shower. And I want more from this. Want to touch Grey, to taste him, to have to every part of him close.

"Let's lie down," I say. Looking into his beautiful lucent eyes, almost silver in this light, the color of raindrops shimmering on a window, I want to drink him in forever, spend hours exploring the lines of his body, taking his strength into me, giving him mine.

"Okay," he says. "Whatever you want."

We turn off the shower and step out, wrapping ourselves in the plush white towels warmed by the heating bar. It's pretty decadent, but we only enjoy it for a few seconds before we move toward one another again, as if propelled, the force between us so strong.

He sweeps me against him to kiss me again, crushing me to him, all of him wrapped around me. Then he lifts me, like I'm nothing, and I wrap my arms around his neck, my legs around his hips, the towel parting across my thighs. I tease his ear with my tongue, telling him things I've never told anyone, about how I want to make him feel, what I want to do to him.

He groans and staggers a little, and we laugh while he carries me to the bed, the two of us still half wet, as he sets me down atop the plush linens. I sit on the edge and reach for him, running my hands along his rock-hard thighs, my fingers trailing beneath the towel, finding his warmth, his hardness, touching him, now, the way I've wanted to touch him.

I look up at him, at his sweet, serious face. His eyes are slitted but sparkling, his mouth parted with the pleasure of it, with my touch making him feel good now. My turn to give him back some of what he's given me.

His breath comes hard, and his fingers move into the wet strands of my hair, stroking it. "Sky, you're . . . This is . . ."

I tug the towel away and pull him down onto the bed. Laughing, we move together to the center, throwing pillows out of the way, tossing the heavy comforter to some corner. He parts my towel, and his eyes on me, on my body, the pleasure I see there, tells me everything.

"You're amazing."

"That's you," I tell him. And it is. His corded muscles, the ripples of his abs, the broad, broad expanse of his chest, his smooth tan skin, the lines and shadows of him. All perfect and beautiful and all mine right now. All mine to taste and touch, which I do.

We kiss and kiss some more, me sinking into him, him sinking into me, tongues and lips and sounds, all so hot and perfect. We breathe into each other, tasting each other. We talk and laugh and kiss and kiss until I'm drunk on him, spinning, and his lips move away to trail down along my body, his fingers following.

He leans over me and sucks first one nipple and then the other into his mouth, slowly, teasingly, firming his hands over my breasts, his thumbs circling, and again so perfect, like he was designed only to make me feel good. Like that's his mission.

"Tell me what you like," he says in a hoarse whisper. "I want you to feel good, Sky. Tell me how to make you feel good."

"You do, Grey. You are."

"What else?" he insists. "What else do you like?" His fingers move down along my body, tracing over my lower belly, plunging farther down. My breath hitches as his warm fingertips close over me, and I rise to his touch.

"This?" he asks, looking up at me, his fingers moving, plunging. His gray eyes pierce me. "Like this?"

"Yes," I say, though it's barely a whisper. He feels so good, and his eyes on me—it's so much. So much sweetness. So much pleasure. So good it almost tips into pain, into the best kind of ache. "Like that, Grey. Just . . ."

He touches me over and over, and his lips move over my body, over my belly, up to my breasts, his tongue making hot circles, his mouth and teeth and tongue everywhere, and we're kissing, and his fingers are moving, moving over me, and it's good. So, so good. I'm trembling under him, this hot spark flaring to life within me, igniting where his fingers move against me, igniting and sparking and flowing out like a wildfire, searing across my body. We're kissing and kissing, and my body trembles against his hand, all of me reaching for that place, that place of heat and light and sharpness.

And then it comes, lashing through me, so hot and intense that I cry out against Grey's soft sweet lips, still pressed to me. And he groans, too, the two of us locked together, this fever burning through me, rippling on and on from a deep sharp pit that unknots and seems to flow outward forever.

Words come from me, and from him, but I can't make sense of them, can't make sense of anything but this beautiful, perfect connection, his hands, his fingers and lips, his sweetness pouring over me, his need. And my own need. My need for more of him. To have all of him.

I push him gently onto his back on the bed. And he smiles, this gorgeous, avid, lazy smile. Smug and adorable because he knows what's coming next. He knows I want him to feel even a tenth of what he makes me feel.

Out of nowhere, he produces a condom and gives me a wink.

"Extra magnum," he says, which makes me laugh so hard while we put it on him together.

I climb onto him, feeling like a feather against the solidity of him. He's slick from the shower, still gives off waves of sweet-smelling heat. I straddle his hips and run my fingers along his pecs, stroking the muscles of his arms, his torso, bending over him to tease my tongue over his smooth flesh, to taste him. I graze my teeth over him, and he groans and grabs hold of my waist, tugging me down, his hips rising beneath me.

"Let me know if anything's not okay," he says. "It's . . ."

"Extra magnum. I'm well aware."

I move down, slowly, and his hands guide us, and he's a lot, but it's so good. He feels so good. His hips move beneath me, and mine move to join his, and we look at each other, just the two of us, caught together in a swirl of white sheets and fading sunlight.

My hair falls into my face, and he reaches up to move it back, holding it away.

"I want to look at you," he tells me. "I want to watch you feel good."

I moan. Because this is so perfect, and because I want to watch him, too, as we move together, as he fills me, as his eyes close, finally, and he throws his head back against the bed, his jaw flexing, all of him tightening beneath me.

His hands take control of my hips, gripping them as our movements intensify, as our breath comes harder and faster. I spread my body over his, my full weight against his massive warmth. I put my hands in his hair, kiss and lick and suck on his lips and tongue, the smooth skin of his shoulders. He groans, and I do, and we move together, faster, both of us trembling, both of us seeking after that light again.

He gets there before I do, his harsh gasps, the sharp movements of his body beneath me, telling me everything, pushing me over the edge. Again, that lashing, exquisite warmth, the ripples undulating like sun-warmed waves, flowing outward and over us, sweeping us along, as we rock together, trembling, sharing breath, fingers locked together now, bodies joined.

We settle, finally, and he takes my face in his hands and leans up to kiss me.

"Sky, beautiful Sky."

"Grey, beautiful Grey."

"Oh, shit." His smile disappears. "I just realized something awful."

"What?"

"We're Grey Sky. I mean, our names together. Grey. Sky. That's awful."

I laugh and kiss him. Then I rest my cheek against his chest, listen to the fierce and steady beat of his heart. "Yeah, that kind of sucks."

"I don't think we can be together," he says.

"No, you're right. Not with those names."

"We should break up."

"Definitely."

"When do you think? Like, three hundred years from now?"

I smile. "Maybe five hundred."

He tightens his arms around me and kisses the top of my head. "Okay, five hundred years, and that's it."

We doze and wake up to kiss again, to touch one another, to whisper all of the things we've spent months not saying. It's like that night in the darkness of my room when he held me, only so much better. Because now his body is mine to explore, now we can pour out our hearts to one another, tell each other our dreams and plans and know, because we're free to say it, that we'll pursue those dreams and plans together.

"Are you sure you want to keep acting?" Grey asks. "I don't like what it did to you."

I smile and slide my bare leg over his. "Acting didn't hurt me. *I* hurt me."

"Still . . ."

It occurs to me that being good at something, that making people happy with a gift, isn't all of it. It has to feed *me*, too. It has to give me joy the way music does. The way Grey does. I'm hungry, I realize. So hungry for so many things. Food, most definitely. But for my music, too. For a life that reflects my passions. That gives me life, makes me burn inside. I've been starving myself in more ways than one.

Mia comes to the door with a couple of carryout containers, which I grab from her like she's handing out fistfuls of gold doubloons. I don't even care what's in them.

"Whoa," she says and peers around me into the room where Grey lounges on the bed, barely covered and smirking.

He gives her a jaunty wave. "Howdy."

"Uh, howdy to you."

I turn back to her with a look I know is the absolute opposite of a poker face. "Thanks for the food. And for everything."

She grins. "So, I should come in, right? Hang out with you guys? You look like you want company."

"Um, that's a big N-O, but thanks again."

"Fine." She gives me a phony pout.

I give her a kiss on the cheek. "I'll text you later."

"You better."

"I will."

I close the door, and Grey is right there, taking the boxes from my hands. "I'm starving."

"Me too." I know I need to take it easy. I don't want to make myself sick. But it's like a switch has been flipped inside me again. I have so much more energy, such a stronger feeling of just plain *life* than I've had in a while. I guess intravenous fluids and a couple of orgasms will do that for a girl.

I start with a container of chicken soup, which is just heaven, and Grey tears into a turkey club sandwich, though he wraps up half for me and makes me promise to take a few bites at least.

While we sit there, I send an email to Parker and Jane, telling them to hold off on scheduling anything for me until further notice. They know I've been sick, but that hasn't kept them from coming at me with messages, phone calls, notes of concern wrapped within reminders of obligation. But I know I need to take care of myself first. I don't need my body to tell me that twice.

Next comes the tougher call—the one to my mom. I sit there and polish away the smudges on my phone screen with the edge of the sheet.

"You okay?" Grey asks.

"Yeah. Have to call my mom. Just not sure what to say."

He leans over and smooths the hair away from my neck to press his lips there, trail kisses down to my shoulder. "Just tell her how you feel."

"I know. I just . . ."

"Just what?"

I shake my head. "It's just hard to let her down."

"Well, don't you think you're letting her down worse by making yourself sick and taking on too much?"

"I guess."

He starts in on the French fries. "So, this thing I figured out, with some help from a friend, is that if you avoid something it just keeps coming at you, over and over again, to kick your ass in bigger and bigger ways."

I sigh. "You're right."

"I am wise beyond my years."

He takes the soup from my lap, clears all the containers from the bed. Then he draws me against his chest and puts his arms around me. Grey kisses the top of my head. "Whatever happens, I've got you. More importantly, you've got you. Believe me."

I feel a tingle in my sinuses that tells me I'm about to start crying. Lately, I'm just a wreck over everything, but I know that'll get better as I do. "I believe you."

Picking up my phone again, I have Siri call my mom. I feel like I forget to breathe as the phone rings once . . . twice . . . three times before my mom answers.

"Oh, honey, are you all right?" she says. "I've been so worried about you. I wanted to come there, but—"

"It's okay. I'm out of the hospital. I'm doing better."

"What a relief. You need to take care of yourself, Skyler. You can't worry me like that."

"I know, Mom," I say. "That's what I want to talk to you about, actually."

Before I chicken out, I tell her I'll always do what I can for her, but I need to think of myself, too.

"I think you should sell the farm," I say. "The land is worth a mint. You could get a nice apartment near Scotty, help with the girls."

She's quiet for a long moment. I feel her disappointment beaming across the miles at me, but at least she doesn't reject the idea outright.

"You don't want me out there?" she asks, finally.

"I don't think either of us wants that, Mom. Not really."

"And you're not coming home?"

"I'll come for a visit soon," I tell her. "But I'm staying in LA. It's where I need to be."

I look up at Grey, and he tightens his arms around me and nods. His expression is so adorable—enthusiastic and encouraging, but beyond that there's a maturity, a look that tells me he understands what this means to me. And he truly does have my back.

I can get used to this, I think. Even if it's only for five hundred years.

Chapter 43

Grey

This is so unusual," Titus says as he pulls the guitar strap over his head.

"Yeah, it is. But it's kind of the same, too. We're still playing music for an audience."

"My parents are out there. With all their lawyer friends."

I laugh. "And I'm counting on them to be our most law-abiding fans."

We're in the back room of Norman's, a club owned by one of my dad's friends. It's crowded in here, a small back office that's piled high with paint cans and blueprints, crates of vodka and industrial-sized cleaning solutions. Titus and I needed a second away from the commotion outside. Just five minutes for us both to process the insanity of the last twenty-four hours.

Yesterday, Sky and I came back from the Virgin Islands to find the entire band waiting at the apartment. As Beth swooped Skyler off to smother her with affection and care, the guys presented to me their idea. It was: Let's fuckin' play anyway!

After so many weeks of preparation, we were primed to play and, without the showcase, everyone felt wired and unsatisfied. We had, as Emilio put it, gig blue balls. Forget the showcase and Vogelson, who still hasn't replied. We *had* to play. Anywhere. ASAP.

I got behind the idea immediately, which started a flurry of activity as each of us reached out to our social networks. I went right to Adam's house, to see my parents. Dad was there; he'd arrived in LA while I was in the Virgin Islands. When I told him what we were doing, he made some calls and got us the venue for tonight, Norman's, which is closed for remodels. That easy. Hey, sometimes it's nice to be a Blackwood. None of us cared if we played on plywood, or if the walls were unpainted Sheetrock. We had a venue.

The audience gathering outside right now is all family and friends, anyone who's rallying to the call we put out last night. Emilio's music students and people from the film crew have showed up. Some of the Boomerang people are here. Nora's yoga class is taking a night off, and I think Shane said his dentist just showed up. It's random and awesome. Totally personal. I think we're almost at two hundred people. Not bad for a day's notice.

And as it's turned out, Norman's is looking pretty swag. Saul, from sound, is finishing up all the amp hookups for us right now out on "the stage," which is really the platform where the raised bar will eventually go. Last I checked, Danny and Alfredo, the grips, were out there setting up lights under the guidance of the director of photography, who's offered to film the show for us. Bernadette and Kaitlin were out there with some of the set designers rigging up colored canvas sheets. About an hour ago, Ethan and Beth were out there holding panels and hammering nails for them. There's more, too.

Mom and Ali were running down some catering. Dad and Adam were on drinks/bar. Mia, as usual, was putting out fires.

About an hour ago, Rez even got some calls from a couple of the local bands we know offering to be our opening act. We have that one covered, though, so they'll be coming just to enjoy the show. It's crazy how many people want to help us. I'm not sure what I did to deserve it, but I'm not going to question it. Just letting the good times roll.

What we've ended up with is an aged-up-music-recital-slash-private-party. Kind of funny. Kind of not showcase-y. But cool. Already, it's really, really cool. And it makes sense that these people, who mean something to us, will be the ones to hear us play at the height of our ability, exactly how we know we're supposed to sound.

Good stuff.

Emilio swings the door open. "Your girl's on in five, Blackwood."

I head out of the small room and find Skyler standing behind a canvas panel that separates the stage from the rest of the club. She's holding her electric cello, talking to Beth and Mia, and has her back turned to me.

Walking up, I wrap my arms around her and bend to her ear. "Hey, beautiful. You ready?"

It's loud in here. The whole place is thrumming with the energy of dozens and dozens of people enjoying themselves, laughing, knotting new friendships from our social web. The sound the crowd's making has a warm vibe. It's different than when we play our regular gigs.

Skyler leans against me, tipping her head up. She's wearing heels, but I can still look right into her eyes this way. "Kiss me," she says, "and I will be."

I turn her in my arms, and we somehow manage to hold on to the cello and kiss. As always, we get carried away.

"Oh-kay. I guess I'll just go find Ethan?" Mia says.

Skyler and I laugh. "You're feeling well enough?" I ask, brushing her soft pink hair behind her ear. Just three days ago, she was in a hospital, hooked up to an IV. And it's not like I've let her catch up on sleep. I've been teasing her lately, telling her that's what she gets for dating a younger guy. Bigger appetite. Just thinking about being alone with her, touching her, the way she looks and sounds and tastes . . . what she does to me . . . *everything*. No way I'll ever get enough of her. Ever.

"I feel great," she says. "Don't worry, Grey. I really do. Actually, I can't wait to play."

"Okay. You're going to kill it."

"So will you."

She rises onto her toes and gives me one more kiss, and then she takes her cello, and moves onto the stage. A cheer goes up from the crowd, and Sky does a little curtsy, some of Emma still in her, I guess, but then she grins, that perfect, disarming smile that's completely genuine, and about as un-movie-star as can be. She plugs into the amp then moves to the microphone stand, and goes still, finding her focus. Her hands settle on the bow and the strings, and then she's off.

Watching her play from my spot "offstage" is something I know right away I'll never forget. What can be better than seeing someone you care about lose themselves so completely in art, in bliss? I never had this feeling, watching her act. It feels like a privileged position. I'm so proud of her . . . so proud of who she is, and *flying* that she's chosen to be with me. That's when it hits me.

I *love* her.

Wow.

Then I'm just tearing up like a total freakin' asshole, trying not to lose it even more.

She moves to another song, with notes that rise like a story, like triumph, and my heart almost busts open when she glances at me. We're making a story now. Together. I know that's what she's telling me.

When she plays the last song and takes her bow, the roar that goes up actually makes me wonder if we'll have cops knocking on the door with a noise complaint. Good thing we have a half dozen lawyers out there to handle things if that happens.

I pull her right back into my arms as she comes off the stage. "How'd that feel?"

"So good. So, so good." There are tears in her eyes. There's relief and joy in them, too. "I love you, Grey."

"*What?* Come on! *I* was going to say that."

"Right now you were?"

"Yes! I was getting to it. I can't believe you just trumped me."

She laughs. "You can still say it. I mean . . . I'd still love to hear it."

"I love you, Skyler. You're incredible. I never thought—"

"Are you guys seriously doing this right now?"

Titus looks like he wants to kill me. The rest of the guys look less friendly.

"What? You guys want to play music or something? Shit! Let's play some music!"

I wink at Sky, and head out to the stage with my band. The club looks incredible. I hadn't seen the completed, jerry-rigged transformation yet, but it's a combination of blue and white canvas, and dramatic lighting. It feels like being in a wave—and that's a place where I'm totally comfortable.

In the front of the small stage, I see my parents. First row of the audience. Mom's outfit—jeans and a leather jacket—makes me smile. It's probably what she considers "rock concert appropriate."

Dad, who was just eyeing the club remodel with the eye of a true entrepreneur, breaks into a huge grin when he sees me and yells, "That's my kid!" to no one who doesn't already know this.

Adam and Ali are right there. Ethan, Mia, and Beth. Skyler, who darts out and joins them. And so it goes, row after row of more friends. People from the film crew, friends of the guys, family members, girlfriends. I see Brooks in the back. Garrett stands near him. He blows me a kiss then he leans toward a guy standing between him and Brooks, saying something.

I've only seen the guy in pictures online, but I know who he is. Vogelson.

Rez, Titus, Emilio, and Shane see him, too. They've met him before. I'm the only one who hasn't. Yet.

We look at each other, grinning. After all the bullshit and heartache, wouldn't you just know it? He's here. But I think we all sort of feel kind of *fuckit* about things. We're here to play music. Everyone we care about is here. Plus Shane's dentist. Vogelson can kiss my ass if he doesn't like us.

I don't know if that's the feeling that powers me as we start in. Freedom. Or fearlessness. Zingyness? A steely finish? Who the hell knows? It doesn't matter. What matters is that I sing with every cell in my body. I sing my goddamn heart out. I sing about the love I wish I'd had in my life. The love I did always have and never appreciated until recently. And the new love in my life, the one that makes me feel like I can soar like a hawk.

My brother is in my voice. His unconditional love and support. Titus. Shane, Rez, and Emilio—the brothers I've picked up myself. Beth and Bernadette and Kaitlin and Nora . . . who've all helped me get here in ways big and small. Skyler.

Skyler Beautiful Skyler.

Everyone's in my voice. I'm who I am because of all of them.

And showing them that, letting them into that, is what I do on the stage. I open up, and bring them in.

We go through the set, building an experience for the audience. We play "Runner," and it's our first time performing it live, but it goes perfectly. Better than in rehearsals. One by one, we go through our songs. Nine of them, all original. It feels like it happens in under a minute, but I know I've been up here for almost an hour. With only one more to go, I pause to regroup. It feels like coming out of a trance.

I'm sweating, I realize. I'm thirsty. I feel invincible.

I grab a bottle of water and take a sip, then look around me. The guys are right there with me. This is it. This is us. All the hard work, the rehearsals, the ups and downs . . . it's all worth it because of this. This moment. This feeling.

Without meaning to, I look toward the back of the club. Brooks is easy to find—he's still there. But I don't see Garrett. I don't see *Vogelson*. And I know that's who I was looking for, despite myself.

Whatever. Screw him.

I come back to the microphone stand, and the applause dies down. It's hot in here. Someone's brought in huge fans in the back of the club. I hadn't even noticed. They make the canvas sheets billow, make the light roll with the material in a way that's hypnotic . . . We're all of us at sea. Free here, in this space. Open. I'm open in a way I've never allowed myself to be.

The whir of the fans is the only sound I hear. I don't hear two hundred people breathing, but it's almost like I *feel* them. Our connection is what I feel. Like everyone in this room has been stripped down to the most honest parts of what it means to be human. We're experiencing life together through music. I'm making that happen. The band and I, we're doing this.

I freakin' love it.

I take the microphone and find Skyler in the audience. "For this next song, our last one tonight, I want to bring up someone you've heard already. Someone who's special to me. This song exists because of her. And, uh . . . I'm starting to think I do, too. What do you say, Sky? Want to help us out?"

She of course jumps up onstage to cheers and whistles. And it's as I watch her grab her cello that I see Garrett standing there, too, with Vogelson. Garrett grins his ass off and shamelessly points at Vogelson, then gives me the thumbs-up and starts the whole thing over. Point, thumbs-up, point, thumbs-up.

Vogelson sees all of this, of course, and laughs. I guess when you're Garrett Allen you get away with shit most people can't. Vogelson tips his chin, acknowledging me. The look in his eyes says, "I like what I've seen," and, "Let's work together."

I don't think I'm imagining it, because I hear Shane behind me. "Oh my *God*!" he yells, and pounds a quick, furious beat on the drums that's made of so much pressurized celebration, it's borderline aggressive.

Skyler takes the cello from Saul and comes over. "That looks promising."

I can't even focus on that right now. I'll have to process that later. "*You* look promising," I say, pulling her in for a quick kiss that draws a dozen catcalls from the audience.

"Now," I say. "What do you say we blow the roof off this place?"

———— *Acknowledgments* ————

First, and always, thanks so much to our amazing readers and supportive bloggers for all of your kind words, support, and enthusiasm. You are the best, plain and simple.

To my fabulous and talented coauthor, Veronica: Thanks for countless laughs and swoons; for some truly disastrous culinary and drinking "experiments;" and for being a model of grace, dedication, kindness, humor, and intelligence. No list of adjectives comes close to describing how much I adore you!

To my amazing extended family—Lisa, Mustafa, Alexandra, Andrew, Dina, Samantha, Abbey, Brenda, Elizabeth, Anna, and Matt—thanks again for being just who you are.

To all my writing compatriots—the other part of my family: Thank you for inspiring me, supporting me, challenging me, and being kick-ass, wonderful, brilliant people. I'm so lucky to know you all.

Last, thanks to Josh and Tracey Adams for all you do; to Tessa Woodward for your editorial guidance and support; to Elle Keck for your enthusiasm and help; to Molly Birckhead and Megan Schumann for helping us get these "babies" out into the world; and to the entire team at HarperCollins/William Morrow for working so hard on our behalf. Sometimes it feels like magic goes into making a book, but I know it's really a ton of hard work! Thanks so much.

—LO

This book was a joy to create from start to finish. Thanks first and foremost to Tessa Woodward for your belief in us, and for your editorial guidance. Thanks also to Elle Keck for all your help in bringing this book to publication. Megan Schumann and Molly Birckhead have both done so much to spread the word on this trilogy. I'm grateful for all your efforts!

Boundless love and thanks to my family and friends for their patience and support. I'm blessed to have you in my life. To my wonderful and talented coauthor: All the Mavericks for you! You're a treasure and I'm so fortunate to call you my friend.

Finally, thank you readers and bloggers for letting us share these characters with you. You've made this so rewarding and fun. Thank you for taking this journey with us. For you, a standing ovation.

—VR

About the Author

What do you get when friends pen a story with heart, plenty of laughs, and toe-curling kissing scenes? Noelle August, the pseudonym for renowned editor and award-winning writer Lorin Oberweger and *New York Times* bestselling YA author Veronica Rossi, the masterminds behind *Boomerang* and *Rebound*.

GET BETWEEN THE COVERS WITH THE HOTTEST NEW ADULT BOOKS